THE HUSBAND

The Husband

a novel by SOL STEIN

Coward-McCann, Inc. *New York*

The law holds that for his work a writer should draw not upon the experience of his life but upon invention. That law is a fiction, as is this book. If any of the characters and events of this book bear any resemblance to real persons and real events, it is coincidental.

FOR PAT
modus vivendi

THE HUSBAND

Chapter One

The office was folding up early. Secretarial desks were cleared, typewriters covered, and the girls were lining up in front of the mirrors in the john to pretty themselves. Account executives, eyes on the clock, were returning client calls and keeping them short. Copywriters and artists had stopped being creative at four o'clock. It was now four thirty, and the only clerical employees of the agency not caught up in the frenetic preparty activity were the two girls manning the Dale, Bowne, and Armstrong switchboard, which they would continue to do until one minute to five, when they'd pull the plugs and connect the night lines, though nobody would be around to answer them. Everybody in the agency, all one hundred and thirty-four employees, were invited to the party at the Biltmore in honor of Old Alex Ragdale, who had reached his sixty-fifth birthday and was being made to walk the plank.

The agency occupied one floor and part of another in one of the skyscrapers in the Grand Central area. The main floor had four corner offices, the plushest for Paul Dale, who owned a controlling interest in the firm and was the only name partner. Legend had it that of the original Dale, Bowne, and Armstrong, Bowne had shot Armstrong over Bowne's wife and had drawn a life sentence. Actually, Bowne and Armstrong are both Dale family names which Paul used to make his fledgling agency sound bigger than it was when he returned from the war and decided to strike out on his own.

The second corner office belonged to Tony Cavallo, the brilliant art director, a very small, wiry, fiery little fellow who hated the big office and actually kept his drawing table facing a blank wall and never used the magnificent desk Paul Dale had provided him with except for interviewing job applicants, a duty he hated and would have gladly forgone if the personnel director had had any gift for judging artists.

The third corner office belonged to Peter Carmody, creative director of the agency, who actually would have occupied the second office except for the fact that he and Paul both felt that their offices should be geographically as far apart as possible.

Paul Dale kept the fourth corner office empty on purpose. His comptroller felt that it was a waste of rent money to keep it vacant, but Paul knew what he was doing: that empty corner office, carpeted wall to wall, was the honey pot that kept the younger executives outworking each other.

The Husband

Peter Carmody called the fourth office Paul's cheap incentive plan. Peter was one of those ageless men who cause comment at long-term school reunions because everybody else has gotten gray or fat or middle-aged in a conspicuous way and Peter somehow continued to look like a slightly older version of the fellow they had known at school. He was just over six feet tall, big-boned, bushy-brown-haired with a bit of a wave in front, pleasant-looking when he smiled, with articulate hands. He wore eyeglasses, but they were in his hands more often than on his eyes; he used them for making a point, for studying when embarrassed or bored, for gesturing at sketches, a kind of baton or ruler or wand. He kept one pair with him, a second in his desk, and a third at home. He'd sooner be caught without a pair of eyeglasses as without one of his hands.

Peter was the only man in the agency who wore a sport jacket and slacks to work, and in wintertime a sweater under the jacket. It was a sign of his easy self-confidence. The careful fellows who wore the latest fashions neatly pressed were unsure how much their talents were needed by the agency. Peter knew. Dale, Bowne, and Armstrong was known not only on Madison Avenue, but in Chicago and L.A. and Houston as very smart, and it had gotten that reputation because of Peter's gift for coming up with campaigns that didn't sell themselves but the product.

When Peter joined the agency nearly ten years earlier, Dale, Bowne, and Armstrong had as many names in its title as it had accounts—three, and none of them big. There were fewer than a dozen employees, counting Paul Dale and the mail boy. Paul felt as if he were run-

ning a retail store and desperately wanted a breakthrough. He consulted a head-hunting firm that found
Peter Carmody for him; he had to pay Peter very nearly
what he paid himself and give him a piece of the action to
entice him. Peter was barely thirty at the time and hot.

Within six months Dale, Bowne, and Armstrong was
making the columns regularly, adding clients as fast as
they could build staff to service them. Peter's work attracted companies who could measure their sales in relation to advertising campaigns and who then stuck with
them in a fickle industry. In the years since, Peter had developed at least four copywriters who, he claimed, could
do anything he could do, but nobody believed that, including the copywriters.

A quick glance at his watch told Peter it was almost
five. Time to go. He was just coming around the corner
of his desk when Elizabeth Kilter came into the room
and shut the door behind her.

He looked at her face, green eyes, black hair, then at
her figure in the deep green dress, then back at her face.

Most young girls, the secretaries around the shop, for
instance, looked soft. Most female executives he had met
looked hard. Elizabeth Kilter was an exception; she
looked softer than any youngster of nineteen. She was
Tony Cavallo's most senior artist. She made a lot of
money for a girl. She wasn't a girl, he corrected himself.
She was a woman.

Involuntarily Peter's eyes strayed to the family picture
at the corner of his desk—Rose and the two children.
Rose had been a beautiful girl, now was a beautiful girl
getting older. Elizabeth, he had discovered in the last

four months, was a woman. It had taken him very nearly to age forty to learn the difference.

"I just stopped in Alex's office," Elizabeth said. "You going to the wake?"

"Paul says I have to make a speech."

"What are you going to say?"

"I don't know yet." His hopes rose. "Want to walk over to the Biltmore with me?"

"I'm not going. I said good-bye to Alex in his office."

"It'll be an awfully lonely party for me if you don't come."

"I can't think of it as a party. Alex looks awful. What's he going to do with the rest of his life?"

"Retire."

"*To do what?*"

"It's company policy," said Peter uncomfortably.

"Screw company policy," said Elizabeth, and she was out the door, gone.

Peter, shaken, walked out around the edge of the bull-pen, past several offices, including Alex's, glad to see a bevy of glad-handers around Alex because he didn't want to talk to him just yet, and went the whole long way around two sides of the building until he was at Paul's open door.

"Come on in," hailed Paul. "Just getting ready to go over. Susan"—he jabbed a thumb out the door—"is closing up and goosing the stragglers over."

Peter made sure he was close enough so he couldn't be overheard by anyone outside. "What's going to happen to him?"

"Who, Alex? He'll be fine."

"His grandchildren live in California."

"So he'll visit California."

"Then what?"

"Maybe he'll move to California. What's this all about?"

"Alex and Martha have lived in Mamaroneck all their lives. Their friends are all there."

"It'll sort out."

"He doesn't like golf."

"He'll find something."

"All he knows is advertising."

"Yeah," said Paul.

Paul was right. Old Alex Ragdale, the first male employee of the firm to reach the mandatory retirement age, was the kind of account executive you trusted with a secure account, who could take clients to lunch or dinner, talk about their grandchildren as well as his own, describe a campaign devised by somebody else, keep the client posted. He couldn't make an ad, or get a new account, or keep an account that was in trouble.

"Let's go," said Paul.

Together they headed for the elevators, where a group of dolled-up typists and executive trainees shushed up the second the boss was in sight, and they all descended to the street in unreal quietness. The Biltmore was just a few blocks away.

Paul marched rather than walked, glancing sightlessly at passersby as if he were a colonel inspecting troops.

"How long do you want me to talk?" said Peter.

"Well, I'll say a few things officially and give him his present. I suppose Old Alex'll say a word or two, and then you can wax eloquent about his contribution to the firm."

"You said that with a straight face."

"Alex is reliable. You don't see much of that in the young job hoppers."

"Why don't we keep him on?"

"Peter, you just can't set a policy and then break it when the first employee reaches sixty-five."

Peter was tempted to say, "Yes, Colonel." He said nothing as they went through the revolving doors into the Biltmore.

They had rented several adjoining parlor rooms, where the partitions could be folded back to make a room large enough to accommodate one hundred thirty-four employees minus Elizabeth Kilter and plus Mrs. Ragdale, the only spouse invited to the affair. Within a short time the cloud of cigarette smoke, not all of which managed to rise, plus the senseless chitter-chatter and clinking of glasses, made Peter want to run for cover rather than circulate. He hated cocktail parties, but he had a duty to do. He watched several of the billing clerks getting the seventeen-year-old handsome Puerto Rican mailroom boy, unused to drinking, drunk. He watched the pairing off of some of the singles, in preparation for whatever was to come afterward. Finally he summoned his courage and went over to the Ragdales, insinuated himself among the well-wishers, pumped Alex's hand.

Old Alex Ragdale, as he was known since his retirement party was announced, was a short man, which meant that he had long ago lost the battle against a paunch, what with the constant lunching and dinnering and keeping up with the clients' cocktails. His hair was white, not gray. His full face had a constant blush from broken capillaries in the cheeks, and his sideburns looked as if they should have grown into mutton chops. Peter liked him. The man had done his duty for the firm and in turn had drawn his pay. But his work was such that he could be easily replaced by someone younger, at less pay, and he would soon be completely forgotten.

Mrs. Ragdale looked very much like her husband—a matched pair.

"I'm sorry your husband is leaving us," said Peter to Mrs. Ragdale.

"Confidentially," she said, "I think he is, too."

Alex stared her down, and she said no more. Peter, helpless at small talk, clapped Alex on the back, a gesture he regretted immediately because it seemed so condescending, and moved away through the crowd.

On the raised platform at the other end of the room, Paul was tapping the mike and ahemming for silence. "Folks," he said, when most eyes had turned toward him. "There, that's better now. Can you all hear me? Good. I'd ask you to be seated, but there aren't any seats." That got a short laugh from some of the younger employees. "So we'll keep the speeches down to size. Today," he said, gesturing at Alex, "we are gathered to pay our respects and to say good-bye, or rather *au revoir*, to the first employee of Dale, Bowne, and Armstrong to reach the retirement age of sixty-five. I am happy that the pension plan will provide our friend and colleague Alex Ragdale and his wife with security for the rest of their days."

This time there was some temperate cheering.

"I know," continued Paul, "that it is customary on

such occasions to give the departing employee a gold watch. However, I know that Alex Ragdale has had a busy business career—twenty-one years of it with this company, I am proud to say—and has not had much time to travel except on company business. Therefore," and he drew a long envelope out of his inside pocket, "I am pleased to present Alex Ragdale, one of our best-loved employees, with a pair of tickets for a round-the-world cruise which sails from New York harbor a week from Sunday!"

There were *Oooh*'s before he finished his sentence, and at the end of it wild cheering, as people parted to let Alex come up to the platform to receive the envelope. Alex's red face was redder than usual. Were there tears in his eyes?

He shook Paul's proffered hand, then whispered, "Thank you" into the microphone.

"One moment," said Paul. "To help Alex keep track of the time while he is on that round-the-world cruise, here also is a gold watch, only in keeping with the times, it runs on an energy cell and you don't have to wind it."

Alex took the watch with both his hands, afraid of dropping it.

"Read what it says," shouted someone from the audience.

Alex tried to check the flood of his feeling. He read the engraving on the back to a hushed room. "To Alex Ragdale from his friends and colleagues at Dale, Bowne, and Armstrong on the occasion of his retirement and in appreciation of his services."

"Go ahead," said Paul, "say a few words."

17

The Husband

Alex Ragdale handed the watch down to his wife and then grasped the microphone with his hands. Peter could see the perspiration beading on Alex's forehead.

"I'm not one of the creative people, and while I can hold my own in conversation with a client, I haven't anything new to say except thank you for your generous gifts and for coming here today and for your good wishes, and I would forgo them—the gifts, I mean—gladly if it meant I could continue working with you all. I miss you, and I hope you will invite me to come around and visit when I return."

He fled from the platform into his wife's arms. There was loud, continuing applause, and then someone whooped up, "For he's a jolly good fellow," and everyone joined in.

Paul's finger beckoned Peter up onto the platform. Peter swallowed the rest of his drink, handed his glass to somebody, and went up.

"Our creative director, Peter Carmody, wanted to say a few words."

You lying bastard, thought Peter.

"Ladies and gentlemen," Peter said, looking about the room at the glazed expressions, "or am I not describing you correctly." It got a laugh. "I could say that Alex Ragdale is an honorable man. But I played poker with him one day on the train out to Chicago." Laughter again. "I could say that Alex Ragdale is a virtuous man, but I have seen his right thumb and forefinger close on a secretary's behind." Mrs. Ragdale's laughter led the rest.

It was at this moment, his mind churning to think of what toastmastering nonsense he would say next, that Peter spotted Elizabeth Kilter at the very rear of the room, near the door. She had come, after all. Why? To see his puppet show on behalf of company policy?

"Now that he is going to retire," continued Peter, "Alex can play golf on weekdays"—someone cheered—"when there's no lineup at the first tee, except Alex admitted to me years ago that he learned golf only to play it with clients and that the game bores him stiff. He could garden—I've seen their lovely garden—but then what would Mrs. Ragdale do if Alex poached on her territory? He could get himself some Sears Roebuck tools and monkey around the house, but after seeing him try to get his office door back on its hinges after the furniture movers left last year, any monkeying he does around his house is likely to make his property values plunge! Seriously—"

It was that word "seriously" that got the big laugh.

"Not everyone is suited to living half a life on half pay. When Alex gets back from his round-the-world trip, when he's had enough of living in a stateroom and hoping the Dramamine keeps working, I think the first Monday back, I think Alex should show up in his old office and get to work and earn the other half of his pay right alongside the rest of us!"

For a moment there was a dreadful quiet in the huge room as people looked to Paul for a cue, then received it from Alex Ragdale, who came back onto the platform, saying, "Bless you," and Mrs. Ragdale was up there beside him, hugging Peter, and Peter, embarrassed, said into the microphone just, "Enjoy the party," and left the platform, catching a glimpse of the artery pulsing in Paul's forehead. Peter worked his way through the pleased crowd to where he had seen Elizabeth standing, but she was no longer there.

The Husband

Peter wanted to get out into the street as fast as possible, but the coatroom woman—she was older than Alex, wasn't she?—moved slowly, and by the time he got his coat and gave her a quarter, Paul was at his side.

"How are we going to get out of this one?"

"Maybe we don't have to."

"You should have consulted me."

"I didn't even consult myself, Paul. It just came."

Paul, his anger flaring, marched back to the crowded room. Peter headed for the subway which would take him off Manhattan Island, Elizabeth's island, to a suburb where Rose kept house for him and the children. He hoped the children were still awake. After seeing Alex Ragdale and his wife clutching at straws, he didn't want to face an evening alone with Rose.

Chapter Two

Peter Carmody opened the door of his home, set down his bulging briefcase, and surveyed his domain. The two children were lying ass-up on the carpet, watching television, and didn't turn to greet him.

Were they ignoring him, or had they simply not heard him come in?

He opened the door again and this time let it slam. Twelve-year-old Margaret whipped over and in a second was on her feet running toward his outstretched arms. Ah, he thought, she hadn't heard me the first time.

Jonathan, a blasé thirteen, turned more slowly so that his eye would not lose sight of the television screen until the very last second. By that time Margaret was swarming all over her father, taking his hat, holding onto his arm as if it were the limb of a backyard tree.

"Hi," said Jonathan.

"Not yet," said Peter. "I haven't had a drink."

In an instant Jonathan and Margaret were both at the alcove bar, their hands moving perilously among the glassware, vying with each other for the martini mixings. The homecoming ritual had begun.

Peter was pleased. Waiters and wives, he thought, regretting the thought almost immediately, are paid to serve you. When children do it spontaneously . . .

It hadn't been spontaneous. He had had to give the signal.

"Before I succumb to the decibels," he said, "would one of you silence that box?"

Margaret left the martini mixing to Jonathan and turned off the TV set. "We were watching the news, like you said we could."

That hadn't been the news he had caught out of the corner of his eye.

"And after the news?"

"A program," said Margaret, playing it safe.

"And then?"

"Another program."

"I'm sure they were highly educational."

Both children laughed. Peter joined in. What the hell, he had long ago lost the television battle.

"If the news intrigues you," he said to them both, "read a newspaper."

Jonathan was pouring the martini off the ice. "Newspapers are a bore," he said.

That was an echo, not a thought originating with Jonathan, a thought remembered. The newspaper strike a year ago had convinced Peter how much of each day he had let drift away, running his eyes up and down columns, across lines, reading news and items that were not news in the hope that they would make his subway ride pass quickly and then discovering, when newspapers were not available, that he did not miss them, that somehow one heard about the important news anyway. He tried a book, a book he did not need to read for business, and surprisingly it had interested him the way books once had when he was twelve or thirteen. He had finished the book on the ride home that evening and felt an embarrassing sense of accomplishment—*I read a book!*—as if it were some sort of achievement, the resumption, after a hiatus, of an old pleasure.

He wondered why those bobbing heads on the subway, when there was a strike and the regular papers were not available, why did they go like lemmings for newspapers brought in from other cities, or the second-rate fly-by-nights, and behind these substitute screens of newsprint, scanning, scanning, before they were quickly or ultimately bored? Why did *they* not try a book? He noticed, with surprise again, that three or four, no, six, actually were reading books. For a moment he felt a bond, as if they were all members of a club, outlanders among the newsprint. Of course he had overblown the experience, the sense of triumph. He actually had a fantasy about millions of middle-class men suddenly discovering on their shelves at home the unread books, the books read by their wives or children or by themselves when they were younger, rediscovering the pleasure of getting lost in a book, as each surely must have done as a boy.

"Did you hear what I said?" asked Jonathan.

Peter, not knowing how long his mind had been distracted, or in fact what Jonathan had said that started him off this way, said, "Of course."

Just then the swinging doors from the kitchen opened, and Rose came through to greet him. Her face was still beautiful in a public sense, a perfect oval topped by auburn hair, a nose that couldn't be faulted, a fine mouth. It was the eyes really that troubled him as the years went on, their restless lack of ease, their defensiveness. Was it a tenderness they protected—Rose had been tender in the early years—or a vacuity? Rose's surface was fine, perhaps brilliant, her clothes carefully chosen—she had even picked perfectly the chic, colorful apron she now wore while preparing dinner—her makeup barely visible as makeup, a ready public smile. But her eyes, the visible body openings, looked beautiful only when they were closed. Open, you saw the floundering within, the lack of purpose, of interior style, of personality one could wear when naked.

"How did things go at the office?" she asked out of habit, and Peter remembered suddenly that the book he had read during the newspaper strike was an English novel called *The Go-Between*. He had brought it home to Rose that night, finishing it on the train, and had told her what pleasure it had given him, and she had said, as he expected, that she would read it at once, that night in bed before going to sleep. As he recalled now, she had read less than a chapter and had never opened the book again.

He hadn't reminded her. Was that a fault? A recognition of reality?

"Isn't this the night what's-his-name got his farewell party?" asked Rose, remembering the special reason for Peter's late arrival home.

"Alex Ragdale," said Peter.

"Yes, of course," said Rose, her accent at its most controlled, a faint hint of carefully cultivated British English that always disappeared within several sentences but caught up again and again during the course of an evening, except in moments of tension, when Rose spoke like her mother.

"Weren't you supposed to make a speech?"

Yes, he would have liked to tell the whole of it, the prelude with Paul, Alex's terror of dropping off the cliff of retirement, what Paul had said, especially what he had said—one wanted to tell one's wife stories of minor courage—but Rose had already declared herself on retirement when the company plan was introduced: retirement was a good thing, devoutly to be worked for.

"I made a short speech and came straight home," Peter said.

She had skipped her ritual kiss on the side of his face, the point she had aimed for when she came through the swinging doors from the kitchen. "Good," she said. "It would have been awful if you got here after Jack and Amanda arrived."

He had completely forgotten. Guests for dinner. Oh well, the Baxters would make four. Four was better than two; it might keep an argument with Rose from flaring. Over what? *Over anything.*

Peter let himself slip down into his armchair.

"The children were perfectly adorable today," said Rose. "They fixed up a tent with blankets in the basement, put up a sign saying 'The Facts of Life' on it, and called all their friends in. They charged a penny admission and let everyone into the tent at the same time."

"What was on the inside?"

"Nothing," said Rose. "Just another sign saying 'The First Fact of Life Is: Know What You're Paying For.' "

"What a dirty trick," he said for Rose's benefit.

The children are a saving grace, he thought.

Jonathan, aping in his speech a cross between his mother's attempt at an accent and a butler he must have seen on television, said three words as if they were three separate sentences. "It . . . was . . . fun." In his hand was the martini, slopping ever so slightly over the side.

"Were the kids mad?" Peter asked him.

"They ran right home," said Jonathan, "to try the same stunt on some other kids."

That's the way it is, thought Peter. When you're conned, you learn how not to be conned exactly the same way next time, but what you relish is using your new-found knowledge to con someone else. How did child-less couples ever learn about life? Oh, well, most couples who had children didn't really observe the behavior of children closely either. Certainly he hadn't until a few years back, when Rose's speeches had become so pre-dictable that he began to look to the children for sur-prise. They had become his university.

Jonathan handed over the martini, and Margaret set a cocktail napkin down on the table.

"Martooni," said Jonathan.

"Houdini," said Margaret.

Then both children together said, "Watch it disap-pear!"

Rose disliked these rituals. They were childish. So they were, thought Peter, but he and the kids liked them. Rose couldn't be suffering as much as her expression pretended. He sipped the drink.

He sipped at it again, watching the children's expression. He smiled. "It's good."

Immediately the children clustered to him, imperiling the drink, which Peter quickly set down, sensing—how do these feelings travel?—that Rose was about to make a short speech.

"Peter," she said, "is it wise to make bartenders out of the children?"

In adolescence Peter hadn't wanted to be the usual things—a doctor, a lawyer—engineering was a big and coming thing, but when he inquired as to what engineers *do*, he lost interest. He really wanted to be a king, as all boys probably do at one moment in time, though with Peter the idea became fixed, an interesting, unrealizable idea: to be in absolute charge. In high school—was it the first year or the second?—his class was given the assignment of writing an essay on a vocation, and it was then that Peter wrote his famous eight or ten pages on kingship which, when it became known, elicited snickers from some of the kids and surprise from the teacher, who gave it an "A" because it was well written and sparkled with quotations from Shakespeare and Shaw and some miscellaneous ones from Bartlett and seemed to have wit even in those parts he had composed himself. The essay was posted on the bulletin board along with the other "A's," which is where it earned its scorn from the other boys, though the girls in the class seemed to have a different view of it and, he later learned, talked about it a good deal among themselves during recess. One girl, a very pretty girl in fact, stayed after school to copy the essay out after asking his permission. He was flustered, of course, wondering why she had asked. Was it courtesy, or did she want to call his attention to the fact that she was copying it out?

Her name was Rose.

Actually Peter was annoyed at himself for suspecting Rose's reason for copying his essay. She was paying attention—wasn't that a good sign? A day or two later, she found her way to him during a recess and talked about his essay. She liked the idea of someone wanting to be a king, or something like a king.

Peter asked her to go to the movies on Saturday night mainly because of the way things were shaping up among his friends at the time. Two or three of them would have a date of sorts on Saturday, all going to the local movie, of course, and the rest would go to the same movie as a pack. There was a distinction in going to the picture with a girl, paying for her, buying popcorn for them both, nodding over at the stags, who had to act tough and restless whenever interest in the movie flagged.

When the boys were together they would talk about baseball mostly, but occasionally about a girl. For instance, there was a girl about their age—her name was B. (they never said her full name)—who was said to have actually had intercourse with three Italian boys on one night (the Italian boys seemed to go in for real sex, rather than just petting like the other kids). It was said of B. that on that night she and the three boys had all been in the room together, two of them watching while the other performed, switching until each had had his chance, and that then B. had actually done something—the descriptions varied wildly—with all three boys together.

The boys also talked about Verna, who was older and not very bright, who had left high school when her pregnancy showed and then afterward worked as a waitress in a place frequented by truck drivers. Verna was said to take one of the younger boys up to her one-room apartment occasionally, and things would go on with the baby right there in the crib.

Sex was beginning to be not only colorful anecdotes for the boys but a matter of economic interchange as well. There was quite a traffic in contraceptives in school. Peter was quite sure that most of the boys who bought them didn't use them but resold them to other boys, even at a slight loss, in order to get hooked onto the bravado train.

Peter had taken a girl named Sally to the movies several times. She was two grades ahead at school, extremely witty and bright, which is the reason Peter gave for going with her; but when he was in the mood to tell himself the truth, his interest in Sally lay in the fact that her breasts were fully developed and she sometimes wore the kind of brassiere which let the nipples show through the dress. He sometimes held hands with Sally in the movies but couldn't try anything else because it would shatter, he thought, the intellectual foundation of their friendship. Peter had a tentative date with Sally, but he was now convinced nothing would come of that, at least nothing to do with the sexual feeling that was preoccupying his days and sometimes exciting him beyond tolerance. So he called Sally and gave some tepid excuse about

having a bad cold and then let his mind stray freely about
Rose, who had agreed to go to the movies on Saturday
night.

Suddenly Peter realized that Sally would probably be
at the movies on Saturday also, would see him. Oh, well, if
it made her jealous it might lead to something, and if it
made her angry, it couldn't be helped. Was that the beginning of duplicity?

As for Rose, Peter didn't see why he should have any
reservations about seeing how he could make out. She
had made the first approach, she wasn't a tramp like B.
and Verna, and they didn't have an intellectual rapport
to spoil. He thought about Rose on and off for the rest
of the week, and by Saturday he was quite prepared to
see how far he could go with her.

It went as far as marriage, though it took seven years.

From the beginning, Rose was quite a feather in his
cap. She was pretty enough to be stared at. She knew
how to dress in a way which attracted a great deal of attention at dances and parties. She admired his ambitions,
which were very large. And there was one other thing.

One evening after they had been seeing each other for
several weeks, Peter had promised to keep Rose company
while she baby-sat for the Burkes. The evening got off
to a brilliant start when Peter picked up Rose at her
home. He greeted her mother in the kitchen and then
her father in the living room. Rose's father was snoozily
reading the *Daily Mirror*, a New York tabloid which
contained very little news of more than local interest,
pictures of car accidents, and publicity stills of Holly-
wood starlets, a newspaper held in contempt by Peter's
family for as long as he could remember. Peter shook

Rose's father's hand, then took the tabloid from him, which surprised her father, and ripped it in two, which surprised everyone including himself. Rose's father was livid, Rose's mother, who hurriedly came in from the kitchen when voices were raised, was amused, and Rose —well, she was overjoyed. Her fellow had taught her father a lesson.

They left the house hurriedly, happily, and got to the Burkes just in time. As soon as the Burkes had left for their bridge game and Rose and Peter were alone with the sleeping baby, she kissed him, a long, slow, exploratory kiss which he broke away from only because he had an erection, which embarrassed him.

Rose put on a record and Peter, mainly to calm himself, made a big do about investigating the Burkes' library, which didn't help because in the course of his explorations he found behind some other books a copy of a paperbound and poorly printed book which Mr. Burke had probably brought back from a business trip abroad. Rose and Peter read the book together, glancing at the clock once in a while because the Burkes were due home at eleven. He didn't know at the time if Rose was being aroused by the book, as he was, or was aroused by his excitement, but they did kiss again, and Peter had to exert every restraint to keep from touching her—until it happened. Rose—he never knew whether it was by chance or will—let her hand come to rest, it was only for a second or two, on his pants at a critical point. He looked at her face, expecting anger, though he had had nothing to do with it, and instead found a beatific expression, or was it admiration again?

It was half past ten. With so little time left, Rose

helped him uncover her breasts, which were lovely, but as he touched them he thought he was going to have an orgasm right then and pulled away. She took this as an affront, so he had to explain, his breath coming hard, and she was so sympathetic and understanding, he was overwhelmed. They were kissing each other in a head-long rush to Peter knew not where, when he suddenly felt her hand moving in a way which alarmed him because it seemed so experienced and yet he was certain she couldn't have had this kind of experience, and before his troubled thought could lead him anywhere, his reservoir of youth exploded.

There was a lot of fixing up to do before eleven but they made it, and when the Burkes returned, the book was back in place and the two of them were sitting on opposite ends of the couch listening to records.

Peter and Rose said very little on the way home, holding hands all the way. Peter was a little leery of going in because of the incident with the newspaper, but Rose assured him that her parents would be asleep. Which wasn't quite true. Her mother did come out in her bathrobe just long enough to say, "Glad you're home. Don't stay up too late," which Peter took to mean he might stay a while. When her mother went back and closed their bedroom door on the father's snoring, Peter kissed Rose gently and learned something he was to know much better as the years went on, that to Rose a kiss was never a kiss but an introduction. Their bodies were very close when they kissed again. All Peter's fears came bounding back, including that of her father's wrath, but Rose assured him with what seemed like serene confidence that in her bedroom they couldn't be heard. For a second

Peter felt she was rushing and wasn't it the man's job to take the lead, but all this was brushed away by a fierce appetite, whetted and now seemingly uncontrollable.

Rose excused herself and came out of the bathroom moments later, wearing a nightdress through which he could see not just the outlines of her body but the shape of her breasts, the nipples, the dark hair where her legs met and, when she turned, her bottom.

"What if they come in?" he made his voice say in a whisper.

Rose simply put a finger on his lips to silence him. She withdrew her fingers in favor of her lips, which brushed rather than touched his, but enough for him to taste the toothpaste she must have used in those seconds away.

When they were both on the bed, he found himself kissing the edges of her mouth and then her lips full on, and finally her now slightly open mouth. He felt an impetus that would not subside.

He raised her gown as if it were a curtain. She turned away, as if in shyness, but in turning revealed more, and soon he found himself kissing her body, and when her gown interfered, she let him take it off. She gestured at his clothes. It seemed to take him forever to get everything off, except his socks, which he didn't think of as curious or amusing until afterward.

Peter felt embarrassed about his erection and wanted to turn the light off, but she took his hand away from the switch. He had a great deal of difficulty at first, though thinking at the same time how automatic it was, how you didn't have to learn. He was kissing her deeply, exploring her mouth as if to focus attention there, when in fact it was the thrust and thrust of his lower body that held his attention and hers, and suddenly the delicious agony couldn't be kept back.

The thought of it broke into fragments in his mind: he had done it, it was wrong, it was the most exciting thing that ever happened to him, they had taken no precautions, and finally, as he slipped out, he saw in a wave of fright and triumph the slight stain that said it had been first for her, too.

Terrified now that her father would rip him as Peter had ripped the newspaper, he dressed quickly and impolitely left Rose as soon as he could, flooded with guilt, shame, and exhilaration. . . .

All of this went through Peter's mind like the shapes of a kaleidoscope as he watched Rose's adult face intent on a question he had not answered.

"Peter," she said, "I'm asking you if it's wise to make bartenders out of the children?"

Peter turned to Jonathan. "Do you want to grow up to be a bartender?"

"I want to be a microbiologist." Jonathan pronounced the word perfectly. Peter would have to find out what microbiologists do, just in case the idea stuck. To Jonathan he said, "Now bartenders talk to nice, relaxed people all day. Microbiologists talk to other microbiologists. You'd better be a bartender. Margaret, my pretty, do you want to be a bartender?"

Margaret shook her head. "I want to be a nurse in a psychiatric hospital."

"You see, Rose, what horrible futures are in store for these children," Peter said. "They'd be better off as bartenders. Jonathan, stop eyeing my drink. If you want a sip, take a sip." He was challenging Rose, and she picked it up.

"Now please don't do that," she said.

"Bartenders," said Jonathan, an arch of wisdom over one eye, "are not supposed to drink." Was his voice changing, or was that just a huskiness Peter detected in his son's pitch?

Peter nodded in the direction of the glass. "Go ahead, try it."

"No, it tastes awful," said Jonathan in his husky voice.

Rose, a slight genuine alarm in her voice, asked, "How do you know what it tastes like?"

"I licked the ice once." Jonathan's face registered a facsimile of disgust.

Margaret was not going to let Jonathan hold the center of the stage for long. "Daddy," she said, her voice a controlled instrument, "Daddy, I love you."

Peter looked skeptical. "What's the pitch? When you say it that way, I want the words behind the words."

Margaret looked defeated. "Daddy, how do you always know what's going on in my head?"

Peter lifted her chin with his curled finger. "Everybody butters up people once in a while. What did you want to say?"

"Are you going to get drunk tonight?"

How do you deal with a child who is so clear, innocent and direct? Jonathan was looking at him. So was Rose. It was a real question.

"If Jack and Amanda are boring," Peter said, "I might."

"What does drunk feel like?"

"Gimme a kiss," said Peter, hugging her.

"What does it feel like?"

"Next time I'm drunk, I'll let you feel," said Peter.

Rose looked hopeful that the exchange might be over.
"I mean it," said Margaret. "Don't joke."

"Well," said Peter, deciding quickly that he had better
try to be accurate, "how you feel depends on what you
felt like before you got drunk. I mean, if you felt lousy
before, you're likely to feel better during, and—"

Rose cut him off. "Almost always worse afterward.
Peter, dear, do put on a clean shirt for the evening." The
accent was London now, with a try for Oxford.

"The Baxters know I've got a clean shirt," said Peter.
"Can't I just show them one?"

"Look at that spot."

Peter suddenly felt very tired. "That's not a spot," he
said, "it's a Biltmore canapé."

The phone rang with a shattering brilliance, as if the
ringing of a phone at this hour in this family was a signal.
Rose knew it. The kids sensed it. Margaret glanced at
her father and picked up the receiver.

Peter watched Maggie as if she were, for that moment,
a stranger's child, a little skirted girl, never again a baby,
though he wanted so to continue babying her, not quite
grown-up but getting there. Getting where? he thought.
And for an instant he remembered Rose on that first
night, just a few years older than Margaret now. Unbe-
lievable!

"Yes, my daddy is home." She sounded frighteningly
grown-up. Margaret put her hand over the mouthpiece,
watching her hand all the while as if to be certain that
all sound were really blocked. Then she said to her father

—was there a secretiveness in her voice, an edge of conspiracy, a confidence?—"It's Miss Kilter."

"Oh?" said Peter, getting up, knowing the intended casualness of his "Oh?" had not really come out that way. He had always thought acting was a snap until Rose —how long ago was it now?—persuaded him to take a small part in a community theater play so that he'd be around to see her perform. He had learned with what seemed a terrible shock at the time that it was one thing to feel nuances and quite another to make them come out in his voice. He had learned to respect acting then as something quite difficult to do well, and really admirable since it was one of those things everybody thought they could do, and so few actually could. He had intended casualness now and had sounded as if he were walking up to a witness box in open court.

He took the phone.

"Hello, Elizabeth. Yes. No, the three members of my august household are immobilized, staring at my canapé spot. It was a soggy canapé. Yes, I'm listening."

There he was in two worlds, one coming over on the telephone, Elizabeth trying to keep a cool voice, asking a necessary question, and his family focused on him. *En famille*, he thought, the real world, and yet the wire running from the phone sang.

"Of course, I looked at it before I left the office," he said. "I thought the first sketch was far better."

He knew what Elizabeth had started to say and cut in quickly. "That's not the first time Paul was wrong today." Again she said what she had to, and he answered, "That's not the first time a client was wrong."

Could they hear the sound of her voice? he wondered.

"That's also not the first time that Paul and a client agreed. Work up the first sketch," he said.

At last Rose moved. "Come, children," she said, "let Daddy have his conversation in private." She took them out the swinging door to the kitchen because it was the quickest escape route. What did the children sense?

"They've taken to the hills," he said into the phone, then, "Let's get fired together."

He liked that thought. Fired. It meant someone took action, got rid of him, made it easy. Easy?

With quietness, with a sense of risk, knowing he shouldn't say it, he said into the telephone, into the wire, through a dozen connections across the city to Elizabeth's ear, "I love you."

The house seemed hushed, and for a moment he wished the television were blaring.

"Yes," Elizabeth answered. Reserved Elizabeth reserved expressions of love for the most intimate moments, when their bodies were locked and moving into the private provinces of joy.

They were connected by silence and by the background imperfections of the telephone system, whose silence was not yet absolute and therefore an intruder. And so, after a time, he hung up gently, not certain whether he had whispered good-bye. Then he cleared his throat—that seemed loud—and whistled the three notes he and Jon used as their identifying sign. From the kitchen he heard Jon's three-note reply.

When they trooped through the door, he stared at them as if they were strangers. Was it because the unit he now belonged to might be with Elizabeth and not here? How much did they sense, how much did they know? The most? The least?

It was Rose's face he was looking at now. It had slack in it, slack and lines. "I suppose it's all right for us to come in," she said.

"I didn't ask you to leave," Peter said in a voice that he realized at once was too loud and too belligerent, but how to control it? "Rose, why don't you have a martini? It'll loosen up the charley horse in your face muscles." He hadn't meant to say anything like that.

"My expression is my business, Peter."

"You can't see your expression. I can." *Shut up, shut up*, he thought.

And there's Jonathan, thirteen years old, heaven help him, and he's going to try to make peace.

"Mommy, Daddy, please don't argue tonight."

"Done," said Peter, suddenly relieved. "In fact, I'll even change my shirt. Now you kids get upstairs and change into your bedtime regalia."

"And bathrobes," Rose called after them.

"By all means," said Peter. "Jonathan, put on your smoking jacket!" *Stop needling her*, he thought.

"I don't smoke," said Jonathan from the stairway, laughing.

A good kid.

"And how is Miss Kilter?" said Rose.

A frontal. Let it pass.

"Fine," he said.

Rose stood there looking at him, lost, he thought, the girl who'd married the fellow who was a hero at school because that was what success was then for them all, and the fellow who needed the prestige of a good-looking girl like Rose on his arm, wedlocked with a house and children, all of their adult lives a common past.

Keep quiet, he thought. *Don't open your mouth.*

"What do you want me to say?" he said. "Look, I'm sorry about that crack. My nerves are on edge."

"Mine are on the same edge. Can't we . . . ?"

She trailed off, passing the cue to him.

"Can't we what?"

"Try," said Rose. "Stop living from day to day."

"How do you want to live, wall to wall?" There he went. *Bigmouth.*

"Peter, I'm serious. We never, you know, spend time alone together anymore. Not really." Too much time, he thought.

"I know how we could do time together," he said, and noticed the look of sudden hope in her face. "When the Baxters get here, let's kill them and get put away in a coeducational jail." *Bigmouth, stop.* "If we kick and scream, we might get solitary confinement together. You and me. Alone."

"What's wrong, Peter?"

Husbands he knew just played the game, said nothing, kept the cork in, the lid on, let things pass. It was easier that way, but Peter had never learned—would never learn?—to stop the connection between thought and speech. For a second he thought he had it under control, but she said again, "What's wrong?" and that did it.

"I know the damn record by heart," he blurted, seeing the surprise and pain in Rose's face. She had not meant anything, had not intended trouble, wanted to soothe, smooth over. *Let it go.*

"I'm bored," he said, and he knew he couldn't stop. "Classically, cumulatively, infinitely, overwhelmingly bored. Another couple of years of this and I'll be hooked on television." He was shaking his fist at the box, knowing that was not what his fist was for. "If you watch that thing long enough, you die sitting up, right there in that chair."

Was she trying to embrace him, or just to plant the ritual kiss denied him earlier?

"I haven't washed up yet," he said.

"I don't mind," said Rose. "I care for you, Peter. You don't believe half the things you say. Why should I?"

Thank heaven people believe what they want to believe.

"I'll see how dinner's coming. Do change your shirt."

"I'll change," said Peter.

Upstairs, like an addict taking the needle out of a drawer, he went for the bedroom phone and dialed. Elizabeth answered before the first ring was over. He didn't have anything to say to her. Why had he called? She was pleased, but why had he called?

"Just making contact," he said into the phone, feeling like a fool.

"Thank you," said Elizabeth. And that was all there was to it. He hung up, blood in his face and his heart going fast. He turned to find Jonathan at the door, dressed in the Coca-Cola costume.

"Jesus!" said Peter.

"Guess again," said Jonathan.

That kid would be all right. Would he, though, if

The Husband

Peter left, went off to live with Elizabeth, came only on visits, like jail or summer camp?

The Coca-Cola costume was one of a hundred thousand distributed in one week, free with six-packs, just in time for Halloween, a hundred thousand walking billboards: Invented by Peter Carmody.

Jonathan went into his act, and Peter could tell at once that it had been rehearsed.

"While Coca-Cola's got the touch
Six full ounces isn't much
Pepsi's got the quantity
But Coca-Cola is the drink for me."

Peter broke up laughing. "Great, great," he said. "I can retire. I'm absolutely replaceable."

And now Margaret was behind him in her Coca-Cola costume, vying for attention. "I'm working on one, too, Daddy. Jonathan's isn't buckeye enough."

"Dad," said Jonathan, "isn't my song buckeye?"

"Where did either of you pick up that expression?"

"Well, see," said Margaret, "you said Mr. Dale likes buckeye."

Damn Paul, thought Peter. He thought it and said it.

"Mommy," said Jonathan, "says you shouldn't damn Mr. Dale in front of us. It undermines our respect for authority.

Damn her, he thought.

"You kids listen to me." He hadn't intended the stern note in his voice. He softened it. "Part of my job is to teach you to undermine some kinds of authority."

There was Rose behind Margaret and Jonathan. Had she heard? Did it matter?

"Daddy," said Margaret, her eyes glistening with mischief, "I want to be in advertising like you."

"A moment ago you wanted to be a nurse," said Rose.

"Oh, well, see, that was for laughs," said Margaret. "Being a nurse is icky."

"Your grandmother was a nurse," said Rose.

"So was Florence Nightingale," said Margaret, so sure of herself. "I want to make up advertising ideas like Daddy."

Peter thought he could put a stop to it. "Advertising," he said, "is no place for women."

"Well, see," said Margaret, "Miss Kilter is in advertising."

The silence lasted what, a second, two?

"Miss Kilter," said Rose, "is a career woman."

Had she wanted it to sound sinister?

"She's not married. She doesn't have a family. She doesn't have a man of her own, like Daddy. You don't want to grow up like Miss Kilter, Margaret."

Margaret, side blinders on her eyes, fixed her vision on Peter.

"You're doing fine, Margaret," said Peter. "You grow up any way you like."

Change the subject.

"Is a career man like a career woman, Daddy?" asked Jonathan.

Peter said sternly, "You were supposed to save that outfit for Halloween."

"Daddy," said Margaret, "do you want me to grow up like Miss Kilter?"

The Husband

How had it gotten out of hand?

Rose put her arms around both children. "To bed."

"Daddy," said Margaret, stalling, "what is advertising?"

"Everybody knows what advertising is," said Rose. "Get ready for bed."

"It's a fair question, isn't it, Daddy?"

Peter touched Margaret's head, her hair. "You ought to be in politics. You're a real smoothie."

"Never mind that," said Margaret, her voice testing to see if she had gone too far. "What is advertising?"

"Well, it's a business," said Peter, hoping to escape. He still hadn't changed his shirt.

"Everything is a business," said Jonathan.

Margaret shushed him. "You keep out of this."

"Business is for men," said Jonathan, refusing to be silenced.

"Miss Kil—" and Margaret stopped. Something had told her she had stepped over the line. How to recoup? "Is Mommy in business?" she went on.

"Well," said Peter, "she's very busy all day long, shopping, buying clothes, returning them, buying more clothes, electric toothbrushes . . ." *Watch your step. Don't needle.* The Baxters would be here soon. They'd drink. All would pass.

But there was Margaret, questioning. "Is business making money?"

"Not all businesses make money."

"Well, see," said Margaret, "if Mommy doesn't make any money, then isn't she in business, too?"

"I give up."

"Now do get to bed," said Rose, the voice in mid-phrase becoming vaguely British again. "You'll never be able to get up for school in the morning."

"Well, see, he hasn't answered what advertising is."

Cornered, Peter tried. "Advertising is . . . a way of telling people . . . about what to buy?" He hadn't meant it to be a question.

"Like on television," said Jonathan.

"Hopefully not always," said Peter, smiling.

"Well, see, don't people *know* what to buy?" Lovely Margaret.

"Sometimes," said Peter, "they buy the wrong product."

"Like Pepsi-Cola?"

"Exactly," said Peter.

"What's wrong with Pepsi?" asked Margaret.

"Daddy doesn't have them as a client, stupid," said Jonathan, scoring.

"I like Seven-Up," said Margaret, Peter immediately clapping his hand over her mouth in jest.

"Shhhh, we must be loyal to the client. Like Paul. Paul is very loyal. He even drinks rum and Coke, the great beginner's drink."

It was Rose's turn. "Paul is hardly a beginner."

Jonathan was looking directly at Peter when he said, "Paul bosses Daddy."

The reaction came from Margaret with her bunched-up fists, and Peter swung them apart. "Now wait a minute!"

"Tell him you don't have a boss," said Margaret, puffing.

"I do," said Peter. "Everybody has a boss."

"Why aren't you the boss of everybody?" asked Margaret.

"The president," said her brother, "is the boss of everybody."

"To bed!" said Rose, and this time, played out, they kissed Peter good night and went, leaving him straightening his tie.

That instant the front bell rang, and the kids escaped from Rose and went charging down the stairs to open the door.

Jack Baxter was older than Peter—not much, he only looked that way. His body, fully clothed, seemed slack, and it was hard to imagine that Jack had played great tennis once.

In the upper reaches of the law, there are lawyers you know in a second handle financial corporate matters, and the only crime they run into in their work is embezzlement. Then there are lawyers who don't really practice law at all, the show business lawyers who are really star-level agents, packagers of talent, deal makers, and leave contracts to junior partners as a near-irrelevance, something to be completed once the deal is made so there will be something in the files to refer to in the event of a breach. Then there are the courtroom performers, the surgeons of the law, who enjoy catching a witness in a lie right on the stand. Few of these, Peter knew, had any special interest in justice.

Jack Baxter was a poor bit of all three types. His corporate clients were very small guys with very small problems and liked Jack because he treated these problems as if they involved a merger of Du Pont and General Motors. Jack also played the show business lawyer, but only for two or three nightclub types he had met along the way. And Jack enjoyed the courtroom bit, but the courts were always lower courts, and Jack felt most comfortable when he knew the judge and when the ploy he was going to try was one he had tried successfully before; so he practiced on people not in the courtroom but in living rooms and bars and trains, where he didn't have to win or lose.

When a potential client paid a first visit, Jack would listen to his story and then say, "You don't want a tough lawyer," at which the new client would always assure Jack that was exactly what he wanted. So Jack made out all right so far as clients went. It was just that he knew now that he wouldn't ever reach the big time, and it got him physically in his appearance, the slackness of a college athlete who now knew he'd never hear the cheering again.

Next to Jack in the doorway, stood Amanda, who in her college days was a very attractive girl but had turned out to be sterile, and that was that. Her growing up from dolls to dates to being the busiest baby-sitter in the neighborhood had been pointed like a rocket toward motherhood. At the moment she and Jack heard the conclusive news from the doctor, Amanda Baxter's main fuse turned off for life. Jack had said all the nice-guy things, such as, it didn't matter, or they could always adopt, or think how free it would leave them to enjoy their own lives, and sometimes he really wanted to believe one or another of these things, but Amanda had thrown the switch on all that. For a while, bride Amanda

47

was in what a doctor described as "an acute nervous condition." Once when she had a very realistic nightmare about having a hysterectomy performed on her, which of course she had not, it looked bad, but within a day or two Jack had the sense to empty out Amanda's closetful of dolls and give them to the Salvation Army, which brought her back to her senses. However, Amanda had been brought up in an atmosphere of extreme religiosity, which of course turned her as well as her sister and two brothers into agnostics, but Amanda was never able really to shake out the idea that sex was for procreation, and she deeply resented, now that she couldn't procreate, Jack's occasional insistence on taking his pleasure.

Amanda was very well liked by her female friends, all of whom had children. Rose liked to be with her, Peter suspected, because Amanda was more like a sister than a friend, in appearance definitely an older sister, very reliable, comforting, and in no way a threat.

This evening Amanda and Rose greeted each other at the door, as usual, with the kind of exclamations and embraces usually reserved for airports and train stations, though they had seen each other within the week. Jack and Peter shook hands. Peter thought that after all these years, he and Jack still didn't like each other well enough to begin a social evening without the formality of a handshake.

Peter shooed the kids back up the stairs and Rose motioned him upstairs, too, pointing to his shirt.

"Can't I make my friends a drink?" Peter thought his use of the word "friends" a definite concession that would please Rose enough to have her lay off. She didn't.

"You've got something to attend to," she said.

Peter, with a look of mock supplication, turned to Amanda and Jack. "See this spot on my shirt? That's a Biltmore canapé. Does it offend you?"

Jack and Amanda were puzzled.

"Okay," said Peter, "I guess it does. I'll change." He made the stairs two at a time.

"What's gotten into him?" Jack said to Rose.

"Two martinis. Two that I saw. God knows what he had at that office party."

"Well," said Jack, "we've got some catching up to do. Rosie, my love, suppose I make the drinks?"

"Rosie is not your love," said Amanda.

"There goes that literal mind," said Jack, "just like Maggie, except it's excusable in a kid."

"Now don't you two start," said Rose. With a gesture, she turned the bar over to Jack.

Jack quickly hung his jacket on a chair, rolled his shirtsleeve cuffs a few turns and, clinking two glasses, asked, "Rosie, what'll you have? I'm having an economy-sized Scotch myself."

"I'll just get myself some orange juice from the kitchen," said Rose.

"Rosie, I think you should have a drink." There was no mistaking the lascivious tone of his voice. "A drink will positively loosen you up."

"I don't need loosening up," said Rose, disappearing through the swinging door. Jack was left alone, pouring Scotch liberally over ice for himself. Alone with Amanda.

"You've got a dirty mind," said Amanda.

Jack was not about to have his spirits squashed. "Everybody's got a dirty mind," he said, "just some people are stuffy about it."

Amanda was screwing her lips together, trying to build an anger she didn't quite feel, when Rose came back in with the pitcher of orange juice and handed it to Jack, who plunked some ice in two large-sized glasses and sloshed some juice over the rocks with the kind of flourishes magicians once used in vaudeville. He handed a drink to each of the ladies and raised his own glass.

"Well, bottoms up," he said.

They all took a sip.

"Well," said Jack directly to Amanda, "aren't you going to criticize my saying 'bottoms up'?"

"This doesn't taste like orange juice," said Rose quickly, wrinkling her face.

"I slipped some vodka in the glasses before the ice," said Jack the magician. "I figured both of you could stand a screwdiver. And here comes one now."

Peter was far enough down the stairs to hear, and knew exactly what kind of evening it was going to be.

"If you don't stop it, Jack," said Amanda, "I'm walking out of—I don't know why you keep—really, all that stag-party talk, it's not necessary. Rose, he's just a big kid."

Jack pinched Amanda's cheek. "Lolita," he said, "I'm for you."

With a flourish he hoped was sufficiently broad to draw attention and change the course of conversation, Peter said, "Ho, happy people, how do you like my clean shirt?" He could hear his idiot voice saying, "Ho, happy people" and hated himself for playing the game, though the words, like the clowning, seemed unavoidable in an evening with Jack and Amanda.

"Mind you," said Peter, "despite the clean shirt I'm not really respectable." He slipped his jacket off, and it was immediately apparent that the shoulder seam of the clean shirt had split. "I'll look like a bum unless I keep my jacket on," he said at Rose. "No, I am not changing my shirt again."

An evening like this, he thought, is like reading all of the Sunday newspaper or sitting in front of the tube for hours on end or going to a funeral of somebody you really didn't know very well but where you had to show your face. A waste of life. He fixed himself a drink at the bar and noticed the silence. All three of them were looking at him. Nobody had said anything. Had they read his thoughts? Of course they couldn't read his thoughts. Was he the culprit? Of what? What had he done now? The drink made, he took a very large swig.

"Number three," said Rose.

She was counting his drinks. Sure, he could stop drinking. He could chloroform all three of them. How was that for a solution?

His expression must have been enough to panic Jack, who headed for the piano, the loudest diversion he knew. Jack had one of those great big voices, good for occasions in which a group of men, all loaded, sing barbershop songs. It was a message voice, getting the message across.

"*I want a girl, just like the girl that married dear old Dad,*" he sang. "Hey, this is a lousy piano. *I want a girl, just like the girl—*"

Rose tried to cut in. "Jack?"

"Next time I'll bring my own," said Jack, banging away.

"Girl?" asked Peter.

"Piano," said Jack. "*Oh, I want a girl, just like the girl that married Artie Shaw.*"

Rose tried again. "Jack?"

"Some people like a roller piano," said Jack, "but I like to roll my own. *Oh, I want a girl, just like—*"

It was Amanda's shrill voice that cut him down. "Jack!"

"Present and accounted for. What do you want?" He continued playing, but with a light touch.

"For heaven's sake," said Amanda, "Rose has been trying to get your attention."

"Well, speak up, Rosie old girl, bellow like Amanda does. It's a sure attention getter."

"Jack," said Rose, "do you handle divorces?"

Jack took his hands off the piano.

Peter was more surprised by the word than the question. Divorce, he thought, is an integral part of marriage, a shadow of possibility, an occasional secret wish quickly chopped down, or a brooding hope lurking in thoughts and arguments. The husband who has not had a fleeting thought of divorce is a liar, to himself mainly. The wife who says she has never had a thought of divorce is also a liar. The word, spoken out loud for the first time not in argument, where it can be a weapon thrust, but in front of friends, the way Rose had asked the question, was more than that: not a gauntlet flung (for a gauntlet can always be picked up) but a line crossed (when you look behind you, the line has disappeared). The public question, unlike the private threat, cannot be repealed. Even if never spoken again, it becomes a permanent fixture of the marriage.

In an instant, Peter noticed the striking difference between Rose's expression and Amanda's. Rose, controlled on the surface, held the muscles of her face in a counterfeit of calm. Amanda looked as if she had been slapped.

"Funny you should ask that," Jack said. "Just this afternoon—"

Amanda whipped into his sentence. "Don't tell it."

"Told *you*, why can't I tell *them*?"

Amanda crumpled into a small patch of brown broken leaves, swept out of sight. Jack, suddenly enthusiastic for his subject, stood up from the piano, put a foot up on the stool and began talking at Rose and Peter with relish, unaware, it seemed, that his wife, for all practical purposes, was no longer in the room.

"I was telling Amanda about my little fun afternoon and didn't finish till we got to the door tonight. You didn't overhear us, did you, Rose?"

Rose shook her head.

"Well," he continued, "I thought maybe you had. You see, there's this fellow I represented on a business deal—drew his will, too, I did—who's been feuding with his missus, and this afternoon the big confrontation scene took place in my office. Armbruster, who's representing the wife, is a nice quiet old guy, never had a fistfight in his life. He brings her to the office and my guy's there because we figure we might patch it up. You see, there're some kids involved."

Peter caught Rose looking at him.

"It seemed like everything was going to go peaceful

when my fellow says something—it seemed unimportant —and the wife grabs the letter opener off of my desk and throws it at him—missed, thank God—and Armbruster looks like he's going to have a heart attack. And my guy picks up a paperweight, and I yell at him, 'Put it down!' The damn fool smashes it down on the glass top of my desk. Smithereens."

Peter got up. "Nice quiet profession, the law. Now why don't we all just—"

"Wait a sec," interrupted Jack. "Haven't finished. I'm going to add the cost of a new glass top to that guy's bill. Not that the poor bastard'll be able to pay, not in this jurisdiction. The husband always gets screwed by the judge more than he ever got screwed by his ex. Sure I handle divorces, Rose, got to. Hate 'em like every other lawyer. Why d'ja ask?"

"Can't we talk about something pleasant?" said Peter.

"What makes you think advertising is pleasant?" said Jack, haw-hawing. "Mind if I pour myself another? Thanks."

The only sounds in the room: Jack's steps to the bar, the clink of the ice, the Scotch pouring.

"Two doubles is four," said Amanda. She hadn't disappeared after all.

Jack had filled the glass too high and leaned down to take a slurp so that he could carry it. "Three doubles is six," he said. "You kids trying to play scoreboard? I tried to tell this guy most people can't afford a divorce. It's not just the trip to Mexico, it's two apartments, double a lot of living expenses, and the husband gets socked for his wife's legals as well as his own, and he's up a tree and can't pay. This fellow who was in this afternoon, I know his business, and *he* sure as hell can't pay—but mostly it's the animus. If you think people are civilized, you haven't seen them tangling in a divorce action."

"Okay, okay, Jack," said Peter.

"You can call me John, Peter, old boy," said Jack, haw-hawing with the pleasure of attention. "You know, every time I settle a damn case where steam's let off, I make a real big college try to get the adversaries to shake hands, and you know where it's hardest? Divorces. They've been playing with each other's breast, bum, and crotch, swallowing each other's spit for years, and then won't shake hands."

Amanda looked as if she might explode. "Jack, stop that talk!"

"Okay," said Jack. "Married people body around together, present company excepted. That okay, Amanda? Peter and Rosie must have gone to bed twice because those two kids upstairs looks like 'em, but we don't have any damn kids, and that's proof Amanda and I never go to bed."

He ended the speech inches from Amanda's face. "How's that, lover?"

Amanda's voice was barely audible. "That's cruel, Jack," she said.

Jack took Amanda by the collar of her dress as if she were on display as a bad example. "I have my personal Legion of Decency right here," he said.

"Lay off, Jack," said Peter.

"Watch your language, Peter, old boy," said Jack, enjoying himself and not noticing Rose coming up to him.

"Aren't there ever friendly divorces?" asked Rose, and Jack could see it was a sincere question, which worried him because the drinks had relaxed him enough to begin noticing other people, and he could see that Rose wasn't being casual at all. He let go of Amanda's collar.

Peter could hear Jack's voice shift gears. "Oh, some divorces are real quiet, but that's usually when one of the parties skips. The only noise you get is a lot of complaining about what a bastard the vanished spouse is, but without the other spouse right there fighting back it's a lullaby compared to usual. Your client tells you his side of the story over and over, and eventually you hear from the fled spouse's lawyer. You pick up her official story. What neither of them tells you is what it's like in bed together. But you always know."

Jack was convinced it was going to be a marvelous evening. When a stranger stopped him in the street and asked the time or directions, he enjoyed it. He loved being a father to the clients who asked endless questions, some of which were questions for a lawyer, some for a doctor, and some nobody ought to be asked. He felt best when he provided authoritative answers, or answers the client would believe to be the result of deep study and knowledge or vast personal experience. A client who asked a great many questions usually was treated more kindly at bill time than the occasional fellow who said to Jack, "Just tell me what the law says and what I can do about it." The pleasure Jack took in magistrating was usually less in Peter's presence; Peter was knowledgeable in so many ways Jack could get caught out on. It therefore heightened Jack's enjoyment now to see Peter's puzzled expression.

Rose was asking how custody worked, and Jack said, "The wife always gets custody. It's the big weapon, and she gets custody unless she's a whore, I mean a real one for money, that you can prove, or a dope addict, and I don't get that kind of trade. As far as my practice is concerned, the wife always gets the kids."

"Doesn't that stop a lot of divorces?" Peter hadn't intended to speak but there it was, out.

"Look, Petey," said Jack, "I'm talking firsthand experience. What the hell do you and I know about the people who never get to lawyers? Maybe kids stop 'em. Maybe religion. No one in Amanda's family ever got a divorce. Maybe habit stops 'em. When they get as far as the law, I know if you can reconcile 'em it's because they can't stop sleeping together, and if you can't it's because they don't, or they're sleeping around, or they'd rather not, like Amanda."

Would Jack ever actually shoot Amanda? The thought would never occur to him. The weaponry of marriage, Peter thought, outdoes anything the Army comes up with. Would he set fire to her dress? Would he smother her with a pillow while she slept? Never.

"Do I read you wrong?" said Jack to Amanda. "I'm sure these fine people would let us use their guest room for half an hour—"

"Leave her alone, Jack," said Peter.

The words washed off Jack's back. "Or we can go to a motel," he continued, inches from Amanda's face, "if you think having people in the house would bother you, or have you got cramps, dear?" He turned to Rose and Peter. "Some Februarys she has cramps for thirty-one days. She'll go to her grave without ever having an orgasm and—"

Amanda slapped his face hard.

That was a wild train Jack had gotten onto, thought Peter. He looked at Rose for having brought up the subject that triggered Jack. Rose moved her shoulders helplessly.

"I need a drink," said Jack.

"I think you've probably had enough," said Rose.

"Hey, Pete," said Jack menacingly, "do I have to go to the bar down the street to get a drink when I'm your guest?" He looked like a kid burning ants.

Peter touched his hand to Jack's arm and said calmly, "We'll have some wine with dinner, Jack."

Jack knocked Peter's hand off. "What a cheap-jack host."

"Jack, you ought to be in the advertising business," said Peter, determined to smooth things over. "In my business everybody tanks up at lunch. Drinks before dinner wouldn't hit you so hard."

"The drinks didn't hit me. She did," he said, jabbing a thumb at Amanda.

"Well, you're even."

Amanda came across to Rose like a cartoon rabbit, walking on the balls of her feet in tiny steps.

"Rose," she said apologetically, shaking her head, "I feel nauseated."

"I heard you!" bellowed Jack.

Mildly Amanda said, "All I said was, I was nauseated."

"You always use that as a goddamn excuse."

"You knew I had rheumatic fever," said Amanda. "You didn't buy a pig in a poke. How many times have I told you that?"

"I didn't see the poke," said Jack.

"Now let it go!" said Peter. He took Amanda by the

arm in almost courtly fashion and walked her closer to Jack, smiling a smile he used with clients in serious situations, a smile that could crack at an instant if its bluff were called. "Hey, can't I get you kids to shake hands?"

The thing that helped the most was strained laughter coming from all of them at once.

Bravely Rose said, "I think I'll have another screwdriver."

"Isn't Petey enough?" said Jack, ho-hoing, hoping now with the rest of them that things would calm down, that he would calm down, because he had felt that angina squeeze in his chest that the doctor said wasn't angina and he himself was sure wasn't angina, only God or Death or Somebody saying, take it easy, bud.

"Petey," Jack said, "what's wrong with women? You make a little joke, let loose, have some fun after a goddamn day full of making-a-living crap, and they go straight, square, and simpleminded."

The cheese stood still in the middle of the room.

"I'll make my own," said Rose, gladly adding the sin of bartending to that of having a second drink voluntarily.

"I'll get it for you," said Peter, feeling kindly toward Rose, toward Amanda, toward all women at that moment. All women: Elizabeth? *Rub the mind blank. Quick.*

Peter took Jack's glass, gave Rose her drink, took Amanda's glass, and when everyone, including himself, was armed, raised his drink: "To alcohol."

"Crap!" said Jack. "It makes strong men weak, weak men strong, all men weep, and nobody ought to be without it. The way the deck is stacked, it takes a strong man or woman to get a divorce. I don't mean just think about it—everybody thinks about it—I mean, go—all the way! Amanda, baby, you're lucky I'm a weak man." Jack toasted her. "Skoal!"

Amanda managed a weak smile.

"Dinner will be ready in less than ten minutes," said Rose out of nowhere, not being sure whether it would really be ready in ten or twenty but feeling compelled to say something.

Jack sidled up to her. "Rosie, how come you're so curious tonight?"

Rose seemed to think about her answer for a long time. She wanted it to sound adult and thoughtful, even abstract, to establish the nature of her inquiry as something less than personal.

"Every young girl is interested in marriage," she said. "I guess every married woman is curious about divorce."

"Hey, Petey," said Jack, "your wife has turned into a philosopher." Jack suddenly felt the platform disappearing from under his feet, his chance at building a spell gone. How to retrieve it? His gaze caught Amanda's, and there were tears in her eyes.

"Oh, come on now, baby," he said to her, "I've just been having some fun. Too much inkohol. Baby, let me get you another drink, okay?"

"All right," said Amanda.

"How about a little kiss for Uncle Jack?"

Amanda shook her head.

"How about a little old handshake? All right?"

Amanda had no choice. Peter watched Jack and Amanda shaking hands. It was the kind of moment you wanted a camera for.

Jack mixed Amanda's drink. "Peter," he said, "tears always get me. Don't they get you?"

"Another word out of you and I'm turning on the television set," said Peter.

"Dinner'll be ready in a few minutes," chimed in Rose.

The exuberance was coming back into Jack's voice. "You know what keeps marriages going these days? Those Connecticut parties. Everybody needs to switch around once in a while. Amanda, why don't you go sit down in old Peter's lap?"

Amanda, to everyone's astonishment, perhaps to her own as well, finished off her drink, set down the glass and said, "I think I will."

She sat down in Peter's lap. It was a very strange feeling for Peter, as if his mother or his sister had suddenly made a sexual approach. He remembered the time he first saw Amanda in a bathing suit—at a beach party it was—and how astonished he had been that she had breasts and hips. He suddenly realized that Amanda had settled in his lap, not the way a stranger sits on the edge of a chair but in a way that brought a maximum part of her body in touch with his.

"Is this the way you mean?" said Amanda, and she kissed Peter, not on the mouth, thank heaven, but softly on the cheek.

"Wow!" said Jack, startled and somehow pleased. "Rose, my hostess, under the circumstances you've just got to reciprocate." He took Rose by the hand and led her to a chair at the other side of the room, plunked himself down in it without letting go of Rose's hand and said, "Now you sit right down on Jack's plentiful lap."

Rose looked at Peter. Peter looked away.

Rose sat down on Jack's lap.

"Isn't this wonderful?" said Jack, his voice having gained the platform again. "Now strike up the band. *I want a girl, just like—*"

"Stop wiggling, Jack," said Peter. "Rose'll fake an orgasm, and it'll go to your head."

"Peter!" exclaimed Rose, genuinely shocked because she hadn't been aware at all that Jack was wiggling.

"Oh, come on now, everybody, we're having fun!" said Jack. "Let's sing! *I want a girl, just like . . .*"

Slowly, hesitantly, they all joined in, and throughout the house there now resounded the voices of Jack, Rose, Amanda and Peter, singing.

"*I want a girl, just like the girl that married dear old dad. A sweet old-fashioned girl with heart so true, a girl who loved nobody else but you . . .*"

It was Rose who first noticed the children on the staircase in their nightclothes.

"Jon!" she said.

"Maggie!" said Peter.

"Ahem, did we wake you?" said Jack.

The adults started to disentangle themselves. Amanda got out of Peter's lap, straightening her dress, and Rose was already up and away from Jack, floundering in dreadful embarrassment.

Peter, softly to the children, said, "It was just a little joke."

Chapter Three

On the way to Elizabeth's apartment, Peter found himself ten steps behind a blond girl whose hips moved in a rhythm that excited him. He walked rapidly, despite his heavy briefcase. As he overtook the girl, the anonymous and interesting blondness changed; in profile she had a rather ordinary face. What was all the excitement about?

He knew, of course. Elizabeth had brought a sense of spring and sexuality back into his life. Now he found himself looking at women as women, not in the fraudulent manner of ogling and whistling—the male way of pretending maleness to other men—but looking at individual women he had never seen before, as if each was someone one might indeed go to bed with. He gave each credit to start with, then took the credit away if he found them unattractive in voice or walk or manner or holding onto some other man in a declarative way. The surprise to him was how many kept the credit, including older women who, he noticed, were likely to have a quick sense of their own sexuality, or the frisky younger ones whose youthful assertiveness was more stimulating than their overkempt bodies, or even women he knew but had never before thought of as possible bedmates. How much fair game there was in the world!

The legend in America was that the women castrated the men, but Peter now knew that to be inaccurate. A good deal of that overt dominance was the result of dismay, the woman in effect saying to the man: if you're not cock-of-the-walk, I will be; there has got to be a cock somewhere.

Since the advent of Elizabeth, Peter found that in the community of females there was a sense of his cockiness. Some women, he was beginning to find out, had an immediate response to the electricity a man felt inside himself. Where had his been so long?

Peter swung the glass door to Elizabeth's apartment building forward with more energy than called for and just made the self-service elevator in which a fortyish woman, armed with groceries, was already pushing a button.

They looked at each other. Does she know I am going up here to get laid?

Would she like to get laid? She probably hadn't thought about it. Was she thinking about it now that she and he were in the elevator alone?

Peter looked her full in the face and was immediately convinced that she hadn't thought about getting laid for a long time. She wasn't unattractive.

The woman got out of the elevator, flicking a look at

him, and he suddenly realized why: he hadn't pushed a floor button. He did, and the light went out. He got the light back on. He pushed the right button. Man, get ahold of yourself!

He let himself in with a key kept not with his other keys but in his wallet, in a small envelope on which he had taken the precaution of writing a fictitious masculine name. To avoid getting caught. Why avoid getting caught?

Elizabeth was lying on the floor, six or seven open books around her. She turned away from the one in her hand as she heard the door open. Her smile had a virtue no other had ever had for Peter.

Some people have a ready smile, which they flick on to say, "I'm smiling, don't worry." It usually *was* a cause for worry, like a salesman's "Let me be candid with you." Peter remembered the school librarian with the perpetual smile—not for him, or over anything, or to anybody at all, just a permanent, frozen expression of pretended happiness. Peter knew an art director who, at age forty-five or thereabouts, had been told that he looked younger when he smiled, and that smiler was now impossible to look at with a straight face. It was indeed rare when a smile was an expression out of the ordinary, showing pleasure short of joy. Elizabeth smiled when she meant it and could not bring herself to smile otherwise. It was a liability in business; it put some people off but never anyone that mattered. Hers was the league of people who felt that a smile was an expression one should not cheat with.

At this moment, Peter and Elizabeth were looking at each other, and he thought how rare that was, too, men and women who already knew each other taking the other in.

He put his briefcase down and flung his coat over a chair.

She was on her back now and slowly raised her legs until they were perpendicular. Then she slowly lowered them. Peter watched her as she repeated the exercise. Was it that her body showed through her clothes more than with other women? Was it perfectly proportioned, or was this another exaggeration, a way of his describing his feeling for her to himself? Ah, the old myth-making machine: my girl is the most beautiful girl in the world. Still, he thought as her legs moved up, then down, what a body.

"You are a remarkable woman," he said.

It was superfluous to compliment a woman like Elizabeth.

It was not superfluous to compliment any woman ever.

When the kids were crawling and toddling around, Peter used to get down on the carpet with them, playing at their level. But as Jonathan learned to walk, and then Margaret, getting down on the carpet seemed undignified. Yet here he was, lowering himself to the carpet next to Elizabeth, and as he put his arms around her, his self-consciousness vanished. He was aware of the warm musk of her lips and mouth, her breasts against his chest, her pelvis thrust forward to fix the body-length bond between them. It was incredible how the whole of him, embracing the whole of her, was instantly and fully engorged. As he kissed her again, he had the definite sense that his organ was reaching out for her as if it had a life of its own, hurrying him along.

His fingers raced to undress her, and himself. He felt the need of more hands, preferably nontrembling hands. How beautiful she was in her nakedness, small and perfect. He pulled her perfection against the bearishness of himself. Why did male desire demand the ultimate at once, and the female, like a soufflé, require gentling and patience?

He kissed the echelons of her body. He stroked her, hoping for gentleness, barely controlling the impulse to grab and fuck. How like the Saxon thump was male desire, how like the curlicues of French was femaleness, the light multiple syllables taking their own sweet time. His tongue moved over the recesses of her neck—he could feel the wild pulse in her body now—and he checked the rush and impulse to force his thrust inside her, and then, quite unexpectedly, her hand was stroking his member as she spread her thighs apart, and the opening was entered.

He raised himself above her as high as possible so that they were joined now only in the one place, and he moved as slowly as possible until her own rhythm forced him faster, plunging with fierceness, anger, love, until finally both of them flooded in communion.

They had been lying quietly in each other's arms for a long time, and he had dozed off for a while.

She was up on an elbow, looking at him.

Smiling.

"Good morning," she said, and his heart thumped until his eyes found the wristwatch on his naked arm and verified that he had slept only minutes.

Elizabeth was now slipping back into her clothes, and

he watched her. Why did he not like to watch Rose dressing? Why was he fascinated by Elizabeth's slow covering up of her body, first the brassiere, the cups to the back and the clasp in front, then pulling the whole thing around, then the panties which seemed so fragile to him, and then the outer clothes and last, stepping into her shoes. Why was he searching for significant differences as if there were a need to assemble bits of evidence for himself? Wasn't the overriding evidence in the joy of it? Was he making a case? For what?

"What'd you do today, elf?"

"Do?"

"Every time I went by your office, it was empty."

Elizabeth lit a cigarette. "Drink?" she asked.

"Yes," he said. "You're skipping the subject nimbly."

"I started out," she said, "by having a wolf for breakfast."

"That was yesterday morning. Wasn't that a brilliant idea, showing up here at the crack of dawn?"

"No."

He had thought she welcomed his unexpected appearance yesterday, letting himself in with the key, with light just beginning to show through the venetian blinds, startling her awake with a kiss, then seeing the glow of her recognition. Love in the morning was not something he liked, but it had been especially good that morning. It was almost always good with her. When would it not be any longer? Only a creep would think that, he thought. Or a man old enough to know that commercials interrupted life, too.

"Were you afraid," he said, "I might find you weren't sleeping alone?"

"If I showed up at your house, would I find you sleeping alone?"

A thought he would rather not pursue. One of the constants of infidelity.

"You started telling me about today."

"Well, this morning I dressed, bathed, went—"

"In that order?"

"Inclusively but not serially. Went for milk and bread and things, looked at last night's painting, decided that I'd have been better off sneaking into a movie with you, then decided the painting was coming along okay after all, so I patted it, washed the breakfast dishes, left some food to thaw for supper tonight and went to work. Are you going to sit there naked?"

"Go on," said Peter, starting to dress.

"Well, I punched the time clock, and I started to—"

"What time clock?"

"Well, I punched something or somebody on my way in. Maybe it was the fifteenth-floor receptionist. You know how irritable I can be in the morning. I hung my coat up, went into my office, discovered it wasn't my office, went next door to my very own office and looked out the window."

"Nice view?"

"Couldn't see. Window washers were washing the windows from outside, and all I could see was the window washers."

"So far I have a feeling you're overpaid."

"In twelve minutes flat I whipped off a first-rate sketch of a Coke Christmas display to go with that mean-looking Santa Claus, and the rest of the day was spent showing off my twelve minutes' work to Members of the Hierarchy."

"They liked it?"

She dismissed his question with a wave of her cigarette. He knew how good her work was.

"Any propositions today?"

"Are you being jealous or proprietary?"

"I know the environment."

"I also did a cover idea for the Helena Rubinstein brochure, and I found out, in midafternoon, that you're not a father."

"I *am* a father," he said.

"Well, then, I'm not a mother."

He said nothing.

"If I were pregnant, you'd send me to the butcher."

"No."

"You'd marry me?"

"Why ever for?"

"Honor. Anyhow, the matter is academic. Your honor is safe for now."

His nerves were spindling off somewhere, and he was trying frantically to get them back in place. He took a long swig of the drink.

"Hey!" she said.

He knew she knew that any time he took a long swig like that, it was a squashing down of something. Thank heaven the radio was a transistor, he thought, as the sound came on at once, and with a turn he found music he could dance to, took her in his arms and danced. Would their dancing silence him inside?

Over her shoulder, he tried to concentrate on the physical objects of the room. The walls always seemed to re-

cede into darkness, probably because Elizabeth kept
paintings, hers and others, lighted by spots inobtrusively
placed against the ceiling, and the paintings therefore
seemed to mark the outer limits of the room; out beyond
them, darkened space.

The couch was convertible; it had to be in an apartment this small. The coffee table was very low, as if it had
no legs at all. Handsome actually when seen from above,
which is how it had to be seen, but no place to park a
coffee cup gracefully. Beauty first. Only bathrooms and
kitchens were for utility, Elizabeth had said.

At that precise moment Peter became aware of the
loud thumps from the floor below. They hadn't been
making that much noise.

"Oh, hell!" he said.

"Ignore her," said Elizabeth.

They continued dancing until the thumps repeated
themselves.

There was no point trying to continue. Elizabeth's dismay showed on her face. The last time they had heard the
noises from the floor below, they had been on the convertible, the distraction had wilted him.

"Do you think she objects to the dancing or that I en-
tertain a man on the premises?"

"You do both brilliantly."

"She gets paid."

"That's catty."

"Perhaps. But true. There's been a petition to get her
out of the building."

"Then to her you're a scab. She'd outlaw free fornica-
tion."

"I could tell her you buy me a lunch and dinner sometimes, and these earrings, and this watch, and you've given me cash I've never returned."

"What are you working up to?"

"Nothing. Depressed by my state of sin."

"Think how stately the sin of the married woman who knocks down a split-level house, a maid, an extra car, and for less comfort than you give me."

"That's an awfully economic view."

"When there's no love, there's barter."

"Why are you so sure Rose is wrong for you?"

This line of questioning, Your Honor, he thought, is irrelevant and immaterial.

"It's the shape of her behind," he said.

"What shape is that?"

"It has no shape. It's the whole of her physically," Peter went on. "She looks right in clothes, but when she's naked it's as if a skeleton were carrying her flesh as a burden."

"You, sir, are that way, too, sometimes."

He couldn't disagree.

"If Rose were an old friend," he said, "I wouldn't see much of her. Our tacks are different. We'd probably have managed to break off. If Rose were a relative, I mean a male-female-neuter relative other than a wife, I'd see her at family reunions and we'd bring ourselves up to date on the number of children we'd had. But I'm married to her, and the children are ours. We have a family reunion every day without the rest of the relatives present for diversion."

Peter took Elizabeth's hand, and gently she took his hand off hers. "When did you know," she said, "about you and Rose?"

"One day long before I met you, I succumbed to television. I mean I sat down to watch some program I thought I wanted to see because the paper said everybody ought to see it, and then I watched the following program, and the program after, and my inertia frightened me. I sat watching, and Rose sat alongside watching, and we died."

"That makes me a necrophiliac," said Elizabeth.

"A restorer of life," said Peter. "The first time we had a drink after work, it was to talk out some business odds and ends, and when we looked up, five hours had passed. Nobody can discuss business for five hours, and we certainly hadn't been."

She knew what he would say. She was watching to see how he would tell it.

"And there was that complicated time we went to bed together, finally, and lying here, my arm under your head, afterward felt as good as during. That never happened to me before. When did you know, elf?"

"Sometimes I'm not sure I know now."

A real question sometimes begged an unexpected answer.

"I've lived alone so long and gotten so used to it."

Elizabeth could see the hurt in his face. "Yes, there was one time," she said. "I was walking by myself downtown on a Saturday morning when you were home with the kids, and suddenly the air raid sirens went off. I didn't know a drill was scheduled, and for five or ten frantic seconds I believed it was an air raid, and I didn't feel frightened of dying." She paused, then said, "Because I was living."

Peter watched her face. "How come you never married, elf?"

"Never been asked," she replied.

"I don't believe that."

"Never been asked by the right man. Not even now."

She saw instantly how much she had hurt him and said, "I'm sorry."

Peter sat her down. "You've never met Harry, have you? America's most ardent advocate of the *ménage à trois*, not in one house but the European system, a wife and kids at home, an apartment for the permanent lady of his life?"

She waited.

"Harry's marvelous," Peter went on. "It's been going on for years. The women sort of know about each other. The wife likes Harry and what Harry calls 'the integrity of the family.' No broken home, no problem with the kids."

"And the other woman?"

"Oh, Harry's mad about her."

"And she's just wild about Harry."

"It's lasted eleven years. I've seen them together many times. They don't sneak around corners the way we do. Most of Harry's good friends see them together, though not at Harry's home, but he's got home friends, too. It works."

The way Elizabeth was looking at him made him want to take back the whole conversation.

"Which of the women," Elizabeth asked, "has the life insurance?"

"I, uh, would be surprised if both women aren't well taken care of."

"I'd like to ask a real question," said Elizabeth.

"Sure," he said.

"Is this a trial balloon?"

Ladies and gentlemen of the jury, I appeal to everyone in this courtroom to believe me sincerely. I love this woman. Is it a sin to like to get laid by the woman you love?

The courtroom shook with laughter.

"A trial balloon?" he echoed, bargaining poorly for time to think. "I don't understand Harry's type of life," he said. He took her hand. It felt limp. "I want to live with you."

She said, "Part time." There was no animosity in her face.

Was she looking for a commitment? He *was* committed, wasn't he? Wasn't he?

If at this moment he had to decide between not seeing her again and living with her—but did he have to make that choice?

He held his left hand before her as if he were showing it to her for the first time.

"Nice hand," she said.

With that hand he gripped her arm and sat her down on the sofa.

Elizabeth watched him pace.

"Did you know I played a beautiful piano when I was six?" he asked. "Good enough to astound some people?"

Elizabeth seemed genuinely surprised.

"When I was seven, a nickel ball we were playing with rolled down the sewer, and two kids helped me lift the sewer cover and another kid went down after the ball. When he came up I reached for the ball, and the other kids couldn't hold the weight alone. The sewer cover dropped on my left hand. Oh, it's all right!" he said to Elizabeth's sudden concern. "I can pick up a telephone."

He stood over her. She wanted to get up, to end the unequal balance of Peter standing and her sitting, but there wasn't room enough to stand up—he was that close —and she wouldn't push him away.

"I could use the telephone, but I couldn't play. I made jokes about being a right-handed piano player. Tennis was the therapy recommended for a kid with fast feet and a good right hand who couldn't play the piano, so I played tennis till it took everybody's mind off my left hand—except mine. How much tennis can a kid play?" he shouted at Elizabeth.

"I decided to be rich instead of a piano player. Did it ever occur to you that wanting to be rich is the perfect substitute? Oh, I wanted to be good rich. My scheme was to be so goddamn rich I could give every kid in the world an extra nickel ball. I wouldn't give to the Red Cross or the Salvation Army or the goddamn Museum of Modern Art. I'd set up a ball foundation!"

"You seem not to have succeeded," she said.

"Getting rich takes too much time. Besides, I saw the others trying, and how they act about money kind of puts you off the game.

"Well, I decided to become a patriarch instead and have a lot of kids and turn them all into great piano players. Isn't that how we use our children?

"Jonathan hated playing the piano. Was I supposed to force him? Well, we had the damn piano paid for and in the house, so Margaret took lessons because she's an angel and wanted to please me. When I finally had the sense to tell her she didn't have to play, she said no, no, it was all right. When I insisted, was she relieved!

"I stopped having piano players. I stopped having kids. For a couple of weeks I thought about politics, but I didn't have the guts to do a Coolidge in a war bonnet. Besides, I couldn't get elected to anything. I'm the kind that gets an appointive office or none at all. And I couldn't buy a South American republic and become a dictator because I couldn't afford it, and besides, I like it here. And they don't have kings anymore, not here, not even in plays. You know what's here? You know what's possible and here and American? Advertising."

Elizabeth laughed.

"Now don't laugh at advertising," Peter said. "What other profession has all the frustrations built right in? A shoemaker makes a pair of shoes, or used to. At least he can fix a pair of shoes, and when he fixes them he knows they're fixed. But what do you *make* in advertising?"

"You're good at it," she said.

"I was a good piano player."

Peter sat down on the sofa alongside of Elizabeth, resting his head in his hands, in the audience with her, avoiding looking at the empty stage of her living room.

He tried to keep all trace of scorn out of his voice. "Advertising moves people. Closer to a store. That's not the way I want to move people."

She was passing him a cigarette she had lit. He held it without smoking.

"My first three years in advertising," he said, "I worked like a fury by day, and by night I wrote something to move people. I wrote thirteen good chapters of a fifteen-chapter book, but I didn't have the guts to take the silence, and I showed the thirteen chapters to Rose."

"Did she like it?"

"She never said. She fell asleep over the first chapter, and I put it and the other twelve away in a drawer."

With unaccustomed intensity Elizabeth said, "You're out of your mind. Why?"

"Because I wanted to kill Rose. I should have! People are more tolerant of murder than divorce."

She said nothing.

"The big myth used to be that you ruin the kids if you get divorced. Now they say you can divorce your wife but you don't have to divorce your children. Is that true? It takes two heroes to make a decent relationship with children possible after divorce, and how many couples are made up of two heroes? Is Rose? Am I? I saw what happened with Charlie Baron and his kids. Charlie's wife remarried fast and she saw to it that the kids' ties with their stepfather, one by one, replaced their ties with Charlie, until Charlie had the role of visiting stranger, and the visits became intolerable because the loyalty of kids is conditioned by toys and holidays and day-to-day things, and most of all by exposure and habitat. Charlie wouldn't have divorced his wife—he swore to that—if he had known he would be divorcing the kids also. It's okay for the guy who isn't much involved with the kids, or never was, or who identifies the kids with his ex and would just as soon not see them, but for a guy like Charlie Baron it was pure hell."

She knew he wasn't talking about Charlie Baron.

The cigarette in Peter's hand had burned itself down

to a butt without his having taken a puff. Carefully he cupped his other hand under the ash and brought it over to the ashtray.

"You know," he said, "Rose never asked to see the novel again. Not out of meanness; Rose isn't mean. She forgot about it."

"You love the kids very, very much," said Elizabeth, speaking against the one possibility she longed for.

"I love the kids and I love you, only you're not their mother."

She didn't seem to understand.

"The kids are my kids, me as nearly as I can make me. I'd give my life for them if ever put to the test. I couldn't bear not seeing them every night."

"You don't see them every night now," said Elizabeth.

"I know," he said.

"If you came to live with me, it'd be worse."

"I know."

"The kids are kids. They need you. And you're not ready to live without them. You should stop coming here."

"I live here," said Peter.

He hadn't understood what he was saying until he said it, and when he did, it seemed irreversible.

"You," he said, taking her hand, "are my next of kin."

He kissed her. It was somehow awkward sitting side by side, and so he pulled her to her feet, and their faces and bodies came together and stayed together.

"I'll be back in a minute," she said and headed for the bathroom.

Necessary interruption. Physiology. Nuisance. No use complaining.

The ringing caught him a step and a reach from the telephone. He had picked it up before thinking. Hang up? Childish. Try a neutral male voice. Say the least.

"Hello?" he said.

"May I speak to Miss Kilter, please?" said the strained voice.

Peter put the receiver down next to the phone. He hadn't wanted it to clatter but it did. He should have said, "One moment, please." He had said "hello"; that was bad enough. His knuckles knocked on the door of the bathroom.

"Hurry up and get the phone."

"Minute," Elizabeth said through the door.

"Hurry," he said, "it's Rose."

Elizabeth opened the door a crack. "It's who?"

"Rose," he whispered, his face white.

"My God," said Elizabeth. She came out. She went over to the phone and then retreated one step.

He motioned for her to pick it up.

She shook her head.

"*I* can't," he said. "Hurry."

I've got to get the hell out of here.

There was absolute fear in Elizabeth's face as she picked up the telephone, visibly mustering her courage. He heard her striving to sound normal, to sound calm, as she said, "Hello? Yes, this is. No, no bother at all, Mrs. Carmody. I'm quite certain. I don't know where he is. No, he's not here. Yes, of course, if he calls I'll tell him to call you, but I don't expect him to call. No, not at all. Good-bye."

Elizabeth hung up. Coward Carmody wanted to avoid her eyes.

"All I said was, 'hello.' "

"Did she recognize your voice?"

"How could she not recognize my voice?" Then, "She has a lot of nerve calling here."

"She has a lot of courage calling here," said Elizabeth. "What excuse did you give for coming home late?"

"The Advertising Council," said Peter sheepishly.

"They don't meet tonight."

He hadn't checked.

It wasn't in an unkind voice that she said, "It's so easy for everyone to come up with a good excuse, everyone but you, I suppose." She turned away from him, saying, "I'll put dinner on," and he knew that she loved him because she wasn't turning away from him but from his dismay.

Peter started dialing a number.

"What are you doing?" Elizabeth asked.

"I'll leave a dime on the table," was his response.

"Stop that. Who are you calling?"

The number was ringing at the other end.

"Guess."

"What will you say?"

"I don't know." It was an honest answer.

"Then hang up."

He did, just as the phone at the other end was being picked up.

"Dinner'll be ready in a minute," she said.

I'm going, he thought.

"I'm going," he said.

"I think you'd better get there after she's asleep. You'll have a scene if you go home now."

Peter put his coat on.

"Are you going," asked Elizabeth, "because you still love her, or you're afraid of her, or because you feel guilty, or all three?"

"That's not fair," he said.

"Who's fair? Do you know how ungodly boring, boring, boring the evenings are when you're not here?"

"What did you do before me?" he blurted.

"I've cut myself off from my friends, I don't go out, I do practically nothing but work and wait here for you. Do you know what that's like?"

They stood ten feet apart, a chasm between them as if he were in a foreign country, and then, knowing what he was doing, he stepped across the border.

He didn't touch her.

"I'm ashamed," he said, "to have gotten this far into life without knowing what love is like."

She said nothing.

She would not help him.

"I want to live, elf," he said, "now and with you."

She didn't move.

"The whole damn world can go to hell!" he declared.

"To hell!" he repeated.

"Do you mean Rose?" she said at last.

"I don't love her."

"You love the children."

"Look, elf," he said, "I don't have to divorce the children." He was buying the myth.

"They won't understand."

"I'll teach them."

"You won't see them often enough to teach them."

"I will."

"Not if you leave."

He started to move toward her, and she put out a hand that stopped him before he committed himself.

"I'll teach them," he said, suddenly in the grip of a wildness he had not felt for a long time, "that you can't live on money things, which is what Rose is teaching them. I'll teach them"—he felt like a fool saying it— "that love is the only damn thing you can—"

Elizabeth interrupted him, her voice very quiet.

"Can you teach them something you don't know?"

Peter looked at her face and thought how lovely it was.

"I'm trying to learn," he said.

"You're a slow learner," she said, wanting to stop him from stepping over the two or three feet of carpet between them, then letting him take her in his arms and kiss her, first on the side of her face, then the side of her mouth, and then on the lips, abandoning herself against any judgment she had, when the telephone shrilled across their kiss and kept insisting it be listened to, even after they had pulled away from each other.

They stared at the intruding telephone until finally it stopped. It could have been a wrong number. It could have been anybody.

Chapter Four

The key wouldn't work in the front door of his house. It was almost three in the morning. The street was empty. The trees at the curb were a military escort leading nowhere. The other end of the street was barely perceptible in the mist.

Peter tried his key again. It went in only part way. Of course it was his house, fake English Tudor, the phenomenal azalea in front, the brick steps.

If a policeman came along, he'd show some identification, driver's license, something with his address on it. He was not breaking in. It was his house.

He went around to the back, careful to make as little noise as possible on the pebbles. Most peculiar if the neighbors saw. Rose asleep?

Rose was not likely to be waiting up for him. Sleep was as essential to Rose as a cigarette before morning coffee to some people. At late parties, along about midnight, a switch would go off in Rose's head and she was for all practical purposes gone. Peter hoped the switch was working.

The most awkward part of dating for Peter as a teenager was his mother and father's insistence on waiting up for him. He'd see their heads out of the apartment window, searching the street in the direction from which he was to come. Once, at sixteen, Peter had exploded at the reception committee, as he called it. His mother had cried. Out of her crying came her confession, a fear she could never shake, that if she went to sleep Peter might not get home safely. His father kept her company, though he was perpetually tired from overwork. And so each minute after midnight was a rock on the cairn of Peter's guilt. No amount of postmidnight fun made up for the sad, unspoken recriminations under his father's eyes. Nor did his mother's obvious relief at his homecoming give him reassurance of her love. It was her superstition, not love for him, that kept her up.

Now, at the back door, an envelope Scotch-taped over the keyhole had his name on it, in Rose's handwriting. *Never darken my door again*, he thought.

He pulled the envelope away from the door.

See my lawyer, he predicted.

He opened the envelope.

It said, "The lock man said it couldn't be fixed and had to be replaced. If you didn't find key under the front mat, don't leave it there all night. Rose. P.S. I tried to call you about it."

His back-door key worked without fault. Peter let himself in, pawed his way across the kitchen, through the dining room darkness, then turned on a lamp in the living room, opened the front door, and retrieved the key from under the mat. He relocked the door, hung the new key in his case, dropped his old key in an ashtray, thought better of it and backtracked to the kitchen and dropped the old key in the garbage. He was halfway up the stairs when he remembered a light was burning in the living room. He went down, turned it off and climbed the stairs slowly.

Upstairs, he looked into Margaret's bedroom. The night light cast a cold blue-green glow across her sleeping face. You'd think a girl would pick a pink night light.

He had always welcomed the fact that Margaret looked so little like Rose. He kissed her forehead gently.

In the other small bedroom, Jonathan as usual was completely under the covers. His shirt was on the chair, but his flung pants had missed and lay crumpled on the floor next to the discarded socks and shoes. No underwear in sight. He must be sleeping in his underwear, against instructions. In the morning Rose would find Jon's pajamas under his pillow, where they had rested all night long.

Peter changed in the bathroom. Pajama-clad, he went into his bedroom for the first time, quietly. His side of the bed was turned down. Rose, asleep, was as far on her side as one could manage. On his pillow lay a penny.

Peter put the penny in his night table drawer, where there were now hundreds of others. On his wedding night, he used to tell his friends, Rose offered him a penny for his thoughts. And many nights since, offered a penny, he had made up thoughts that would satisfy Rose. It was easier than refusing.

The Husband

He lay stiffly under the covers, wondering if Rose, out of habit, would at some point come snaking across the bed and entwine herself with him. She didn't move. He raised his head slightly to make sure she was asleep. She was.

If she was awake, or would now awaken, would he take her to absolve his guilt? Out of one bed, in another. Henry had boasted once about sleeping with three women in one day, his mistress in the morning, a matinee at lunch with a woman he had just met and never saw again, and his wife that night. Why was it called making love?

He was falling asleep. Thank heaven.

Rose had heard Peter stumbling about downstairs and had been awake, ever so slightly, when Peter came to bed, but she pretended to be asleep because she knew they would argue. She must have dozed off because when she awoke, Peter was asleep in that straight facing-up position she couldn't stand because it reminded her of a corpse in a coffin.

It had been a successful day, Rose thought. She had avoided the temptation of daytime television. Margaret had skinned her knee. Rose had handled the wound washing, the Bactine application and the two large-sized Band-Aids expertly. She had baked a cake, creatively she thought because she had improvised on the ingredients. There was a good chunk left over for Peter if he was home for dinner tomorrow.

If Peter was home for dinner tomorrow had not been a problem until recently. During the day, when the insurance man had come about the missing camera and stayed to talk, obviously interested in her, she had thought of seducing him. It could have been easy, but in her heart she knew she couldn't sew shirts for a stranger or go to bed with one even if she felt it would somehow stop for a moment the gnawing she felt about Miss Kilter.

She knew that Peter and Miss Kilter seemed to have some kind of professional bond. She had felt that way ever since she had dropped into Peter's office unexpectedly while shopping downtown one day and found Miss Kilter there, and Peter and Miss Kilter, after acknowledging her presence, had gone on talking as if Rose were not there.

Rose felt pretty realistic about the whole thing. She knew most men had affairs sometime or other, and she knew no reason why Peter should be exempted from that affliction, but she just couldn't picture Peter going to bed with anyone. That is, she just couldn't conjure up the visual image of Peter nude and a woman nude and going at it together.

She didn't think Miss Kilter was all that attractive, certainly not in that way, and she didn't think Peter liked that type at all. He had said so many times, hadn't he?

Now she felt her nerves going, as she thought of it all, and remembered Peter's suggestion that if she ever felt that way at night she should turn on the pinpoint bed lamp and read, but the truth was that she hated reading because it left her so alone, as a child and now. She preferred the theater to reading because in the theater there were people around you enjoying the same thing at the same time, but Peter hadn't taken her to the theater all season, and she just couldn't bring herself to join Amanda's Wednesday matinee excursions with those other ladies. The strained babble of women at a Wednesday matinee was so different from the comforting, convivial noise made by men and women at an evening performance.

She wished magazines weren't so full of articles about satisfying your husband sexually. There must be interest in the subject or the magazines wouldn't keep running the articles. Those letters-to-the-editor from women brazen enough to put their initials to thoughts about their marriages.

She reached over for Peter.

For as long as possible, Peter tried to ignore Rose's hands, to feign deep sleep.

But it wasn't possible and finally, with sadness, he turned to pay an installment on his wedlock bargain.

Chapter Five

Peter let himself into Elizabeth's office and closed the door behind him. He was leaning against it when she looked up.

"Paul's taking me to Chicago with him," he said.

"Oh?"

Couldn't she give him more than that? Yet there was a fascination in her giving so little. He gave too much. Talking, he put all the details on the line. Better her way. Left a touch of mystery.

"When?"

Good, she had spoken again; he hadn't been forced to fill the void. Man, you're grabbing at straws.

"Now. Paul says we'll be stuck through tomorrow, and I don't have a thing with me. I'll have to buy a pair of pajamas in Chicago. Look, will you call Rose for me and tell her?"

She looked at him as if he were insane. "I think your secretary'd better phone."

Elizabeth call Rose? What was going on in his head?

He felt the door in back of him moving and eased away from it just as Big Susan poked her head in.

"Don't let me interrupt," she said, interrupting.

Peter was rather fond of Big Susan. She was five feet ten or so, which wasn't so gargantuan, just that her method of attack, her presence, was so formidable. No one called Big Susan that to her face, partly out of courtesy and partly because of her position. She had been Paul's right hand as long as anyone in the agency could remember. She had once been his secretary, but hardly anyone remembered that. Big Susan had a secretary of her own, as had Paul, and if you wanted to get the word on anything to Paul, you didn't drop it to Paul's secretary but to Big Susan's. That was the line of communication to the top.

Big Susan lived well. It was said her salary was higher than most of the account executives, though no one knew exactly because her check, like Paul's, was made out by the comptroller himself, not by the bookkeeping department. When Peter came to the agency, his first impulse was to dislike Big Susan, but he was won over by her wit and charm. Naturally he had wondered if she was a dike, but had decided not, mainly because he found her attractive despite her size and couldn't imagine being attracted to a girl who wasn't straight. "Girl" was a term one had to stretch these days when thinking of Big Susan because she was surely forty, maybe forty-five. One sometimes had the sense that she governed the agency, though her suggestions were always transmitted in Paul's name.

The Husband

"I hate to break this up," she said, "but Paul's almost ready." She passed an overnight bag around the edge of the door. "I'll brief you on the plane. Between drinks." Winking, she said, "You've got thirty seconds," and left.

Peter put the overnight bag up onto Elizabeth's desk. Inside were a pair of size "C" pajamas, a pair of stretch socks, two white shirts, one size 15-34 and the second size 16-35, undershorts sizes 34, 36 and 38, one medium undershirt, a toothpaste, toothbrush, and razor kit. Inside the top bag was a Scotch-taped note scrawled with a felt marker in green: YOU LOOK LIKE A 15-34 AND A 34 WAIST TO ME, BUT I'M ENCLOSING OTHER SIZES IN CASE I'VE GUESSED WRONG. KEEP WHAT YOU WEAR, LEAVE THE OTHERS ON YOUR DESK. MY GIRL'LL PICK UP. RETURN THE CASE WHEN WE GET BACK. CHEERS. SUSAN.

"That's what I call a perfect office wife," said Peter.

"Paul's. Be careful."

"I'll call you tonight from Chicago."

He left without a further word, hurried to his office, took out the bigger shirt and the two pair of larger shorts, thought they looked awfully silly on his desk and stuffed them on top of the out box, slipped a paperback off the shelf into his briefcase and there was Susan at the door, saying, "Time."

He followed seven or eight steps behind her toward Paul's office, and as they passed Elizabeth's she was at the door and whispered to him, "Don't fight with Paul. Unnecessarily." Big Susan turned around and said cheerfully in what Peter thought was much too loud a voice, "He'll only be gone one night!"

The elevator behind Paul's office dropped all three of them nonstop to the basement garage, where Paul's chauffeur took their bags, and in seconds they were limousining through New York traffic toward Kennedy Airport. The Chrysler Imperial rode beautifully, which had one disadvantage: the silence inside was excruciating. Somehow Peter had gotten between Susan and Paul, and for a moment he wanted to shift to one of the jump seats, then thought the better of it; let it pass.

He cleared his throat.

"Chicago must be the Bermar account."

"Right," said Paul. And nothing else.

Peter wished he could turn and look at Paul, but that would have been impossibly awkward, so he tried to reconstruct Paul from memory. How little one remembers the specific features of someone known for years. A craggy face, visible cheekbones, a larger than average face, conspicuous ears, eyebrows thick like wild black weeds, a strong face. Did the skin sag at the jawline? Paul was past fifty now.

"Yes?" Paul was saying.

Idiot, he had actually turned to look at Paul. Make up something quick.

"What about Bermar?"

Susan put her hand on his arm. "I'll brief you on the plane."

It was unlike Paul to be so silent. The Bermar account was in trouble, but why was Peter going along instead of Coolidge? Coolidge was probably in Chicago already; maybe Coolidge had sent for Big Daddy to help. Big Daddy took Big Susan. Why Peter? He knew about Bermar mainly from a few quick words at meetings and from the ads themselves, which weren't the agency's best, but what could you do with a car rental system that was third

when the number one and number two were playing
cutsy with each other in the public prints and had five or
six times the money to spend?

Why was Paul so damn silent?

While they were checking in at the airport, Paul went
off to the men's room for a moment, and Peter quickly
asked Susan what the hell was up with Paul.

"He takes two Marazines," she said, "which he
shouldn't, and two Miltowns, which he shouldn't, but
flying still frightens him, and the combination turns him
off long enough to get there."

So pills accounted for Paul's silence! Peter had thought
Paul was angry at him, that Paul was worried about the
Bermar account or some mysterious agony. The answer
was so simple, reasonable, and yet—he looked at Susan.
She was lying. There was something else on Paul's mind.

They entered from the front of the plane, where some
faded stretch of red carpet led to the stairs. Some promo-
tion man, somewhere long ago, had thought of that. He
was probably working somewhere else, maybe for another airline, trying to come up with something to sell in
the ads because fares were the same, and if you couldn't
buy price, what else could you buy except destination
and some gimmick?

The first-class seats were much wider than the ones
Peter was accustomed to. He was struck by how easily
Big Susan had managed to get Paul into the seat in the
row behind them so that Peter and Susan would sit together. So Paul could eavesdrop? It didn't make sense.
What could Peter give away? He didn't even know why
they were going.

First class really didn't make sense either, considering

the price difference. A short time in a wider seat, a bit
more attention, drinks served faster, off the plane a bit
faster, not much really.

It wasn't money they were spending, Peter thought.
You didn't build equity in an advertising agency. An
agency sold service, ideas, built nothing solid that could
go on independently of the people who created the ideas,
performed the services. An agency was as good as its people, who played musical chairs because you got ahead by
switching agencies, not climbing within one, and after a
while the money didn't matter, only the power, the freedom, and there wasn't much of either because power was
really in the client's hands. An agency was as affluent as
its clients, but they could leave quickly, one, two, all,
and how many had a sense of loyalty or even habit strong
enough to resist the Pied Pipers from other agencies, the
new fads, the "in," the chic, the popular? And so if an
agency made money, it spent it on such things as first-
class fares because it gave the beneficiaries a brief sense
of importance as they headed toward their clients, where
deference was expected.

The plane was starting to move, and Peter was suddenly startled by Big Susan's hand terribly close to his
lap. Then she pointed up. He hadn't observed the seat-
belt sign. He quickly buckled his, thanking her, and
wished the hostess would hurry the first drink.

It was early to be drinking. Thank God it was customary in airplanes.

The jet engines were now at a maximum; he knew the
sounds well enough. And then they were hurtling down
the runway, gathering speed as they went past the point
of no return, and he had the sudden feeling that every-

thing he knew about flying had come from stories and that planes loaded with nearly a hundred passengers, as this one was, couldn't possibly get off the ground, and yet the speed increased and it would only be seconds before they'd smash into the barriers at the end of the runway, and what would be left for Rose and the children? He had not bought insurance at the airport and it was now too late, the tail elevated, the impact inevitable, and suddenly the ground outside the window started to fall away and he knew that they were airborne.

How many generations would it take before a man felt natural in the air? In the thirties, when Peter was a boy, the infrequent sound of an airplane overhead was always cause for the kids to stop, even in the middle of a ball game, and look up until the plane had passed. Kids no longer looked up unless a jet was particularly noisy or a helicopter flew particularly low. Would Jonathan and Margaret fly with greater ease? The statistics were in favor of flight; mile for mile cars were more lethal, and yet cars, like trains, traveled on the ground. The fear of flight was in the mind, impervious to statistics, resistant to fact.

The suburbs of New York were now game-sized rectangles of row houses laid in parallel lines, neat as the fields would be farther west.

"Good morning," said the loudspeaker, "this is your captain. We will be flying at twenty-three thousand feet against a slight head wind and should be landing at O'Hare in two hours and five minutes. There's a drizzle in Chicago but it may be gone by the time we get there." The sound clicked off. Bored voice, the captain's. Flying for him, thought Peter, once held the greatest excitement; now a taxi driver, New York to Chicago, Chicago to New York. Planes were metal, clouds were weather, and what waited at the end of the line was not adventure but retirement.

"Same," he said to the stewardess when Big Susan ordered Scotch.

"Before you get sotted," said Susan, "let me fill you in."

"Fill," said Peter.

"In Chicago, Paul will refer to you as Dr. Carmody."

When Peter was still in school, before the war headed off his Ph.D., he had looked forward to being called "Doctor," not as a learned title but as an appellation likely to be mistaken for its medical equivalent. Years of exposure to doctors tarnished the effect. Turning his sudden title over in his mind, he found none of the old pleasure in it.

"Hey, come back," said Big Susan.

"Sorry."

"H. Q. Wilson, who—"

"I know who."

"Okay. He's the reason we're going to Chicago." She turned to see if Paul were listening. Peter wished he could turn, too.

"H. Q. Wilson runs Bermar with two tight fists. Bermar's doing all right, thank God, but H. Q. owns a big slice of a semiconductor business on the side in Texas, and the competition in semiconductors has been ferocious. All the competing semiconductors have about the same quality, and haggling is all on price or payoffs. H. Q. doesn't run the Texas company, he just counts on it for his biggest money. And so now he takes it out on Bermar, which means us. He also takes it out on his wife and kids and has been going to a headshrinker for nearly two years. It's one of those late-in-life loves when a noneducated, nonintellectual like H. Q. gets involved with Freud after fifty and becomes completely shrink-oriented. He discusses our proposed campaigns on the couch and admits it. It's like going to a fortune teller, you know? H. Q. is Coolidge's account, but Coolidge told too many headshrinker jokes to H. Q. before H. Q. got the bug. Coolidge hasn't any face left. That's why Paul is flying out with an industrial psychologist like you."

Peter looked at Big Susan as if she were nuts.

"Why are you looking at me like I'm nuts?" she asked.

"What the hell do I know about industrial psychology? I couldn't open my mouth."

"Paul doesn't want you to open your mouth. He'll introduce you, make his pitch, and every question he asks you will have an obvious yes-or-no answer. You can even shake or nod your head if you're shy about one-word answers. Look, all you are on this trip is a warm body that happens to look like an industrial psychologist.

"Why couldn't Paul just hire one?"

"Too risky. He might say something."

She patted his hand. "Leave it to Paul."

Peter couldn't help it. He turned around. Paul was fast asleep, a half-finished drink in his hand.

"The nap is good for him," Susan said.

The drizzle hadn't cleared Chicago. The plane came in under the ceiling, straightened up, cut its airspeed a bit too fast and came down with a bump the passengers didn't appreciate. It woke Paul, who leaned across the top of the seat and with surprise in his voice said, "We got here."

"Dr. Carmody is fully briefed," said Big Susan.

Paul nodded his satisfaction, yawned. Bit by bit the fissures in his face started to fill with intelligence and life at the prospect of success in Chicago.

By the time they reached the hotel in the Loop, it was cocktail time, and Paul suggested they stop in the bar. Big Susan took just a moment to check all three of them in, and from the room numbers Peter had a fleeting impression that Big Susan and Paul had rooms next to each other. Probably connecting doors.

He regretted having thought that. He knew, everyone knew, that Paul and Susan were a package. He assumed, everyone assumed, they weren't just pals. It was none of his business. He couldn't care less. Really.

Two doubles apiece, ordered quickly, drunk quickly. Paul was obviously celebrating his intact arrival. He actually seemed jovial.

"You see, the honest thing about Bermar," Paul was saying, "is that number one in car rentals is going to stay number one and number two is going to stay number two, and there's one helluva gap between two and us. The only real way of narrowing that gap is for Bermar to get locations in third- and fourth-level towns, maybe two, three hundred within a year, because car rental is convenience, not a model's face in the ad. But that would take more working capital than H. Q. can come up with now or in the foreseeable future, and he knows it. So we're going to have to play games."

99

The Husband

Peter could swear that Susan had put her hand on his thigh for a split second without any attempt to conceal the move from Paul.

"The game I'm throwing him at our dinner meeting this evening," said Paul, "is the kind of idea he expects from an advertising agency, an idea he'll think of as a breakthrough since he can't come up with more branches. I'm going to propose a Car-of-the-Month Plan. You sign up with a Bermar dealer and once a month you get a different car for the weekend. Your choice off a list of available cars; one weekend a Thunderbird, the next an MG, the next maybe a Toronado, you know, a family fling around the neighborhood trying out all the cars the average fellow dreams about and seldom has the guts to buy. If he signs up for a second year, the first month he gets something really special for the weekend, say a Lincoln Continental, and maybe the third sign-up gets him a Rolls. If you organize things right, you won't need a lot of fancy cars to make things work, and what Bermar'll be doing is renting cars on a regular, predictable basis, on weekends, when business is off anyway, to guys who don't really need to rent a car. That's the key. This Car-of-the-Month idea will bring Bermar a lot of new customers and put them on a steady sign-up basis, and the capital investment for the new cars'll be a fraction of what it would cost to set up a couple of hundred or more new franchises. Also the ad campaign for Car-of-the-Month will glamorize the whole Bermar operation, pick up a lot of industry comment, and maybe even get H. Q.'s mind off the electronics business in Texas." Paul laughed.

Peter was impressed.

"As for you," Paul continued, "whenever I mention some phase or other of the plan, all you do is nod approvingly, and if you want to be a nice fellow, you'll pop out once in a while with 'Very sound psychologically' or some such, okay?"

The United Nations types one runs into in New York are always saying everyone in the world is really the same. Where in Africa or Asia, thought Peter, in what Welsh coal mine or Slovak village, did any human being even think the way Paul just did? Everywhere? Or did most of them emigrate to America?

At the elevator on the twelfth floor, Paul and Susan went right, jangling their respective keys, and Peter went left. There were two hours before the scheduled meeting. Ease off. Call home.

In his room, Peter was unable to find his suitcase. He phoned down to the desk and was told the bags had gone up as instructed when they checked in. He dialed Susan's room number.

"No, you're not bothering me," she said. "Wait a minute and I'll look."

She came back to the phone and said, "It's here.".

"I'll be there in a flash."

"Five flashes. I need a couple of minutes."

Peter hung up and stretched out on the bed, careful to get his shoes on the footboard and not on the bedspread. Good boy gets check mark for being considerate to hotel bedspread. Mother had been dead eighteen years. He was still keeping score for her.

He closed his eyes and thought that while home was

nice, another city, even if not a strange city, was good, change was good; all the senses needed a new locale from time to time.

Better get up, he thought, you're dropping off. He was on his way down the hall when he remembered again that he hadn't called home.

Peter knocked twice on the door of Susan's room. He smelled the perfume even before he entered and headed for his suitcase on the luggage rack with the thought of getting in and out fast so as not to intrude. The lock click made him turn. Susan was leaning against the closed door, and the shock of what he saw made his right hand sweat on the suitcase handle.

He lowered the suitcase to the floor.

Susan was wearing something chiffony, covering her from neck to toe and yet transparent enough for Peter to see the darkness of the areolas of her breasts and the hair where her legs met. Over the years, he must have seen Susan dressed in a hundred different garments, suits mostly, and they flashed through his mind now, but never had he suspected that the large, well-proportioned lady was anything like the woman leaning against the door.

With a pleasurable sting, he remembered the hand on his thigh in the bar.

He felt himself thickening.

"Did you like," she said, "Paul's plan?"

Susan passed very close to him, headed for the open bathroom door, turned the shower on, and as she did so, dropped the negligee at her feet.

"You could be an angel," she said lightly, lightly, "and soap my back."

He took the bar of soap like an automaton as she stepped into the shower.

"You'll get your jacket wet," she said, facing away from him and letting the water rivulet over her.

Peter hung his jacket on the knob of the door and rolled up his right sleeve. "Let me borrow that," she said, taking the soap from him and covering her large self with a white film that turned to lather and then ran off, swirling into the shower drain. She handed the soap back and turned her back.

Peter was sure it wasn't happening.

"A little lower," she said, and he did.

His mind was observing in fragments: the lather swirling into the drain, the shape of her right hip as it curved toward the front, and then the fact of the second door; it *was* a connecting bathroom, and the door into the other room wasn't locked. If Paul had wanted to, he might even have heard their conversation. Peter touched her shoulder and gestured toward the second door.

"He's a gentleman," she said. "He'd never open without knocking first."

Susan's wet face was close to his. Suddenly there was the commitment, her lips on his mouth, a rousing excitement that was frighteningly unbearable. She glanced down and smiled her pleasure that her attentions had had the desired effect.

"Dry me," she said, her voice meaning "please" also. He never had before. Not Rose. Not Elizabeth.

"Lightly," she said.

It was unbearable.

In a moment Susan had gone into the bedroom, on the lightest of feet, it seemed, as if dancing, and let herself down on the bed, a Maya, Odalisque, and the thumping inside him would not be put off. His clothes fell where they fell, his pulse like a river now, and he was kissing her, preparing to let an enormous lust loose, when the second door had the promised knock and before Peter could think a thing, Susan had said, "Come in," and Paul was standing there in a bathrobe watching them.

Chapter Six

Peter's first feeling was the expectation of violence, Paul picking up some lethal object and smashing him for trespassing, revenging himself on the errant son caught in the mother's bedroom. This sense of immediate punishment was reinforced in an instant by the sure knowledge that his days at the agency were over; he was suddenly out of a job, with no reference from his employer possible.

Instead, Paul said nothing.

"Paul won't hurt you," said Big Susan softly, touching him to retrieve his downfall.

In that second he felt surely Big Susan was lying; Paul was ready to smash.

Peter wanted desperately to buy a moment's respite to think, but Big Susan's experienced hands and lips kept after him.

The Husband

In the same moment that Peter began to understand what was happening, Big Susan pronounced it: "He only wants to watch."

Everyone knew about voyeurs, but Paul seemed so *normal.*

It was the word *normal* that careened around in his head as he saw Paul standing there, the impassive exterior cracked by just a trace of anguish, and Big Susan frantically trying to make things work out—for whom? For him? For Paul? For herself? Certainly not for him. For Paul then?

Was the whole trip to Chicago planned for this, a grotesque camping-out seduction? Was the meeting with H. Q. Wilson at Bermar just the excuse?

He looked down at Big Susan, who was trying to work things around to a solution, as she must have tried in countless previous experiences with someone as unprepared as Peter. What a threatened way to live, Peter thought. Or were they used to it?

It was then she repeated the harmlessness of it all in the same words. "He only wants to watch."

Peter couldn't do it. There are moments in childhood when you want the trapdoor to open, the instant escape from what is happening. You never give up the hope of such trapdoors. He needed one now.

It was his body refusing. If Peter were capable, he might have gone on with it, as men have with women and women with men in countless instances, on with it because of the disappointment on Paul's face and because Big Susan seemed so desperately to want to succeed.

He looked at Paul and moved his shoulders as if to apologize.

Paul left the room without a word.

The door to Susan's bathroom closed. Peter could distinctly hear the second bathroom door close and lock.

Big Susan turned off the main light, leaving the room in the softer glow of the bedside lamp. The voyeur gone, the visibility could decrease. Was it her disappointed, angry vengeance he would have to face now, as he had Rose's on those occasions when Rose had been disappointed in herself and had turned her disappointment on him?

Susan's face seemed softly honed in the lesser light. She kissed him very gently on the cheek. As if it were a rare distinction, she said, "You're a wife fucker."

That wasn't true, of course, and Susan knew it because she knew about Elizabeth. But was it in some sense true? If it was, why had he gone as far as he had before Paul came into the room? Because a man is a physiological instrument, subject to the whims of chance? He felt affection for Susan, built over the years. Had he been attracted by the sudden sight of her nearly nude and feminine in a way he had not imagined her before? Or was there a law of sexual opportunity which affected men differently than women?

No matter. It was no go.

He dressed in silence, as quickly as he could, took the suitcase and stood a moment at the door. Susan had not moved, and now that it was over, he saw as he had before how lovely she could be. He felt pity for her in the role she pursued.

"I'm used to it," she said, getting off the bed and coming over to him at the door. "The funny thing is how often it works out."

Peter wanted to say something helpful, but all that came out was, "Wouldn't Paul get the same kick out of watching blue movies?"

"Would you?" said Susan.

She kissed his cheek again, as if to grant reassurance of some kind, and Peter followed his impulse, which was to kiss her not on the cheek but on the mouth, and it was the same mouth he had kissed before and the same excitement came over him. He could feel her body through his clothes, and the insanity of it was that in a second he was locking the bathroom door and shedding his clothes again. He couldn't tell whether Susan wanted to with him, and for an instant, it was only an instant, God help him, he found himself using force, and then he knew she wanted to also, and he did. It brought him great physical pleasure, and a welcome release for them both. What kind of animal was he, he thought?

Their joy was barely subsiding when he thought of Paul in the next room.

Where would this lead to, or was this merely one of those sexual transiencies other men talked about that had no repercussions whatsoever?

Paul knew.

Susan knew.

He knew.

It could not be erased. *Play it by ear*, he thought, and knew that playing things by ear was not his life-style. He found his security in planning. Now someone else's plan had been unleashed in his life.

As he dressed for the second time (that meeting with Bermar—that improbable meeting—was so soon!), he saw Susan watching him and wished that he could read her mind. He wanted to blow her a kiss, knew it might look foolish, and so he simply picked up his suitcase (the traveling salesman, he joked to himself) and when he closed the door of her room, he stood outside just long enough to hear her unlocking her bathroom door to let Paul back into her world.

Peter had the key in the lock of his own room when he heard the phone ringing and remembered that he had forgotten to call home. He got the door open as quickly as he could, shut it behind him, dropped the suitcase and headed for the phone. When he picked it up and said, "Hello?" he wondered if his voice betrayed him.

"Here's your party," said the telephone, and then he heard a woman's voice in New York say, "Thank you."

He really didn't want to talk to anyone. He wanted time to think.

"Peter," said Elizabeth, clear as if she were in the room with him, "you've been cheating on me."

After an interval, she said, "Are you there?" and he realized that though his brain had been clacking away, his voice had been silent. He said he was there.

"Anything wrong?" she asked.

"No, no," he reassured her. Then, thinking he had best carry this lightly (why do we think mind reading is possible when we know it is not?), he said, "I can't be cheating. Rose is in New York."

"Did you call her?"

He had forgotten. He would right away.

"You sound distracted."

"Well, the meeting's very soon. I'm supposed to play industrial psychologist."

Elizabeth laughed.

Then she said, "Why do you sound the way you do?"

"How do I sound?"

"Removed. Not yourself."

"Sorry. Been a bit hectic since we got here."

"How hectic?"

He wished the conversation would stop. He was trying to say innocuous things and instead was getting in deeper.

"Peter, when you're home where Rose can hear you, you say the most indiscreet things. Now that you're in a hotel room alone, we talk like strangers. Or aren't you alone?"

If he said he was alone, she'd expect intimacies on the phone. If he invented somebody's presence, it could lead to complications. Things were complicated enough already.

"Are you there?"

"Yes, sure."

"Are you alone?"

"Yes, I am, but, elf, listen, I've got to get set for the meeting. My mind's in a whirl."

He could tell that she was put out. The range and pace of his talk had been artificial. He wished the whole conversation could be recalled and tried again. He said goodbye. As he hung up, an onrush of guilt flooded him for the first time since he left Susan's room.

He stretched out on the bed, hoping that if his body

could relax his mind would, too. The phone rang. It was Susan.

"Meet in the lobby in ten minutes, okay?"

He was used to Big Susan giving instructions. Now she was asking.

"Paul be there?" he asked, feeling foolish about the question.

"Of course," she said.

He was tempted to say, "The show must go on." With temptations like that, say the least.

"Ten minutes," he said.

Peter called Rose and explained as quickly as possible about the sudden trip, the industrial psychologist bit, he'd be home tomorrow.

Rose interrupted. "Is Elizabeth there?"

"She's in New York," he said, trying to sound surprised at the question.

"I'll let you talk to the kids," said Rose, and in a minute he was listening to Margaret jabbering away, and then Jonathan, and when he hung up at last, he remembered almost nothing of what had been said.

He spotted Paul and Susan across the lobby. He wondered if Paul was thinking about firing him. Not now; he knew about Paul, Paul knew about him and Elizabeth. A blackmail standoff, even up. His clue would be what Paul would say.

Paul said merely, "Let's go," and they did. The limousine was out front. The pilgrimage to Bermar was made in silence.

Paul was brilliant at the meeting. The Rent-a-Car Club

seemed a sounder idea than at first. Peter nodded and yessed on cue, and at the end of the meeting H. Q. Wilson seemed genuinely pleased and even made a big do over Peter's "contribution."

Peter had lost his sense of time but knew it was quite late when they got back to the hotel. They didn't stop in the bar for a nightcap. Nobody suggested it.

He wondered if they were supposed to make another try at it now that everyone knew his role. Would Paul risk it?

Peter wondered what else would have happened that night if the first pass had worked. A second round? Does twice make a confirmed habit?

Big Susan had said other attempts had sometimes failed. He looked to her for a cue.

"Good night," she said as the elevator reached their floor. "We'll see you in the morning." *Would* Paul retaliate? There was a sadness on Paul's face as he and Susan turned off to their rooms.

As he lay in bed, Peter tried to imagine the conversation that might be taking place between Paul and Susan. He wondered if anything else besides conversation took place. Probably couldn't; that was the problem, wasn't it? Did Susan tell Paul earlier what had happened between them? Would she now, or ever?

It must have been close to morning when Peter finally fell asleep. He dreamed one of those transportation dreams in which you can't get a cab, the trains go in the wrong direction, you try to walk and things get in your way, and you get increasingly alarmed about never reaching your destination. The phone, not the dream, shattered him awake.

It was Susan's voice.

"We're dressed and headed out to Bermar to finish off the basic budget questions. Paul thinks maybe you'd better stay here. Things went so well at the meeting we might as well leave well enough alone."

It was her old way of talking.

Since he couldn't get back to sleep, he got dressed and ate some waffles in the coffee shop downstairs, then roamed around Chicago, feeling superfluous. When he got back to the hotel, they still weren't there.

He imagined that Susan and Paul had been in a terrible car accident, wiping out the incidents of last night without trace.

Susan and Paul finally showed up, packed quickly, and the three of them were sped to the airport. The accident will happen now, Peter thought. All three of us will be wiped out, that's the way it's planned.

The plane took off on time. He sat behind Susan and Paul, who talked during the trip as if they were old and very good friends staging a reunion. Peter could make out very little of what they said. All he could see was the heads bobbing from time to time. On this leg of the trip, he was the voyeur.

Chapter Seven

Angled on Peter's head was his seldom-worn bowler hat, a signal to those who knew him well that he was in a manic state. He led Elizabeth by the hand ("Not by the hand!" she said, but he paid no attention) down the tree-lined street on which he lived, his legs moving faster than a walk and yet not running.

"Peter," she said, "you're out of your mind."

"Out of breath," he answered, "and well out of my mind. Have you ever been in my mind? It's terrible."

"Not a step farther." She had stopped abruptly, catching Peter in midstride and nearly throwing him off balance.

"Hey," he protested.

"It's insane. I won't do it."

He couldn't tell how serious she was. A moment before, she had seemed to be sharing his madcap exhilaration, but now, half a minute from home, she stood braced against his tugs, determined.

"If you won't move," he said, "I'll carry you."

"*That* would really be insane. A streetful of people would see us."

They both looked. There wasn't a soul on the street.

"But anyone could come out at any time," she protested. "Look, something sensible. If you have to go there, go, but I'll just disappear quietly around the corner and have a cup of coffee."

He had made the mistake of letting her hand go, and she was now walking off, dashing his plan and his spirit.

"Please!" he said. It was the sound of his plea that stopped her. Elizabeth enjoyed so his manic states, and knew how quickly they could disappear.

"It means a lot to me," he said. "Please come."

"You're looking for trouble."

"I don't think of you as trouble. You came this far," he said. "It's just down the block."

"I didn't think you'd go through with it."

"Are you daring me?"

"No, heavens, no."

"Then come with me."

She gave him her hand again. *Insane.*

They stopped in front of the three steps leading to the front door. Peter dropped Elizabeth's hand, let himself in with the key, disappeared into the house for half a minute to make a quick check, and then motioned her in.

Elizabeth went up three steps like an automaton, then stopped as if there were a curtain of air at the open door. "The children will hear us," she said.

"They're asleep. I checked."

"What if they come down?"

"I'll tell them you're my visiting-nurse service. To hell with that," he said suddenly and with the strength of his arms alone lifted her up over the threshold. "I feel great tonight," he said as he set her down and closed the door.

"What if Rose comes back?"

"When she goes to gab with Amanda, she always stays all evening."

Once or twice Peter had heard about this form of insanity from other men, taking a woman to your own house, to the stronghold itself, the ultimate boyish dare. But—he had rationalized the danger away—there were things he wanted to show Elizabeth, and what other way was there?

"This the kids call the daddy chair," he said, sprawling in it.

"It looks decrepit and comfortable," said Elizabeth, her voice still forming a high thin edge to her nervousness.

"My father's," said Peter, glorying in the depths of the chair. "Never reupholstered, made before I was born."

"Is this the mommy chair?" asked Elizabeth, her hand on a greenish, thin chair Peter had always thought of as an inanimate lady-in-waiting.

"Rose doesn't have a particular chair."

"She sits in your lap."

"Now don't you start."

A quick glance at each other told them both this couldn't be happening.

Elizabeth, to her relief, recognized a painting on the far wall and let loose an appreciative sound. "How do you ever afford a Buffet?"

Peter perked proudly. "Bought it years ago. Instead of eating. That's not true. Instead of drinking. It cost ninety bucks. Ninety could have bought two cases of Scotch in those days."

"It's probably worth several carloads of Scotch now."

"I adore it," said proud Peter proudly.

"It, or the fact that you bought it cheap?"

He smiled. "It's very difficult to lie to you." Leading her away, he said, "This one, elf, I got for nothing."

"I wondered where you hung it. It's not my best. Doesn't Rose mind?"

"I don't think she knows who did it," said Peter, sorry he lied, sorrier that Elizabeth knew it.

"She can read, can't she?"

"Hey, never mind," said Peter, "come look at this. Meet the hobby I had before I had you. It's stereophonic, multiplex, ambidextrous, hydraulic, and psychotic. It's got a woofer, a tweeter, and a first-class rug beater. The automatic changer changes seven-inch, ten-inch, twelve-inch, and diapers. Put it together with my own hands."

Like a boy about the set, she thought. Was he like a boy about her?

"Nice hands," she said. Response to a litany.

Peter tried to put his arms around her.

"Not here," she whispered.

"Want a drink?" he whispered back.

"No, no, not here."

"Want two drinks?"

"Peter, you're insane."

"I've got some marijuana in the closet."

"I don't believe you."

"Would skeletons do?"

"Peter, I've got the creeps. Let's get out of here. This was a crazy idea to start with."

"Will you spend the weekend with me?"

"Here?"

"Course not. In a motel."

"With Rose's permission?"

"Okay, then, in a revolving door. Separate compartments. Who can criticize that?"

"Please let's leave."

"I wanted you to see me in my natural habitat, elf, framed by my worldly possessions."

"It feels like a cage to me."

"I go in and out at will," he said, a shadow edging across his voice. He was sliding off the manic wave, a surfer hitting the beach. "This, m'lady," he said, "is my warehouse. Devoid of emotional content. Except that my children sleep here."

"Peter," she said, "this is the place where *you* sleep."

He was trying to think of something clever to say to her when they both heard the car in the driveway.

Peter's face went gray. "That's our car."

"You said—"

"Get upstairs."

"What?"

"Quick. Up the stairs and turn to the right. The bedroom."

"Hide in your bedroom?"

"The kids are in the other bedrooms. Now hurry. I'll think of something."

"I won't hide!" she said, green determination in her eyes.

Peter, his heart thundering, heard the front door open.

He expected anger on Rose's face. Instead, it had the lines and pulse of surprise and fear.

"Oh," was all she said.

He cautioned himself. *Play it safe. Say the least.* But he found the words running. "I thought you were—I mean, you said you'd be—weren't you supposed to be at Amanda's for the evening? How is she?"

"I was."

"She has those . . . again?"

"It wasn't cramps."

"Rose, you're shaking."

"Here are the car keys. Jack's there now with a bunch of the family. Go over and keep him company."

Lightly, lightly. "I really don't feel like Jack tonight, really. I'd rather not."

"Please. He needs you."

"What's the matter?"

"Could you get me a glass of water?"

"Sure, but why don't you—?"

"Never mind the water." Rose folded herself into a chair, her bony knees raised high, her shoulders hunched, making her chest seem convex.

"My mouth is dry," she said. Peter went through the swinging door to the kitchen to fetch the water, wanted or unwanted, to give himself time to think, but the image of Elizabeth and Rose unspeaking in the same room stayed in his mind until he came back quickly and gave hunched Rose the glass. He noticed the black smudge of mascara, wet, at the right eye. Outside, he heard the horn of a passing car. He didn't realize Rose was talking to him, ignoring Elizabeth, until Rose had said a sentence or two.

"And when Amanda phoned, I said I'd finish watering the garden. That was when I phoned you at the office so you'd know where I was. I finished watering the garden. The hose needs picking up, I forgot to put it away. I changed my clothes. It was an hour between watering the garden and calling and changing and driving over, and I rang. I thought she might have gone out to the corner for something, you know? I tried the door and went in and there, right on the other side of the door, going into the kitchen, a chair was knocked over and a glass dribbling all over, and Peter, she was against the counter, her mouth open. I wanted to scream, she looked so awful. I mean, her teeth looked so false and one breast was hanging out, I mean, completely out of her housecoat like a limp bag. I found the doctor's number pasted near the phone and I called, and he said not to worry, he'd come right away, and he came. Peter, Amanda is dead."

Rose hadn't touched the water in her glass. Suddenly she was looking at it with revulsion, as if it reminded her of the spilled water in Amanda's kitchen. She set the full glass down on the carpet next to her chair.

"The doctor said it was a heart attack, not a belly-ache. The symptoms are sometimes the same, he said— but that's not fair! Amanda's just halfway through life, she's my age. Go, go, Jack's waiting for you. I tried to make him come here, but the relatives wouldn't let him."

It took a second for Rose to rise from the chair and to put the sticks of her arms around Peter, sobbing, "Peter, tell me you love me!"

Peter stared over Rose's shoulder at the expanse of the gray carpet and Elizabeth at the other side of the room.

"Peter, you'd better get over there," said Elizabeth, speaking for the first time.

"What is she doing here?" said Rose, her voice rising, her face a red blemish of anger.

Elizabeth, very quietly said, "Please don't look at me that way, Mrs. Carmody."

"What is she doing in our home?"

"You're upset, Rose," Peter said.

Elizabeth asked, "Can I get you anything?"

"What did she say?" Rose asked Peter.

"Can I get you anything?"

"I'm not a visitor here," said Rose, trying to flatten the piercing sound of her voice. "I'll get myself—Peter, where is that water?"

Peter got the glass from beside the chair. He found a Miltown in his pillbox.

"Can I help you?" repeated Elizabeth.

"Don't let her touch me!"

"I wasn't going to touch you. Your husband and I finished the afternoon at a client meeting, and he suggested he might show me his home."

She turned to Peter. "You knew I wouldn't be home."

"Take the pill, Rose. Drink the water. It wasn't on purpose. It happened that way."

Rose swallowed the pill with some water.

"What was that pill?" she asked.

"A pill."

"Tell me."

"Arsenic," said Peter.

"Peter, please," said Elizabeth.

"Vitamins," said Peter.

"Stop that," said Rose.

"It's a placebo," said Peter. "It'll help quiet you down."

The phone rang.

As Peter turned to answer it, Rose grabbed his arm. "Don't leave me, Peter. Let your secretary answer the phone."

Peter stopped. "She's not my secretary."

The phone insisted on being answered.

"Yes, yes, I know," said Rose. "I'm sorry. Do you want me to get the phone, Peter?"

But Elizabeth was already at the phone and answering. "Mr. or Mrs.?" she asked. "I'll get him."

"Who is it?" asked Peter.

"Some excitable lady."

Peter got to the phone, listened for a minute, then said, "I see. All right." He hung up. "One of the relatives. Jack dropped a coffee cup and got pretty hysterical and lit out of there like a lunatic about five minutes ago and drove off. They say he said something about coming here. The relatives are pretty angry."

"Why here?" asked Rose.

"Where do you expect him to go," snapped Peter, "the American Bar Association? You're Amanda's next of kin."

"I'd better go," said Elizabeth, pulling on her gloves.

"Please," said Peter, "I want you to stay."

Elizabeth looked at Rose. "Is it all right with Mrs. Carmody?"

Rose stood motionless.

"Mrs. Carmody is not the only resident in this house," said Peter.

The doorbell buzzed, silencing them. In a second, Peter was at the door, opening it. Jack walked in, stopped in the center of the room. Peter avoided touching him, as if death were catching.

In a quiet voice, very unlike himself, Jack acknowledged their presence simply with their names. "Peter. Rose."

"This is Miss Kilter," said Peter.

"A business associate," added Rose.

Peter said, "I'm sorry, Jack. Rose just told me."

"Hope you don't mind my busting in."

"Oh, no, no, I was just coming over when they phoned."

"Damn son of a bitch relatives," said Jack quietly. "Amanda and I never see them except at funerals. What the hell did they want to come to the house for? I guess it's my fault. Thought I had to let them know. Had to make coffee for all of them. Bastards. I can't make coffee. Amanda makes coffee."

"Want a drink?" asked Peter.

"No, thanks. Mind if I sit?"

"No, no, go right ahead."

"How do you feel?" asked Rose.

"What's that?" said Jack absentmindedly.

"Never mind," said Rose.

"When I'm here," said Jack at nobody in particular, "I can't believe anything happened there, know what I mean?"

"I know," said Peter.

"I feel dead," said Jack.

"You're tired."

"I know when I'm tired. I'm not tired. I feel like nothing. Dead."

"It's the shock," said Rose.

Jack scratched his temple. "With her having rheumatic trouble since she was a kid, while I was coming home from work, I sometimes used to have a feeling I'd find her dead. You know what I mean? The truth is, I always felt that way when I was mad at Amanda, and I hoped I'd find her dead. Tonight I didn't think anything of the kind. I just wanted to eat and watch television. I wasn't mad at all, at anybody, and I came in and there's Rose and the doctor and a sheet. Why the hell do they put a sheet over her face?"

"I don't know," said Rose.

Jack turned to Peter. "Do you know?"

"No."

Jack swung around toward Elizabeth. "Do you?"

"No," said Elizabeth.

"Don't think about it, Jack," said Rose.

"You know," said Jack, "it's ten years, ten or eleven, since I been to church. Damn sermon-preaching minister was just a kid. I guess he's ten or eleven years older now. Do you think Amanda's dead, I mean, like a doornail? No heaven. No hell. I guess not. I feel stupid crying. God, I haven't cried in a long time. Amanda! I mean, do you think I'm crying because of Amanda or because of me?"

"Can I get you something to eat?" asked Rose.

"Like what?"

"There's some ham and cheese."

Jack shook his head.

"Beer?" asked Rose, thinking Jack might like some beer. Peter always said Jack was a beer man by temperament, even if he liked hard liquor.

Jack declined the beer.

"I could warm up some beef stew," suggested Rose.

"I don't want anything. You know what I want? A grown-up son. Isn't that crazy? I want to put my hand on a grown-up boy's shoulder and say, 'It'll be all right, kid,' and we'd both look at his mother, and the kid and me'd be a real comfort to each other."

Rose said, "Your brother Frank's boy is over there with him."

Peter noticed the first sign of emotion in Jack. "That kid's a car thief!" Jack answered in anger. I don't mean that. I mean a son of mine! You know something, Rose, Peter, I'm fifty-six and I'm never going to have a son! Maybe I'm never going to have a wife again. I'd like to have a wife like you, Rose."

"Jack!" said Rose.

"I mean, if you weren't married. Do you know what I'm saying? I don't know what I'm saying. Why did I come here? Rose, you're Amanda's best friend."

"Yes, I suppose so."

"In some ways you're like her."

"I am?"

"Will someone shut me up?" said Jack. "What I mean is, sometimes on Sunday mornings Amanda sleeps late and you know me, restless, so I'd get up and fix breakfast, and go out for a walk and buy the Sunday paper, and if the weather is nice I'll read the Sunday paper in the park, and when I've read all the goddamn stinking ads, I watch the kids playing hockey the way they do,

and it's noon before I get back, and there is Amanda still
asleep and when I looked at her I'd think she was dead."
Jack was weeping freely now. "When," he asked, "is
Sunday?"

Peter had to wait until the small stone of silence slid
down his throat. "Day after tomorrow," he finally said.

"What am I going to do on Sunday? I mean, can you
think of your life completely different? My father was
eighty-four when he died and he wasn't sick much, but
we'd all been waiting for him to go, I guess, 'cause it was
about time and he bored everybody, including himself.
He kept postponing it from year to year and then he
died, and it was like finishing reading the newspaper—
but who expected Amanda to die? You knew her, Rose.
Did you expect her to die?"

"No," said Rose.

"Did you, Pete?"

"Miss," he said to Elizabeth, "I forgot your name."

"Kilter," said Elizabeth.

"Well, you didn't know Amanda at all, but would you
expect a woman not yet fifty to die without warning
me?"

Elizabeth shook her head.

"I mean, you're all sitting there like you don't know
what to say, and what I want you to say is, if Amanda
weren't dead I'd have a chance to treat her different."

"Sure you would," said Rose.

"That's a fucking lie," said Jack. "I'm a lousy husband."

"You're not a lousy husband," said Rose.

"I'm a lousy widower, that's what. Peter, I bet you
didn't think of that. Next time I'm asked, 'Married or sin-

gle?' by some jerk with a questionnaire, I say, 'Widower.' That sounds like a woman, not like a man. Widower. Amanda's still in the house. I'd better get back to the house. Those goddamn relatives will be screwing up the funeral arrangements and getting Amanda someplace in a dog cemetery or having her cremated. Remember how Amanda was afraid of fire? She used to hate lighting the damn stove. It'd be a sin to cremate her."

"I'll come with you," said Peter.

"The hell you will. You got company."

"I was just leaving," said Elizabeth.

"Hell, no! I feel better, really I do. I'm going for a ten-minute drive, and I'll be back at the house. Maybe all the relatives'll have died too, wouldn't that be a present! Where's my hat?"

"You didn't bring a hat," said Rose.

"I always wear a hat. Amanda likes hats. I tell her it makes me bald, but she likes hats. Liked. Got to remember."

At the door, Jack turned. "You know the goddamn government won't even pay burial expenses because she didn't have Social Security and wasn't a veteran? I hate the goddamn government. So long, kids."

"Take care, Jack," said Peter.

"You take care."

When Jack left, there was a moment in which no one said anything, and then Rose said, "Jack's a nice man."

"Just because Amanda's dead doesn't make him a nice man."

"You're not very diplomatic," said Rose.

"I don't like Jack," said Peter.

"Well, don't shout at me," said Rose.

"I'm not shouting."

"All I said was, you could be more diplomatic."

Peter could feel the careening downhill, gears shredding, no traction, no control. "A diplomat," he said, "is about as disconnected from reality as a man can get. You know me, Rose, don't you? Can you imagine me stalling around for months pretending to be talking while somebody else makes up his mind about what I'm going to say? That's what a diplomat does. Well, I think sometimes what you think and what you say ought to be closer together, like now!"

"And what do you mean by that?" Rose said, frightened.

Peter turned away. *Coward*, he thought. "Rose?" he said, the catch in his voice barely noticeable.

"Yes?"

"Sudden things build, and tonight's capped it."

Elizabeth tried to signal to him to stop. "Keep out of this," he snapped to her. "I'm speaking to Rose. All the time Jack was talking—Rose, pay attention—all that time you weren't thinking of Amanda dead, you were thinking of yourself dead."

"That's not true!"

"Well, I was thinking of myself dead, and regretting it! When death comes whoosh I don't want to get caught where I am now. I want to be living when I die. Rose, I'm moving out of the house."

"Peter!"

He started up the stairs, carried by the momentum of his words. "I'm going to pack a bag and leave tonight.

I'm going to get a divorce as fast as I can get a divorce."

"You've lost your mind," said Rose.

"There may be a lot of things I'm going to lose, but not my mind."

"You're not being realistic," said Rose to Peter, who had already disappeared from view at the head of the stairs.

She heard his reply loud and clear. "Maybe I'm being imaginative for the first time since I got into advertising."

"Peter, what are you doing up there?"

"Putting some things in a suitcase. A shirt and underwear," came his voice, "for tomorrow. Another tie. Want to check and see what I'm putting in?"

Rose looked at Elizabeth. "It's the shock of Amanda's death," she said calmly.

"Yes," said Elizabeth.

"He'll get over it," said Rose. "We've been married a very long time."

"I know," said Elizabeth.

"He'll get over you," said Rose.

"Perhaps," said Elizabeth.

"Don't you talk so casually to me. Don't think I don't realize what's caused all this. I didn't have any trouble, not any real trouble with Peter before he met you and your slimy—you heard me correctly, I said slimy—"

"I'll wait outside," said Elizabeth, heading for the door.

"Oh, no, you won't!" said Rose, grabbing Elizabeth's arm hard.

"Please," said Elizabeth.

"No, I want to see what you threw in his face to make him want to leave me. What do you do when you come into his office and close the door? Do you grab for his pants right away?"

Elizabeth tried to struggle free. "You're hurting my arm."

"Do you kiss him, I mean, stick your tongue down his throat? Do you shove your tits in his mouth? Are they nice? Come on, let me see!" With a sudden fury, Rose tried to rip Elizabeth's clothing. Elizabeth tried fending her off but couldn't get the hand off her arm; she felt the nails and then heard the unmistakable sound of cloth tearing. Peter came bounding down the stairs.

"Rose!" he yelled.

Instantly Rose turned on him. "Does she kiss you? Show me where she kisses you. Is it all over, everywhere, is that how she got you?"

"Rose, what's gotten into you?"

"Nothing's gotten into me for a long time," shrieked Rose, "because you've been getting into her! How is it, better than me? Is that why you're leaving, so you can go to bed with her every night? Is that it?"

Into the silence, Peter said the irretrievable. "I love her."

"That slut? Don't make me laugh!"

Elizabeth couldn't stop Peter in time. He slapped Rose's face.

"Oh, he can't hurt me," shrilled Rose, "not by getting into your pants, he can't, not if you do—" She was stopped by Peter's second slap.

"I'm going to marry Elizabeth," said Peter.

Rose, holding the back of her hand against her flushed cheek, said quietly, "Marry? What about me? You're married to me." The enormity of it must have reached her then, because she was suddenly at Peter with her fists. "I'll kill you first!" It took all of Peter's strength to hold her arms.

"Let's get out of here," he said to Elizabeth.

"No, you won't," said Rose, and in full voice yelled, "Jonathan! Margaret!"

"Now stop that," said Peter.

Louder now, Rose yelled, "Jon! Maggie! Come down right away!"

Peter pleaded with her for silence, but this only encouraged her to tear away from his grasp and bound up the stairs, yelling, "Jonathan! Margaret!" until the children heard and were sleepily, frightened, saying, "What is it, Mommy?" and Rose was dragging them, uncomprehending, down the stairs to the living room.

"Hold your daddy!" she screamed. "He's leaving, he says he's leaving forever!" The children seemed completely disbelieving. "Ask him, go ahead, ask him," shouted Rose.

The children went to Peter, who took them in his arms.

"Well, why don't you ask him?" said Rose.

"Where are you going?" said Jonathan.

Peter wished he had had time to think, to prepare. "You don't want to see me arguing with Mommy all the time, do you?" he asked Jonathan.

But it was Margaret who seemed to understand immediately. "Daddy, don't go!" she pleaded.

"He's going to divorce you," said Rose. "He said he's going to divorce you!"

"That's not true," said Peter to the children. "I'll never divorce you. I can't. I don't want to. I love you. I'm just going to live somewhere else."

"You liar!" Rose shrieked.

"Rose, please," Peter said, "what are you doing to the children?"

"Have you asked yourself that? What are you doing, you—you and that—whore!"

Peter let go of the children. "Let's get out of here," he said to Elizabeth.

"Please don't go, Daddy," said Margaret.

"He's a monster!" shrieked Rose.

"If you don't stop that this minute, Rose, I'm going to take the children with me, right in their nightclothes."

"I'll call the police."

"Oh, no, Mommy, please don't," said Jonathan.

"Daddy, who is this lady?" asked Margaret.

"This is Miss Kilter," said Peter.

"She is?" said Margaret, wide-eyed.

But Rose was now screaming, "Whore! Beast! I hate you, I hate you. . . ." and Peter desperately tried to kiss the children, to love them and leave them at the same time, and they clutched at him and even at his suitcase, struggling to prevent him from leaving by their show of force, and they were left hopeless as Peter and Elizabeth closed the front door behind them.

Chapter Eight

The next week was the first that Peter and Elizabeth lived together.

They did one or two daring things.

They had their first quarrel.

They nearly got killed.

On Saturday, Peter rented a room from an ad in the *Times*. The ad called it "a small furnished apartment." It was a furnished room with a pretense of a kitchen behind shutters on one wall. When he opened the shutters, two roaches scurried for cover. It didn't seem to matter. Elizabeth's apartment was only a short walk away.

Peter arranged with the superintendent to phone him at the office if any telegrams arrived. He sent Rose a note giving her the new address and saying to send a wire if the children got sick or something. He transferred some clothes from his suitcase to a shopping bag and took it over to Elizabeth's. On Saturday afternoon they listened to every side of every Mozart record she had. Then they went out to a local record shop and bought three Mozart records she didn't have—this was going to be an all-Mozart day—and picked up a bagful of Chinese food on the way back. In late afternoon they fell asleep listening to Mozart. When they woke up two hours later, they took a walk along the river. The wind was whipping up and there weren't many walkers, but they didn't notice either the other walkers or the wind or see much of the river. They talked in inconsequentials of lovers. They held hands in public. That was Saturday.

On Sunday morning Peter asked Elizabeth to hurry breakfast. They left immediately afterward and hailed a cab, which Peter directed to the Pan Am Building.

"On a Sunday?" Elizabeth questioned.

Peter stretched his legs, crossed them at the ankles, remained silent.

"Okay," she said, too happy to question further.

The Pan Am Building, like any other office building on a Sunday, seemed a mausoleum until they came to the elevator taking people to the rooftop heliport.

"I've never been on a helicopter," she said.

"Neither have I."

Peter made the ticket arrangements in less than two minutes, while Elizabeth stood to one side, trying to deal with the whisper of fear coiling inside her.

"Will they take us without luggage?" she asked.

"It's not a hotel. Cash in advance, no questions asked."

The loudspeaker announced the next flight to Kennedy International Airport. Behind glass, they saw the arriving helicopter settle down, its idling rotors stirring up a whirlwind of dust and pebbles. The arriving passengers held onto their hats, instinctively ducking, though the rotors turned safely above their heads. To Elizabeth, the helicopter looked like an up-angled bus with attachments. The limp, flexible rotor blades certainly didn't look strong enough to lift the huge, awkward machine off the ground.

"It's something out of Dr. Seuss," said Elizabeth as they clambered aboard. "Does it work?"

Peter himself was quite unprepared for the takeoff, the sudden increase of noise, the whirlwind of dust again, and then the roof and all of New York slipping away underneath them with an unexpected suddenness. He remembered the first time, as a boy, he had been up on top of the Empire State Building and how fearful he had been that the building might move. Now it was moving.

He looked at Elizabeth. She seemed really apprehensive.

"What's the matter?" he asked.

"You can't get out and walk," she said.

He laughed.

"You're a fatalist," she said. "I don't like taking unnecessary risks."

"How do you know which risks to avoid?"

"Well, the ones that make me nervous, like this."

"You smoke cigarettes."

She nodded.

"You cross New York City streets dozens of times a day."

She nodded again.

"You breathe our immeasurably polluted air."

"I was about to say those were necessary risks—"

"But you thought better of it, clever girl. This helicopter ride is a necessary risk in two senses," he lectured, making it up as he went along. "If our object is to go somewhere, getting there becomes a necessary risk. But in another sense, it is a necessary risk for some part of every generation to expose itself to the hazards of new things until they become old things. In the nineteenth century—listen to the professor, elf, you can look out of the window later—those cross-continental trains were hazardous. If an accident didn't get you, the Indians might. Well, the Indians and accidents got some people, not most, and today nobody's scared much of trains or Indians. But at the beginning of the century, nearly everybody was leery of those put-put automobiles. People reacted just as the horses did to the horseless carriages. Nowadays we kill fifty thousand or more people every year in those horseless carriages, but you don't panic if I ask you to step inside a car, do you? You get used to the hazard, so you think the hazard disappears. We barely got used to traveling in airplanes and they come up with these freak helicopters, which don't move the way we expect planes to move, and go so damn slow, and land on top of buildings. Well, somebody's got to get our generation used to it. You can look now. That's Brooklyn."

"We've crossed the East River?" she said, astonished.

"We'll be coming down in a couple of minutes. The trip only takes seven."

They spotted the racetrack, a large oval in the midst of the long rows of toy houses, which began to thin out, and then the helicopter was lowering itself in among the hangars and terminals of Kennedy. The airship seemed to squat rather than land in its yellow-rimmed target. Out the window Elizabeth could see the dust and stones swirling as, its front end raised, the monstrous metal praying mantis they were in taxied to the discharge point.

Peter's firm grip on her arm signaled they were to sit still as the other passengers got off. When the stewardess drew alongside, he flashed his ticket and they sat still while several passengers boarded, and off they went to the yellow circle, where the noise overwhelmed them as they lifted off.

Elizabeth found herself relaxing. Peter let her enjoy the startling experience of approaching the skyscrapers of lower Manhattan from an angle that seemed neither up in the sky nor down on the ground but midway, and equal to the grand edifices. They landed at the Wall Street Heliport and then in a few minutes were off again, across New York harbor to New Jersey and Newark Airport, where everybody except them disembarked, some newcomers arrived, and they were up and off again, approaching Manhattan from the west, catching an instant's fantastic view up the Hudson River, and then they were settling with finality atop the Pan Am Building, where their journey had begun.

As they descended the four steps from the copter, they felt the upsucking air lift their hair. Elizabeth laughed at Peter's appearance and he at hers. Hand in hand, they went inside the tiny terminal.

"Marvelous," was all she could say.

"Now, dear veteran of helicopter travel," said Peter, "you are a generation ahead of your time."

She had to admit that at the last she had gloriously enjoyed it.

"A new experience a week for the next forty years

will guarantee you a long life," he said, both of them laughing at the falsity of the promise. As if to belie the lie, Peter said, "Next week it's sky diving." They both knew that was a line another generation would have to cross for them.

On Monday after work they had a couple of drinks in a posh bar around the corner from the office, unafraid that any of the people in the office might see them together, though none did, and then went to a movie for the first time without ducking. They had seen some films together during the preceding months and discovered its hazards. If you were seen going into a movie or leaving a movie with a woman not your wife, it was as sure a sign to some people as witnessing you in bed. Once indeed he was stopped on the way out—carefully not holding Elizabeth's arm—by a woman who had been a friend of his mother's way back and didn't even know he was married, it had been so long ago. He had started to introduce Elizabeth —"This is"—not knowing where the sentence was going, when the woman interrupted, saying, "I know, I know." Which she didn't, of course, and it gave them a laugh afterward. Another time, however, it had been Jack ambling toward the subway, but luckily Peter had spied him in time to turn around and walk right past Elizabeth back into the theater, much to her momentary puzzlement. But now they both walked into the movie house, clearly together, and enjoyed that as much as they did the film. He could tell Elizabeth was relaxed by the amount of popcorn she ate.

His sexual appetite that week, and a capability to

match, astonished him. They were late to work on Tuesday morning and only at a hurried breakfast in a coffee shop realized they had not eaten dinner at all the night before.

On Tuesday, after work, they tried an experiment. Elizabeth rang up a friend she hadn't seen in quite some time and invited Peter and herself over for cocktails, with only the most perfunctory of excuses. Georgina was very married, four young children, a full-time mother. When her husband Ralph arrived home from work, he found the interlopers there and into their second drink.

"Elizabeth, how nice to see you," said Ralph, shooting a look at his wife.

"Good to see you, Ralph," she said. "Meet Peter Carmody." Just that. No explanations of any kind.

Ralph knowledgeably glanced at Peter's hand. Luckily Peter had never worn a wedding ring.

They chatted about the children, advertising, the film they had seen the night before, nothing.

When Peter and Elizabeth left an hour later, Elizabeth let go a sigh of relief.

"What did you expect to happen?"

"Inquiries, prodding, prying. She's a terrible gossip. That's why I tried her."

"She'll have to invent all the gossip. We gave nothing away, did we, elf?"

"Nope."

When the phone rang in Elizabeth's apartment later, she said, "Georgina" at once, and it was.

"She was fishing," said Elizabeth once she was off the phone. "I didn't give her a thing."

They laughed. They were testing.

"Maybe in a week or so we'll have them up for a drink and see what happens."

After work on Wednesday, Peter took Elizabeth to the House of Chan. He felt in the mood for a tremendous meal, and a Chinese meal didn't involve the penalty of extra calories.

He said the right things to the headwaiter, palm to palm, and they got an excellent corner table. Elizabeth ordered a martini, extra dry with lemon peel and on the rocks.

"In an ordinary Chinese restaurant," said Peter, "which means most Chinese restaurants except this one, martinis are hopelessly drowned in vermouth. I order gin on the rocks, vermouth on the side, then I stir in a few drops of the vermouth. It's wasteful because the rest of the vermouth doesn't get drunk unless I'm with Rose."

Rose's name hung in the air.

"What I meant was," said Peter, trying to brush it aside, "she prefers vermouth to what she calls real drinks."

Elizabeth concentrated on the menu.

"Drinkers," said Peter improvising again, "cover the range from A to Z. A's don't drink on principle. B's think they need to have absolute control at all times. They've tried liquor and don't like what it does to them. C's are mostly women who don't like the taste of whiskey. Their favorite drinks drown a minimum of alcohol in something long and sweet. D's are C's who get off the sweet mixers like Coke or ginger ale and conceal their small doses of alcohol in Bloody Marys. Danish Marys test the bartender and the restaurant. Virgin Marys get you back to A without announcing it in fourteen-point type."

Elizabeth did not seem to be paying attention.

"I'm being clever," he said, "and you're not paying attention."

"You're being academic."

Something, thought Peter, has gone wrong. He looked around the room. He wished the waiter would hurry up with their drinks. He felt he had no option but to continue.

"To continue," he said.

"Do," she said.

The word withered him. "At the other end of the scale," he said, depressed now and wishing he hadn't started, "are the fellows who take their poison on the rocks with a splash of soda or water. You know, the barest splash. One step farther you have the serious drinkers. On the rocks, period. Then those who sip whiskey neat. Then those who down the shot in a gulp. After that come only the guys who drink out of a tumbler at home. Or out of a bottle in the street."

The waiter was just putting the martinis down in front of them.

"Does that," she said, "conclude Professor Carmody's catalog?"

He felt the flush of color in his face. He waited until the waiter left.

"What's the matter?"

"I didn't say anything was the matter."

"You were being caustic."

"Let's drop it, shall we?"

What had brought that on, the mention of Rose?

They drank their drinks in silence.

When the waiter reappeared, Elizabeth turned down a

second drink. Peter defiantly ordered two martinis, and when the waiter brought them, Peter moved both drinks over in front of himself. Elizabeth moved one of them back to her place.

"I thought you didn't want another?"

"I'd rather have a second than sit and watch you have three."

"Look, are we having a quarrel?"

Elizabeth thought a moment. Then she said, "I'm sorry." She raised her glass, clinked his and said, "Skoal."

He ordered fried wonton as an appetizer for them both, and an order of shrimps in lobster sauce and barbecued spareribs for them to share.

"Do you want to talk about what's bothering you?"

"Not really."

"Will you anyway? To please me?"

"It's just that it's unfair."

"What?"

"The setup. Don't press me."

"What setup?"

"The deal."

"What deal?"

"The deal a girl gets. A fellow can get out of school," she said, "begin a career, look around, case the scene, date around, take his time. A girl can't."

"Can't what?"

"Find out who she is and what she wants before settling down. She dates. She gets a job. Maybe she likes working. Maybe she likes the smell of a career."

"So?"

"So the girls around her are dropping like flies."

"Getting married."

"Right. Right and left, until the one who doesn't get married fast is conspicuously single, you know what I mean?"

Peter stayed silent.

"You date a fellow here, there, maybe get serious, find out he's not right, date another, and before you know it you're in your late twenties and all the men of the right age are married already."

"You're exaggerating," said Peter.

"Not a bit. By the time I found out I liked my work and my painting and what kind of fellow was right and what kind was wrong, the field had changed."

"What field?"

"Men. The field had narrowed down to the uglies, the cranks, the mamma's boys, the fairies who know it and those who don't, and the miscellaneous types with large, unresolved problems like impotence. What a choice!"

The intensity of Elizabeth's feelings reached him.

"You know what a girl of thirty or thirty-two runs into? The date who studies you. He's got a pattern for a girl all cut out, and he's measuring you to see if you fit the pattern. If you don't fit, finished. Or the date who turns out to have a mother at home he wants you to meet right away and you say you hardly know *him*, hold off on Mamma, and he gets insulted because he's looking for a daughter-in-law, not a wife."

"Are they all like that?"

"You'd be surprised at what's floating around."

"Where does that leave me?"

"You," she said, "are already married."

She stirred her food around with her fork. "It may sound bitter, but it's true. The girl over twenty-five *has* to prospect among the married men if she doesn't want a nut. And taking up with married men, that's a universe of its own. You meet the explorers who always want to go home after a trip, the gutless ones who may hate their wives but wouldn't leave home if you carried them out, and—this is the really large group—the ones who want you *and* their wives."

Hadn't this all grown out of an inadvertent mention of Rose?

"When you tempt a married man who interests you," she continued, "—and don't tell me a girl doesn't have to tempt, she does—your unhappily married friends turn on you as if you were stealing their husbands, and then their husbands suddenly get ideas about you. You're battered by guilt and self-disapproval and the disapproval of everybody else. It's a nightmare."

They were both silent until the waiter brought them hot towels. Elizabeth removed the sparerib grease traces from her fingers carefully, then took the other hot towel and wiped Peter's fingers one by one. Then, their hands clean and dried, Elizabeth put her hands on his and said, "Here I am, supposedly grown-up, in love for the first time in my life, living a reckless week with you, supposed to be feeling marvelous and actually torn to hell."

Peter carefully disengaged his hands and put them on top of hers.

"Thanks," he said.

"For what?"

"For explaining. It may help. Better said than not said."

"A sure road to ruin," she said.

He knew she was right.

Out of habit he paid the waiter in cash in order to keep the bill off his Diners' Club card. Outside it was drizzling. Luckily latecomers were arriving in a cab, and Peter held the door for them and let Elizabeth and himself in before the driver could flip on his off-duty sign.

"I'm through for the day," said the driver.

Peter glanced at his watch. It wasn't shift-changing time. "You'll be through after you drop us," said Peter. The driver, ready to argue, saw the policeman on the corner at the same time that Peter did. "It's only a short distance," said Peter, giving him the address.

All the way home, the taxi meter ticked like a metronome.

At their street the driver said, "Mind if I drop you on the corner? I can go straight up Park."

"Sure," said Peter. They got out, and the man lowered his window so that Peter could pay him. As Peter put the wallet back in his pocket and the cab roared off, he noticed Elizabeth's attention riveted on a shadow against the wall.

The shadow moved toward them.

"Git over here," the shadow said. "Outa the light."

Peter's eyes adjusted to the semidarkness. The shadow was holding a pistol. He couldn't have been more than twenty. He was wearing a badly soiled Ike jacket. He licked his lips.

"Wallet," the voice said.

Peter obeyed.

"Gimme the bills."

Peter removed the bills, leaving a ten behind.

"All of 'em," said the kid. "Put 'em on the ground."

"They'll blow away," said Peter, his voice husky.

"Step on 'em," said the kid.

The kid put his foot next to Peter's, holding the bills down. "Move back," he said, waving the pistol.

Peter and Elizabeth stepped back.

The kid spread the money like cards to see how much there was. "Gimme the pearls," he said to Elizabeth.

"They're just cultured pearls," said Elizabeth.

"Gimme 'em," said the kid, licking his lips again.

"Give him the pearls," said Peter. "Junkies get desperate."

The kid laughed. Elizabeth held the pearls out to him. He snatched them from her hand, breaking the string, and the pearls scattered on the street.

"Shit," said the kid.

Peter started to pick up the pearls.

"Never mind that," said the kid. "Gimme your watch."

It was a very good watch.

"I'll give you a check made to cash for fifty dollars if I can keep the watch," said Peter, hoping a policeman would turn up somewhere on the deserted street.

"Fuck the check," said the kid. "Gimme the watch."

Peter handed him the watch.

"You scared?" said the kid.

Peter thought. "Yes," he said finally, "I'm scared."

That pleased the kid.

"You, missus," he said to Elizabeth, "your watch, too."

"I don't have a watch," lied Elizabeth. Her watch was on a pin she wore on her dress.

"The snatch don't have a watch," said the kid.

Anger rose in Peter. *Think, think, be careful.*

"You better go get your stuff," he said to the kid.

"I could kill you," said the kid casually, the gun bobbing in his hand.

"Get your stuff," Peter ordered.

The kid turned and ran. They watched him run all the way down the block and then a second block and then around the corner out of sight. Peter bent down to pick up the pearls. Elizabeth helped. It seemed to take forever. Some of the pearls had rolled into the gutter, in the wet dirt.

"I hope we got them all," he said finally.

"Never mind," she said.

They walked down the street to her house.

"Are you going to call the police?" she asked.

"It's pointless. They'd never find him now, and we'd have to identify you and identify me, and we don't need that."

She took his hand. His hand was cold, too. She squeezed it. She approved of the way he had handled things. *An easy form of bravery*, he thought, *compared to what's coming up*.

Inside the apartment, he went directly to the phone. "Rose," he said when she answered, "I thought I'd drop by at ten on Saturday and pick up the kids for a few hours."

After a long silence, Rose said, "All right."

"Good night," he said. When he hung up he saw Elizabeth, still in her coat, standing near the door where they had come in.

Chapter Nine

At ten o'clock Saturday morning Peter found himself standing in front of the door of his own house, feeling as if it had an "off limits" sign.

Wouldn't be right to use my key, would it? he thought.

His finger pushed the bell button.

He wished they'd hurry; he wouldn't want a neighbor to see him standing on his own doorstep that way.

Finally he heard steps. Margaret opened the door gingerly.

"Hello," said Peter.

"Hello, Dad," said Margaret flatly.

He had expected her to leap up in his arms. Instead, she kept her physical distance.

"Won't you come in?" she asked.

The expression on her face was studied, noncommittal.

She knew there was a war on, that he and Rose were on different sides.

He took one measured step into the house. The occasion seemed very formal.

"I'll be ready in a minute, Dad," said Margaret.

At that moment Jonathan came down the stairs. "Hi, Dad."

Peter nodded.

"All set," said Margaret, her coat on.

Jonathan stood at the bottom of the stairs.

"Coming?" Peter asked.

"Well, Frank and I were going to do something today 'cause it's Saturday."

"Like what?"

"You know, swing around the block, see what the kids are doing, maybe listen to the new Jimi Hendrix record over at Frank's house. You know, Saturday."

"Jimmy who?"

"Hendrix."

"I see," said Peter. He didn't see at all. The point was that Jonathan wasn't coming.

The surprise stung Peter.

"Margaret and I should be back about five. Maybe I'll see you then. We could walk down to—"

"Frank and I'll probably be at the movies, Dad."

He had been planning to take both children to the movies after lunch. Now he'd better not take Margaret. If they wound up at the same show as Jonathan and Frank, it might be embarrassing.

Rose was nowhere to be seen or heard. *Planned that way.*

Peter fled from the house with Margaret. What was the

boy doing? Had Rose put him up to it? Or was it personally aimed as well as kicked?

He took Margaret on the subway. The ride itself was always fun for her. For himself it provided subway faces to stare at, insufficiently distracting to keep him from thinking.

They got off three blocks from Adventureland. Margaret gave him her hand to cross the street, which made him feel a bit better. Adventureland's slot machines, the forty pinballs, the car-driving apparatus, and the new simulated ski machine could always keep the kids busy for an hour.

Peter armed himself with five dollars' worth of dimes. As always, the memory flicked through his mind: how much a single dime had meant when he was Maggie's age. Depression days. Today he was quite capable of spending five dollars in a bar with a friend. Or with Elizabeth.

That was the first thought of her since he arrived to pick up the children. Child.

Something ventured.

Something gained.

Something lost. Well, not necessarily. It would work out; it had to.

Margaret was staring up at him, palm out. He gave her some more dimes. "Having fun?" he asked her.

"Oh, yes," she said, "but you look gloomy. Do you feel all right?"

"Yes, nurse," he said, smiling. "I feel all right."

There were two car-driving machines unoccupied, side by side, and he slipped into one next to Margaret.

"Race you," he said, slipping a dime into the machine.

He gripped the wheel as the road on the drum in front of him started to meander. Every time he ran off the road, a red light went on and a bell clanged to announce the recording of a penalty. Margaret could hear his bell going off regularly. Peter tried very hard to concentrate on the road and to keep up with its twists and turns, but his co-ordination seemed off, or his attention, though he was fixing it with all his power, and before he knew it, the ride was over and Margaret was grinning at him because her machine registered a score of "Good" and his said "Sunday Driver."

He bought her a Coke and then, sensing she had had her fill of Adventureland, reminded her that their favorite bowling alley was practically around the corner. Within minutes, they were picking up their score sheet and rented bowling shoes at the counter.

Margaret liked bowling because it was the only sport in which she seemed able to compete effectively with Jonathan. Peter enjoyed bowling with the kids (kid, he reminded himself, you've only got one with you). Rose never joined them. She thought bowling wasn't dignified. Peter's friends and business acquaintances all played golf—for the exercise, they said, though they used an electric cart. The few friends who admitted to bowling always went along with their own kids. Adult bowling without kids was for beer drinkers, not college men and professionals. Peter never understood how sport got organized in America along class lines.

They were lucky to get an alley right away on a Saturday, though they had to share a scoring stand with two teen-agers showing off for their girl friends, which was quite a clatter. Peter supposed that a father with a twelve-year-old girl in the next alley was a nuisance to the teen-agers, making them even.

Margaret found a ten-pound ball that fitted her small hand. She was especially pleased that it was a red and white speckled ball rather than an ordinary black one. Peter settled for the first sixteen-pounder he could get his fingers into. That was a bad omen. When he searched around for the best ball he could find, it meant he would try hard to play well. To hell with omens. He'd try hard anyway.

Margaret bowled first. Her ball spun into the gutter before reaching the pins. Peter reminded her to keep her thumb in front, told her to swing the ball back and forth a few times with her thumb in the right direction. The instruction helped. On her second try she knocked down six pins.

She gave Peter a spontaneous hug for his help.

"If you get six every turn, you'll end up with a score of sixty, which isn't bad, little lady."

"I'll do better than that," she said.

Peter held his right hand over the blower to dry the damp. Didn't *usually* sweat.

He stepped to the foul line, holding the ball up. He waited until the bowlers left and right of him had taken their turns. Moving forward, he felt uncoordinated, as if the string connecting his limbs to his body had gone slack. The minute he let the ball go, he knew it was off. The ball spun right, too sharp a curve, then curved left and just managed to clip off the seven pin before careening uselessly against the backstop.

"Here, Dad, let me show you," said Margaret. "Keep your thumb in front. Practice it a few times so the ball will go straight up the middle."

They had a good laugh together.

At the halfway mark, Margaret's score was 41 and his own was 70. At least he wouldn't have to face the ignominy of not breaking 100.

Margaret asked for a dime. He offered to go to the candy counter to get her what she wanted.

"I have to phone," she said. "Mommy said I was to call by noon to tell her if I was having fun."

Margaret went off to make her phone call. "Don't take too long," he shouted after her. "The management doesn't like people to take intermissions."

Was Rose afraid he'd be unpleasant to his own daughter? Did she want to disrupt the first outing?

When Margaret returned, Peter covered his thoughts with a smile.

"She says to be sure I get back by five," said Margaret.

"Your turn," Peter said. *Fuck Rose.*

Margaret's near-perfect shot took nine pins down. With more force behind it, it would have been a strike. She aimed for the lone pin very, very carefully. The ball went down the alley in slow motion. It hit the remaining pin smack on.

"A spare!" she clapped her hands delightedly. He recorded her score and gave her a resounding kiss on the cheek.

Peter thanked God for the game of bowling, which gave the kids a fair chance against adults.

If he intentionally lost the game to Margaret, she would know it. He'd play it straight.

She got a spare on her next turn also, and he wondered if he could win even if he wanted to.

His steps as he released the ball this time were in perfect synchronization, and his eyes didn't move from the pins ahead as the ball hit the pocket between the one and three balls perfectly, and they all came splattering down. The teen-ager in the next aisle nodded his approval.

Margaret's final score was 101, a record for her. Peter's 118 seemed smallish in comparison.

Margaret's happiness pleased him more than the score because as she was playing, a new thought had begun to crawl through his mind: instruction, the tutorial in all things, was a necessary part of fatherhood. Sometimes it was fun for the kids, and sometimes not. From now on, however, fun would govern. If they didn't have fun, they would not look forward to his visiting days. The thought coiled in him: he was an entertainer first now, instructor second.

They bowled one more game, then turned in their rented shoes and their score sheet. The cigar chomper behind the counter short-changed Peter twenty-five cents. Ordinarily Peter would have made an issue of it. The last thing he wanted was to disrupt the day. He said nothing.

He took Margaret to lunch at Nathan's, where every item behind the counter seemed a kid's delight: the best-tasting hot dogs in the world, hamburgers, sweet corn, huge French fries, and a place where you could dump on all the ketchup, mustard, sauerkraut you wanted. And afterward there were the great thick shakes, strawberry as well as chocolate, and cakes wallowing in berries and whipped cream, served in huge portions. Peter and Margaret ate across the table from each other, sloppily, the only way possible to really enjoy such things.

A fat man bumped against the table. The waves in Peter's coffee cup sloshed over the side. The man turned, expecting a harsh remark and quite prepared to quarrel.

"My cup runneth over," said Peter.

The fat man pointed to the vacant chair at Peter's table. "Saving that chair for the missus?" he asked.

Peter shook his head. "Go ahead, take it."

The fat man took the spare chair over to a nearby table, where his three fat children sat with their very fat mother crunching away at their food.

"We," said Margaret, leaning over to whisper, "are better-looking than they are."

Peter nodded in affirmation. An idea occurred to him. "How," he asked, "would you like to see my so-called apartment?"

The idea seemed to delight Margaret.

They passed the superintendent on the way upstairs to his apartment. The man stared at Margaret. Peter hoped the man didn't think he was kinky for little girls!

Margaret surveyed his room. Expressionless. She opened cupboards and the closet, checked things out methodically like a woman shopping for a house. The refrigerator, when she opened it, proved to be nearly empty. Finally she said, "You can't live like this."

Margaret got a basin from under the sink, let water run into it, put a capful of detergent in, asked him for his most run-down undershirt, tore it into rags and proceeded to clean house. For Peter it was a spectacle.

At one point he asked her, "Are you sure you want to be doing this . . . on your day off?" He covered with a laugh.

"It has to be done," she said. She didn't laugh.

Peter stood around, tense and nervous.

"Why don't you relax?" she said to him over her shoulder.

He couldn't, so he called Elizabeth. Thank heaven she was home. He gave her a one-minute summary of Adventureland, bowling, Nathan's, and what Margaret was now doing.

"Can I talk to her?" asked Elizabeth.

The girls chatted on the phone. Then Margaret put her hand over the mouthpiece. "Miss Kilter wants to know if we can come over," she said.

Peter glanced at his watch.

"She says she lives very close," said Margaret.

"Let me talk to her," said Peter.

On the phone he said, "It's after four. I have to get Margaret home by five."

He saw the film of disappointment over Margaret's face.

"Look," said Peter into the mouthpiece, "compromise. Can you meet us downstairs in five minutes?"

They agreed. Margaret quickly finished putting things away. She instructed Peter to get the refrigerator filled. And to keep the place clean. And to open the window a crack when he was out so the room would air out.

"I think more dirt comes in than air," he said.

"Never mind."

Elizabeth met them downstairs, and she talked with Margaret all the way to the subway.

Here's where I leave you," Elizabeth said.

Margaret shook Elizabeth's hand, then looked for Peter to do the same. He did. He wondered what Margaret was thinking.

They descended into the subway. Their train came along in a minute and wasn't crowded, so they were able to sit side by side. At one point Peter put his hand on Margaret's, not casually the way he used to, but self-consciously. He quickly withdrew his hand, wondering, when parents separate, what do children feel? They must blame whoever does the leaving.

He had not wanted to be a villain in Margaret's life. He wanted nothing to change between *them*.

"Penny for your thoughts," he said, putting the copper into her hand.

She returned it, saying nothing.

Was she biting her lip?

Was she trying to keep from crying?

They got out of the subway and walked in silence to the house, where, on impulse, Peter lifted Margaret under the arms up the three stairs to the door, something she had always liked him to do. She was like wood in his arms. He put her down.

Peter rang the bell just as Margaret turned the knob. The door was open.

Rose was coming through the door from the kitchen.

"Is Jonathan around?" he asked.

"He's not back yet," said Rose.

Peter turned to go.

"I'd like to show you something," said Rose. "Margaret," she said, "Janie is playing out back."

Margaret took the hint.

The Husband

Rose beckoned Peter to follow her up the stairs. A small alarm went off in his senses.

He followed Rose into the bedroom. She went around behind him to close the door. He heard the sound. He turned to see her pulling the zippered front of her one-piece outfit completely open. She hadn't a thing on underneath. She stepped out of the suit and came over to him and did something she knew out of long practice would arouse him instantly.

Chapter Ten

Thoughts strode through Peter's head like lectures.

A woman who has successfully seduced a man before, however long ago, can do the same again.

In sexual relations, past experience with an individual counts more than past experience with other individuals.

If a woman tries to get something by means of sex, and if sex has never been of special moment to her, then what she wants must be important.

Peter thought of fighting back the temptress, as it might have happened in an old movie, with the man all stilts and bones jerkily moving about, getting back into his clothes, fleeing against one wall and then another, hiding under the bed, inside a closet, while a piano banged chase music into every corner of the house.

But Peter, being Peter, was fleeing his own way, by

letting her do what she wanted, while his lecturing mind ran wild with propositions.

A rejected wife has the seductive power of a stranger. Not exactly. Reframe.

A rejected wife has the seductive power of a stranger, plus a catalog of experience.

Rose, he thought, was going through every item in the catalog. If only she knew how distracted he was.

"Why don't you relax?" she said into his ear.

Why do people say "relax"? Sex was one of the least relaxed experiences mankind was capable of, ordinary people performing an olympian event. *Relaxation is not the route to orgasm.*

"Peter," she was saying, "Peter, Peter, Peter."

"Rose," he was tempted to say, "Rose, Rose, Rose," but it would be too funny. He thought of stopping, getting off the bed, dressing, tipping his hat (what hat?), and leaving.

Sex once begun was the least frustratable of sequences. Unless the equipment failed. Why was his equipment not failing? Why did his body want to finish the process, the sooner the better, but finish?

For the first time he could remember, he thought, *it's only a lay.* He had heard that from so many men who were regularly and unimportantly unfaithful to the wives, men who kidded him for, as they put it, not getting a piece now and then from another store.

Was Elizabeth his new wife? Was he now, at this moment, committing adultery with Rose?

Peter started to pull out when Rose began a very low rolling sound. Her eyes were shut but her mouth was moaning. He had never seen her fake excitement quite that way. Had she learned it? Had she studied, practiced, was she conscious of what she was trying to do?

He had better stop.

It was too bold a performance to stop.

Get it over with. He plunged on. *What am I doing here?* On and on, and then, suddenly, the clear sound, footsteps bounding up the stairs.

He stopped.

Rose's eyes were open with alarm.

Was the door locked?

A knock at the door. Another knock at the door.

"Get up, quick," said Rose.

Her recovery was instantaneous.

"Yes, yes," she was saying to the door, fixing her clothes hurriedly and motioning him to get his on as well.

"Hurry up, Mom!" Jonathan was yelling through the door.

"What is it?"

"Hurry up, something's in the laundry room."

"Something's what?"

"Burning in the laundry room. Hurry up!"

Rose closed the door behind her as she left. Peter was still adjusting his clothes. He glanced in the mirror. Okay.

He opened the door.

Jonathan was following his mother down the stairs. Hearing Peter, he stopped and turned. He was obviously startled to see his father coming out of the bedroom.

"Go ahead," said Peter. "I'll follow you."

The boy clattered down the rest of the stairs, Peter

following, and then on around through the kitchen and down the basement stairs. Smoke was pouring out of the laundry room.

Rose stood, paralyzed. In a second Peter saw what must have happened. An armload of clothes had been dropped on top of the dryer, and over at the corner, where the dryer-flame burner vented, a part of some garment had caught and was blazing, and now the rest of the bundle was smoldering. He always had said there should have been a second fire extinguisher *inside* the house, not just in the garage. Damn! Peter quickly got to the other side of the basement and the garage doorway. He yanked the small extinguisher, intended for emergencies at his workbench, out of its holder and quickly tried to remind himself of the instructions as he hurried back to the laundry room.

"The fire alarm is on the corner," said Peter to Jonathan. "Pull it. Hurry."

"Go to the front door," he yelled at Rose, "so you can direct the firemen down here when they come."

She watched him turn the extinguisher on and went up the stairs. The smoke smarted his eyes. He didn't seem to be able to get close enough to what was burning. Now the damn extinguisher wouldn't stop. Maybe it's not supposed to, once it's started. With one hand he got out his handkerchief and held it under the tap, and then, holding the soaked handkerchief against his face, he got closer to the burning bundle. He remembered to aim not at the smoke, but at what was causing the smoke, zeroing in on the point of combustion, barely able to see for the tears streaming out of his eyes, coughing terribly, wondering how much the flames would spread before the firemen got here. What was keeping them? It seemed interminable, as he had to back off more and more because of the choking smoke, his small extinguisher no longer effective at that distance. What to do?

A strong arm yanked him back and motioned him out of the way.

The fireman in his helmet seemed a giant as he leveled a large extinguisher at the flames. At the laundry room door, there were two others, one with an ax. Peter hoped he wouldn't have to use the ax.

The third fireman, he now saw, was holding the neck of a gigantic hose, which wound its way up the stairs. Peter went up the stairs to what he wanted most—fresh air.

Margaret and Jonathan were near the door, where another fireman was guiding the large hose snaking out to the street and being connected to the hydrant. Peter gulped the air. The neighbors were out in force, especially the children, all of whom seemed excited by the turn of events, with the singular exception of Jonathan, who was looking at his father in a very strange way.

"Are you all right, Dad?" asked Margaret.

He nodded, wiping his face now with the wet handkerchief. "Just smoke."

Peter sat down on the stairs at the front of the house. Some of the neighbors knew, didn't they?

As soon as Peter felt his breathing coming normally, though ever so deeply, he went back inside, out of the way of the stares. He slumped into his chair. He didn't have any idea how much time passed till he looked up and saw one of the firemen, the one with the ax, coming around from the kitchen.

"It'll be okay, mac," said the fireman. "Gotta watch those gas dryers."

Peter hadn't really thought about gas dryers even when he was living with one, but the fireman was being friendly, and he couldn't say that was the woman's department or that he was just upstairs for a quick one with the lady of the house.

"Are you the owner?" asked the fireman.

Ah, Peter could have given a long and complex response to that unanswerable question.

"Yes," he said.

"You better let your insurance company know."

"Thanks," said Peter and went downstairs to the basement.

The two firemen in the laundry room looked like they were washing clothes. Each was bent over one of the twin sinks, kneading away at blackened garments. One of them said, "You always gotta do this on a laundry fire. Burned clothes rubbed so every cinder is out dead. Otherwise, we leave and then the fire starts up all over again."

"I see," said Peter.

"Then it's our necks in the wringer," continued the talkative one. "They find out who covered the first alarm, and did they rinse and wring the clothes."

"You're doing fine," said Peter.

"Almost finished," said the fireman, wringing a wet bundle that had once been a nightdress of Rose's.

As they finished up, Peter himself checked around to make sure there wasn't a spark left anywhere. It would be some mess to clean up.

He offered a five-dollar bill to the talkative fireman. "I

do appreciate you fellows coming to the rescue. Here, get some cigars for the guys."

"We're not allowed to," said the fireman, taking the money. "But, okay. Thanks."

"Thanks," said the second fireman, his sole verbal contribution to the proceedings. All three of them, with a last look at the hopeless mess in the laundry room, went upstairs, Peter leading the way.

The hose was almost completely gathered up by that time and was being reloaded onto the huge red truck. It seemed an awfully big vehicle for the job that had to be done. Well, thought Peter, you never can tell the size of the job in advance, can you? And the men had to get there somehow; might as well be on the fire truck. He wondered how much it cost the city to douse his laundry room.

The fireman who seemed in charge, and who had not once stirred from the command car which had followed rather than preceded the truck, now came up to Peter with some advice. "Those dinky extinguishers don't do much good. If I were you, I'd get a Blazebuster unit. Keep one in the basement and one in the garage. Get two." He handed Peter a leaflet on Blazebusters. Peter thanked him and noticed the code key rubber stamped on the corner of the coupon. He wondered how much of a commission the fireman got for each of the extinguishers purchased this way.

The neighbors were dispersing. One or two waved at him, and he waved back.

Peter closed the large front door of the fortress. It seemed very quiet in the living room. Rose, sitting in her favorite chair, seemed remarkably cheerful. The kids waited for him to say something. He was very tired.

"I guess it's okay if I sit down," he said, half to himself.

He wondered how he would describe *this* day to Elizabeth. Would he ever?

"You were real good, Dad," said Jonathan.

"Thanks," said Peter wearily. "When I was six or seven, I wanted to be a fireman. Just didn't think I'd have to wait this long."

Margaret and Jonathan's laugh was tense. Peter sat still.

"Well," said Rose.

The children recognized the cue. "I guess we can go out," said Jonathan.

"There's quite a bit of cleaning up to do," said Peter, who wanted them to stay.

"I could get a garbage can down to the basement," said Jonathan, "and stuff all the burned things in it."

"You can take a can down," said Peter, "but you'd better let Mom make an inventory of the things before they're thrown out. The insurance company will want to know what was damaged and how much each item cost."

Rose seemed genuinely grateful for his practicality.

"Thank you," she said.

"Sure," he said. *Sure, what?* It sounded stupid.

"Peter?"

"Uh huh." He was completely unprepared for what she said.

"Could you arrange to move your things back this evening?"

She was out of her mind. No she wasn't; this was a natural response for Rose. Like the virgins in school who after the first time want to know when the engagement will be announced. Was it the fire, the momentary threat of danger to the house, that brought them together?

No, for Rose it was the near-sex, or whatever it had been in the bedroom, his going along, lending himself to Rose's design. Did she think it committed him to anything? *Not on your life,* he was tempted to say. That kind of thing doesn't have the force of union, much less marriage.

Rose wouldn't understand.

Peter was silent for a time, taking in the room as if with a camera, snapping this wall, that wall, recording familiar objects, storing the views away for later.

"Were you about to say something?" asked Rose, her tone mellow. He even thought there was a note of pleading in it.

Could he tell her—hadn't he already told her through word and deed—that their marriage had been a mistake which they now had a chance to rectify? Partnerships made sometimes had to be dissolved. Few friendships lasted a lifetime. Few lasted over the years. Was marriage so different from a friendship that didn't last? You didn't have children with friends; yet that wasn't completely true. Sometimes you'd get close to a friend's kids, and some of that closeness would remain when you saw the kids or thought of them, even when the friend himself was rarely seen and rarely thought of.

"Are you feeling all right?" asked Rose. "Is the smoke still bothering you?"

He shook his head.

The Husband

Peter didn't want to be rude. But above all, he didn't want to lie now, not a fundamental, soul-crushing lie. He gathered himself together. He closed his eyes for a split second so that the camera would stop recording, lifted himself from the chair, and went out the door without saying a single word.

Through the closed door behind him he could hear Rose crying, not the fake tears he had heard from time to time in the long years of their marriage, but sobbing grief because she had been so certain and her hopes had been so high.

As he went down into the subway, he realized he hadn't said good-bye to the kids. There were lots of other things he hadn't said or done, not only today but over the years.

The past is past, he thought, knowing it wasn't. If it were, why would he be thinking now of his own childhood, and his parents, who had stayed together as most parents did in another age?

He put the token into the turnstile and hurried his steps because he could hear the roar of the incoming train below.

Chapter Eleven

"When's the son of a bitch getting here?" said Jack.

Rose watched Jack pace on the far side of the living room. She had noticed his glances at the bar. This late in the afternoon the whiskey mechanism was rumbling in his head, wanting that first after-work drink. She had not offered Jack a drink. Work would not be over until after Peter left.

"When's the son of a bitch coming?" repeated Jack.

Rose sighed. "Please don't call him that."

"Call him what?"

"Son of a bitch," said Rose a bit hesitantly.

"Why the hell not?"

"I don't like that word."

"You just said it."

"I want him to come back."

"Well, you won't get him out of the sack with Miss

what's-her-name by sitting around the house moaning."

"It's been three weeks since I've seen him."

"You've got to leave things to me," said Jack.

"He just walked out of here without saying a word. A word."

"Look, Rose," Jack said, taking her hands in his, "why don't you buy yourself a new hat or girdle or low-cut dress or something? Isn't that what women do when they're down?"

Rose gently took her hands out of his. "Do I look that bad?"

"Jesus, Rose, you look fine, fore and aft. I'm no close-range expert."

He was getting ready to take her hands again. Rose quickly said, "You're close enough, Jack."

He slumped into the nearest chair. "I didn't mean to rush things."

Rose came around behind the chair and put her hands on his shoulders. "You're galloping."

"At my age," he said, and Rose had never heard his voice so linty with weariness, "all you see at the end of the line is the glue factory." Jack was tempted to look around at her, but it was safer not seeing her reaction.

"I've had a yen for you for a long time," he said without turning.

Your job, Rose thought, *is to get Peter back here with the kids and me.*

"Remember when you sat in my lap that time?" asked Jack, his voice subdued.

"I remember."

"Well, my lap didn't forget."

Rose had always thought she was good at pity for other

people, but pity for herself so filled her now it was no use trying.

"I guess I'm blunt," said Jack.

"A little."

"I guess I'm fat, too."

"A little."

"I guess I just don't cut a figure like Peter."

"I wish he'd get here," said Rose.

"What time'd he phone?"

"Ten. That's when I called you."

"I don't like the two of you talking on the phone without witnesses."

"Oh, Jack, please! He's my husband."

Jack stood up, a high color in his face. It was barely a whisper when he spoke. "You're an exciting-looking woman, Rose."

"We'll find somebody for you, Jack. Just give us time."

He looked forlorn.

"I need your help, Jack."

Slowly he let the lawyer's mask slip into place. "Okay, kid," he said, "but leave things to me. Promise?"

"I have to."

"If he'd done this to me," said Jack, the gristle returning to his voice, "I'd have killed him." He pursued Rose to the corner of the room. "I don't understand you, Rose. Don't you want to punish him?"

"There's still a lot of feeling left."

"For that half-assed idiot?"

"I can't get the cobwebs of that many years out of my system in one sweep."

"*He* did."

"Don't be so sure."

"You're soft, Rose."

It was a moment before she said, "If I were soft, he might not have left."

They froze at the sound of footsteps outside. "You better let me do the talking."

The doorbell rang.

"Okay?" asked Jack.

The instant she kissed Jack's cheek, she knew she shouldn't have, but there was no reversing. "Okay," she said, trying a smile that was supposed to convey a promise of good behavior.

Jack let Peter in. Peter closed the door of the cage behind him.

"Hello, Jack," said Peter.

Jack ignored Peter's extended hand.

"Hello, Rose," said Peter.

"Hello, Peter."

"You feeling all right?" he asked her.

"I suppose," she said. "Under the circumstances."

"Now, Peter," said Jack, "sit down over here."

Jack gestured at a chair Peter never sat in.

"You mean exactly here?"

"Yes," said Jack, "it'll be better if you sit there and Rose sits here and I sit in between you."

"Sounds like a properly run dinner party," said Peter. He thought he saw a flicker of appreciation in Rose's eyes for the lightness of his comment.

"Now this isn't a time for levity," said Jack. "I'm here as Rose's attorney, but she's asked me to act as a friend also, and to see if some attempt can't be made at—reconciliation, see."

"You really hate that word, don't you, Jack?"

"I thought with your being away three weeks," said Rose carefully, "you might have had some second thoughts."

"I've had many thoughts, Rose. I didn't mean to give you pain. I didn't mean to have any pain either, and I've had a lot of it these past three weeks."

"Well," she said, "if you're genuinely sorry—"

"I am," said Peter.

"And if you're through with your fling—"

"It isn't a fling. You were pretty rough on her."

"Look what you did to me. I was desperate. I was fighting for—"

"Was it that much of a surprise? Was everything so great between us?"

"—for my life," said Rose.

"Not your life with me, you weren't."

"Hey," Jack intervened, "don't you start turning things around."

"Shut up, Jack," said Peter. "Keep out of this. Rose, you're feeling alone, but not because of me."

"You're out of your mind. There's no one else—"

"Anyone who'd take on the *job* here. You want a breadwinner."

"Of course," said Rose.

"A man around the house."

"Of course."

"Someone to go to bed with."

"Is there anything wrong with—"

"Someone to take you to the movies, serve as an escort, change the snow tires on the car, someone, anyone, but not necessarily me. Rose, you don't love *me*. I mean me in particular. You're just used to me in the job of husband around here."

"That's not true!"

"Well," said Peter, toning down, "I was used to the same thing till I met Elizabeth."

"What has she got to do with us?"

"I love her. *Her*. She loves me. *Me*."

"Then what right do you think you have to come back and talk about reconciliation? Do you think I'd take you back while you're carrying on with that woman?"

"I didn't come to talk about reconciliation," said Peter. "I wanted a chance to say I'm sorry about what happened on the day of the fire." He caught the puzzled look on Jack's face; she hadn't told him. "And I'm sorry I brought Elizabeth here. It was stupid of me. I'm sorry about that scene. Most of all, I'm sorry I didn't recognize us sooner. Fifteen years sooner. Mainly I came because the thing that's killed me most, Rose, is not seeing the kids. Are they upstairs?"

"The kids?" Rose whispered.

"Yes."

"Not me?"

"Seeing you still hurts."

"You do feel guilty."

"Of course I do!"

"Cut the psychology crap," said Jack, "both of you."

"Wait a minute, Jack," said Rose. She was very close to Peter. She spoke as if Jack weren't in the room. "Isn't there anything left?"

Peter, his hands clasped, saw his knuckles whiten. "You don't just slide out of one life into another, Rose.

Sure, there are memories. Feelings. You may not stay in your hometown, but you never forget it." He turned toward the stairs. "Can I see the kids now?"

Rose quickly looked at Jack. "No," she said.

"Well, we'll see about that," said Peter, but Jack had already reacted; his hand was on Peter's shoulder. "No," he said.

"I'm going upstairs." Peter shot a fierce look at Jack's hand. Jack removed it.

"They aren't upstairs," said Jack.

Peter turned to Rose. "Are they up there?"

"No," said Rose, glancing anxiously at Jack, wishing he would take charge.

"Outside?" asked Peter, his anger rising.

"No," said Rose, imploring Jack to speak.

Jack said, "Now look here, Peter, the fact is, you're not going to see the kids."

"What the hell—you said—"

"I wanted you to come by to get some important things straightened out. That's why I told Rose you could come out. And Rose needed to get this reconciliation crap off her mind."

"Please don't talk that way," Rose's voice begged.

"Jack," said Peter, facing him, "you don't have to try to win the vulgarity cup. You're a natural."

"I don't give one damn what you think about me. I'm here representing Amanda. . . ." His voice choked its error. "I mean Rose."

Peter turned to Rose. "You sure you want this kind of representation?"

"Jack's a very good lawyer."

"Our problem has very little to do with the law."

"You'll find out," said Jack.

Peter flicked a murderous glance at Jack and asked Rose once more, "You sure you want him representing you?"

"Yes," said Rose, her voice cracking in desperation.

"Okay, representative," said Peter, giving Jack full face, "listen carefully. I haven't seen my kids in three weeks."

"That's your fault," said Jack. "Nobody told you to leave."

A wildness raged through Peter's head. "Rose, where are they?"

Rose remained silent.

"That's none of your business," said Jack.

"They're my kids!"

"I haven't kidnapped them," said Rose.

"I want to see Jonathan and Margaret. Now. They're my kids."

"You abandoned them," said Jack. "That's the law."

"I aban—you're out of your mind. You know where I'm staying. I've sent a check each week."

"The first two," said Jack. "Rose didn't get a check this week. That's one of the reasons I'm here."

"There's money in the joint account, Rose. I told you that."

"How about the check for this week?"

"Look," said Peter, "I have to straighten out some embarrassing things at the bank. It'll take a little time. I had to put down a month's security, plus the first month's rent for a small apartment."

"The kids have to eat," said Jack.

"Now cut that, if you want me to take you seriously.

There's stuff in the freezer to feed an army for a month."

"You didn't send a check this week."

"I sent enough dough each of the first two weeks to keep a baseball team in steak."

"Out of guilt!" said Rose.

"Maybe," said Peter. "More than I could afford, anyway."

"We want a check for three hundred thirty dollars every Monday."

"Where the hell am I supposed to get it? I can't argue the amount, but don't kid yourselves, I think it's outrageous. But even if it were thirty-three bucks, I don't know where I'd get it right now, and there's no emergency."

"Get a salary advance from your firm."

"I wouldn't dare ask. It's hard enough at the office for Elizabeth and for me, too, after all the rotten stories Rose told Paul!"

"I told?"

"He said you did. You were excited. I'd hate to tell you what else he said."

"Sell some stock," said Jack.

"Come on now, Jack, you know my stock position."

"I always said you were a jerk as an investor."

"That's not an indictable offense. I told Rose about the margin calls. Now listen, when do I get to see the kids?"

"When we've settled the money business, buster. When you're paid up to date."

"You're holding them as hostages?"

"Three hundred thirty dollars every Monday."

"I'm not a counterfeiter."

"Borrow."

"I have, you son of a— What the hell do you think I've been living on?"

"Borrow more."

"I'm trying. Oh listen, you two, I had the first really lovely experience of my life asking a good friend, somebody I've known for years, like you, Jack, for five hundred bucks, and he said no and gave me a business reason, so I asked for two hundred dollars and he said no. I asked for one hundred dollars and he said, go back to my wife!"

"Some people don't like what you've done."

"You know damn well why what I did makes them feel uncomfortable."

"Don't skip the subject," said Jack. "Three hundred thirty dollars every Monday."

Peter's bobsled words came rushing. "Twice I went to see old buddies in other agencies to see if I could get more money by switching jobs, and they wanted to know if the rumors about what they called 'my personal life' were true, and didn't I think I ought to get my emotional problems squared away before taking on new responsibilities. Crap! I tried to get a bag of chocolate-chip cookies at Gristede's on my way here just now, and the son of a bitch—I've had a charge account since we moved into the neighborhood—he asked me for cash and held onto the goddamn paper bag. What are you doing, Rose, telling everyone?"

"If you quiet down," said Jack, "I'll tell you a few things."

"Like what?!"

"The property settlement," said Jack.

"I'm getting out of here," said Peter.

"You'd better listen," said Jack, squaring himself in

front of Peter, knowing this was the time to drive it home. "Rose has possession of the car. She needs it for taking the kids to school and shopping."

"So?" Peter tried to step around Jack.

"We want you to turn over the car to her by endorsing this registration certificate."

Peter looked at the certificate and then up at them in bewilderment. "Is this another condition for my seeing the kids?"

Jack and Rose were soundless. Peter ripped the registration certificate in half.

"That won't do you any good," said Jack. "I can always get a duplicate. Now the house."

Rose felt her hands trembling. "Do we have to do all this now, Jack?"

"Please keep quiet," Jack told her. "Peter, you both own the house jointly."

"That's for tax purposes."

"Well, we want you to sign a quitclaim deed for your half of the house. You wouldn't want to rip the house up the middle, would you, Petey?"

"I put all I had left from my first job and from my father into the down payment on this house, and I've been paying back the mortgage a long, long time. I've got a lot of equity in this house. It's my way of saving."

"Rose and the kids have got to live in it," said Jack with finality.

"Nobody's saying no."

"We want it to be hers legally."

"And how the hell am I supposed to make a new life for myself if I turn everything over to her? You know what the advertising business is like. Maybe Paul will drop me. Maybe I won't be able to get a new job. Maybe I'll have to start a small agency of my own. I'll need some time and some collateral to borrow money. Like a second mortgage on this house."

"The house is hers, not yours. And so is everything in it."

"Now look, I was a grown boy when I married Rose, and I brought some of these things into the marriage. Those paintings are mine. I bought them. Rose hates them. They just hang there because we didn't divide the walls into his and hers."

Rose spoke. "You can have Miss Kilter's painting and that's all."

"That Buffet's mine," said Peter. "I discovered it."

"Rose says it's worth a lot of money now," said Jack.

"Rose hates it."

"Oh, that's okay, we'll sell it."

"Over my dead body."

"Then drop dead," said Jack. "If it has a lot of sentimental value to you, you can buy it from Rose."

"I can *buy* it from her?"

"Sure," said Jack. "We'll get it appraised. You can buy it at the present market price."

"With what?"

"That's your problem. The same goes for the hi-fi set."

"Rose!" Peter turned on her. His face sagged with disbelief.

"Never mind Rose," said Jack. "I've discussed it with her. Don't play on her weakness because she's a woman."

"I built that set," bellowed Peter. "Its value is mostly my labor."

"You should have thought of that before you took off."

"She doesn't listen to it," said Peter.

"That's not true," said Rose.

"Now come on, Rose, this is Peter. Who are you kidding?"

"If you keep this up," said Rose, her voice trembling, "you're not going to get your chair."

"That's my father's chair."

"Your father is dead," said Jack. "Now it's the common property of this household, which you have abandoned, and household property in this state goes to the wife."

"Everything?"

"Everything," said Jack.

"I don't believe you," said Peter. "I'll get a lawyer. Someone who's as big a louse as you are."

"Good. I don't care who you get. He'll tell you how the courts deal with husbands who abandon their wives and children. He'll tell you you abandoned yours the day you took your suitcase out that door. I hope you get a really experienced matrimonial type who knows the cases and knows damn well what husbands get in court. Get a big-ass lawyer. He'll take half your hide in fees. You'll have to keep the payments to Rose up, pay him, and pay my fees, too."

"I pay *you* for putting the screws on *me?*"

"That's right."

"Now I see why some men skip."

"You just try," said Jack. "You'll never see the kids again."

Peter felt his limbs go slack. He hoped it was only

resolve draining away. "I'm not that kind of man," he said quietly, hoping for control.

"We know what kind of man you are, Peter. Stick to the facts. We want half the net value of the stock when you've met the margin requirements, the joint checking account, the cash in the savings account—the war bonds belong to the kids anyway—the house, the car, the furnishings, and three hundred thirty dollars a week paid before ten A.M. each Monday or you don't see the kids that weekend."

Peter walked closer to Rose. She couldn't be frightened of him. Not now.

"Rose, who's doing this to me? Are you?"

"Now never you mind," snapped Jack. "Stick to the property settlement."

"What you want isn't a settlement. You're judging me and laying down the punishment."

"I don't give a damn what you call it. You want to go screwing around, you've got to pay. That's the law in this country."

"And if I don't?" asked Peter quietly.

"I'll have you in Domestic Relations Court on Monday. Nine out of ten couples who appear before that judge speak Spanish. Not a very middle-class place, except for the photographers and newsmen. Everybody loves a scandal if Madison Avenue is involved. And with a Madison Avenue chick thrown in, it's worth a lot of space. Would that be enough of a handle for Paul to give you the old heave-ho?"

"You wouldn't dare."

"Oh, wouldn't I?"

With a gesture just short of a flourish, Jack removed a piece of paper from his pocket and handed it to Peter.

"The judge who signed that is a Catholic, and you know how they feel about divorce. You'll walk out of court with your skin, period. Have fun with the newspapers. Or settle with us."

The legalese on the paper swam in front of Peter's eyes. "If there's a lot of dirt in the papers," he said, looking up, "I'll never keep a job in my trade that'll pay the money you're asking for."

"Read that paper," said Jack.

"I've read it," said Peter, lying.

"Monday, ten A.M., Domestic Relations Court."

"Now Jack, for old time's sake, listen to me."

"I'm listening."

"Don't make me beg."

"Peter?" It was Rose.

Peter looked at her. She seemed the Rose of long ago, the pretty face before it had hardened.

"Come back," said Rose.

Peter spoke very gently. "You don't want me, Rose, even if I could." He turned to Jack. "I need something left. I'll need to furnish a place, even the minimum."

"I'm not interested in your problems," said Jack.

Rose again. "Peter, come back. We'll work something out."

"We can't, Rose."

"We've fought before," she said.

"This isn't a fight, Rose. I'm going to get married again."

"You can't," said Jack.

"I'm a free man," said Peter.

Jack laughed. "You can't get a divorce unless Rose agrees."

"I'll go to Mexico."

"The absent party has got to agree. Even in Mexico."

Peter turned to Rose. "What good does it do to keep me from getting a divorce?"

"Nobody's keeping you," said Jack.

"I'm talking to Rose," said Peter.

"You're talking to her lawyer right now. Nobody's keeping you from getting a divorce. All you have to do is settle the property our way."

"Or else?"

"No tickee, no washee."

Peter felt his forearms linked to his arms, linked to his shoulders once again; bones in operation. "Both of you listen. I'm going to marry Miss Kilter, and nothing's going to stop me."

"Goddamnit," said Jack, "I'm not interested in hearing about your next marriage until you pay the price of this one. You're going to get squared away with Rose before that Miss Kilter's lawyer gets after you."

"What the hell are you talking about?"

"I know your kind. You never stop. What'll you do after you marry Miss Kilter? Whose pants will you want to get into when you're married to her? Who'll be next?"

"Don't talk that way to me. You got rid of Amanda the easy way!"

After a moment of staring at Jack's crimson face, Peter said, "I'm sorry. I didn't mean that." He turned to Rose. "When do I see the children?"

"Hire a lawyer," said Jack, the high color draining.

"I'm through talking to you. Tell your lawyer to call me. He'll tell you what you have to do to see the kids."

"Rose," said Peter, "do you want it this way?"

There was a moment's silence. "You deserted me," she said.

"We deserted each other a long time ago," said Peter. "We've been playing marriage a long time. We made a mistake, Rose. I did. You did. Maybe somewhere in back of our minds we sensed that parting involved something like this. Maybe that kept us together. Or habit. That's even worse. I don't want to make love out of habit ever again in my life."

"Monday," said Jack. "Domestic Relations Court. I'll settle my personal account with you later."

"I suppose it had to end this way. I'm sorry." He directed the words at Rose.

"I'm sorry, too, Peter," she said.

"If you want to talk to Rose," said Jack, "tell your lawyer to call me."

Rose took Jack's arm. "Be sensible, Jack. He's the father of my children."

Jack was steel. "The law says they're both wards of the state unless you people reach a settlement."

"I don't believe that," said Peter.

"Hire a lawyer. Ask him. In the absence of a custody agreement," said Jack, "children are wards of the state."

My God, thought Peter, looking at Iron Jack, at Rose near tears, and around at the objects in a room he had lived in for so long.

He left quietly. In his mind there raced the engine of a car going too fast and suddenly the screech of brakes, the smash into the stone wall, the wild metal and the broken glass, and he was holding onto what was left of the wheel, waiting for the ambulance.

He walked around the block, wondering whether he should go back in. A neighbor waved. He waved without thinking. If he waited till Jack left, would Rose let him back in? Could he reason with her, or would she try the bedroom scene again? If he staked himself out here on the block somewhere, invisible to passersby, would he see the kids come back home, if they were coming back home? Could he waylay them, would they come with him, and if so, for how long, an hour, a day, where would he keep them, what about school? *What if they didn't want to come with him?*

Chapter Twelve

The drugstore was just one block down and one over. Peter thanked heaven no one was there except Elton, the owner.

Peter always thought of Elton as a "nice Jewish boy," though Elton must have been between thirty-five and forty. As the phrase occurred this time, Peter wondered if Negroes knew how many different kinds of "boys" there were in the warehouse of people's prejudices. There were the white Anglo-Saxon sixty-five-year-old runners on Wall Street, who were always "boys." There were the boys between sixteen and eighty who delivered Western Union telegrams. And here was Elton, proprietor of the local drugstore, confidant to the neighborhood, custodian of its small talk and its secret ills, doctor-in-waiting for the minor accidents of small boys, prescriber of reducing regimens for the local matrons, himself the father of two boys and a girl displayed in Polacolor near the cash register, and to Peter always a "nice Jewish boy."

"Surprised to see you, Mr. Carmody," said Elton, extending a hand from behind the counter.

Elton's hand had liver spots. They didn't go at all with his cherubic face and small boy's waddle. "I thought . . ." he said, and thought the better of it.

Thought what? Peter wanted to say. "Tin of Excedrin," is what he actually said.

"Oh, headache?" said Elton, shuffling a tin onto the counter.

"Premenstrual tension," said Peter.

Elton laughed too loud.

"Can't keep up with the handkerchiefs these days," said Peter, taking a pocket pack of Kleenex from a counter display and putting it beside the Excedrin. Then he got to the point. "Elton, I have a Seconal prescription on file here for some time which I'd like to renew."

The cherubic face formed a question mark, the mouth a large pink dot. "Do you have the number or the date?"

"Sorry," said Peter.

"I guess it'd be inconvenient to stop back when you look it up on the bottle."

He knew, damn him, he knew.

"Probably threw the bottle away," said Peter. "You know how it is. I'd say it was about a year ago."

"You know, we're not allowed to renew barbiturates after six months now under the new law."

"I'm sure you can stretch a point for a regular customer."

Doctor Elton consulted his muse.

"It'll take a bit of time to look up."

"I sure appreciate it," said Peter.

While Elton busied himself with the old prescription books, Peter went to the phone booth in the rear and dialed Elizabeth's number.

He let it ring ten times. Impossible there was no answer. Probably misdialed. He tried again. Still no answer. Damn.

"Found it," said Elton, beaming as Peter came out of the booth. "It was more than a year ago. Fifty, hmmm."

Elton was counting out the red pills when Roberta Prinn came in the door. Mrs. Prinn was a prime source of information for Elton. Her twelve-year-old girl sometimes played with Margaret.

Mrs. Prinn looked directly at him, waiting for him to speak first.

"Hello, Mrs. Prinn," said Peter.

"Mr. Carmody," she acknowledged without the "hello." "In the neighborhood?"

Peter cracked a cracked smile at her.

"I'm sure Mr. Carmody wouldn't mind," said Elton, "if I wait on you first."

"I won't be long," said Mrs. Prinn, ordering six or seven things and then leaving a prescription with Elton for delivery later.

"Sorry about that," said Elton when Mrs. Prinn was gone, having good-byed Elton and flashing what Peter was sure was a reproach at him. "You see," Elton said conspiratorially, "I didn't want a witness to the Seconal. It's a favor, not strictly legal, you know." Elton smiled his smile; Peter could have crushed Elton's head against the wall.

Elton put the bottle of red pills next to the other items on the counter.

"No label?" said Peter.

"Better that way," said Elton.

"I thought," said Peter, "the prescription was for fifty."

"You've got a good eye, Mr. Carmody. Not trying to short-count you. Charging half."

"What's wrong with fifty?"

"Well, this is kind of a joke of mine, Mr. Carmody, but twenty-five a stomach pump can handle; fifty is too much. Whenever a customer of mine is down in the dumps, I watch out for things like that. A friend of humanity."

It took all the reserves Peter could summon to refrain from picking up one of the bottles of egg shampoo directly in front of him and flinging it at the cherubic face.

"Charge?" said Elton. He always would have charged it automatically.

"I guess so."

"Mrs. Carmody's charge, or shall I open a new account for you?"

"Never mind," said Peter, putting a five-dollar bill down on the counter. He wanted out of there fast.

Elton came around from behind the counter, holding on to the five-dollar bill. "I hope you don't mind me saying this, Mr. Carmody. You get to be a bit of a philosopher minding store here. In the old days before the pill, you'd see a high school kid come in for rubbers and order some toothpaste first, sort of to make the purchase ordinary, if you know what I mean. Like you order Kleenex to go with the Excedrin, or Excedrin to go with the Seconal, who knows?"

Peter motioned to the five-dollar bill.

"Getting your change," said Elton, not making a move toward the cash register. "I get birth announcements in the form of someone coming in for a case of Similac before the baby's out of the hospital. Steady prescriptions of codeine means arthritis; if it's for an old person, it means worse. People know how much I know. Otherwise, mothers wouldn't come in asking me if their daughters have a prescription for pills. I always tell them that kind of thing gets filled at Walgreen's. More anonymous. Mrs. Carmody's been in with dark glasses in the mornings. I filled a prescription for sedatives for her. I asked your son."

"You what?"

"It's only natural to ask about a neighbor, a friend, a customer. I'm not a dispensing machine, I'm a human being. You see, I learned a long time ago that a hole is a hole. I figure this way: when a guy gets married, the hole has got a lot of glamor around it, especially at first, and then sentiment. A lot of husbands feel sentimental about their wives, you know. Then, after some time, they still feel special about the wife's convenience to reassure themselves they didn't make a bad deal in the marriage. It's not bad to feel that way about the wife, even if sex gets a bit monotonous, I say, because if you pick up something on the side, there are always problems."

He made as if to go for change again, but halted.

"If you take up with a young girl on the side, it's good for the ego. I don't mean a virgin. They all get rid of that in high school. I mean a girl in her early twenties and you're in—well, my age or yours. It's new, so it's good, and she treats you like a wise father for a while, but if she likes sex—and a lot of these young girls do these days—it gets a little tiring keeping up with them, especially if you have a go at the wife once in a while on the side to keep things quiet at home. Sometimes there's the humiliation of her finding someone *her* age, and you're no competition for a seventeen or a twenty. With a middle-aged girl, it's a problem too, because if she's got some money —and a lot of the unmarried ones seem to these days, not like in the Depression—they think you're interested in their money instead of the sex novelty. The not-so-good-looking ones are worse because they're sure it's the money and they won't relax enough to have fun at it, so they drop you. If she's your own age without money—I mean a girl who's unsuccessful in getting a husband and money, like at Grossinger's—it's tough because before you say hello, she's got you divorced and married back to her, and every time you get her in the sack, it's like negotiating another clause in the contract. Takes most of the fun out of it. My own inclination— I'm speaking of my personal preference—is to change around with the local married women, because you get all types and ages for variety, and the convenience is perfect. I've been helped a lot by the pill. The married ones all get theirs here, and if you refill the prescription when there's no one else in the store, except the delivery boy maybe in back, it gives you real leads. You don't have to offend anybody or get into trouble. You just say, 'I can see these work,' and you look at her belly. They all laugh. You'd be surprised the kind of conversations you get into.

I'm averaging about two new ones a month, which isn't bad for a fellow who isn't exactly a movie star. Never in back of the store. That's for kids. I never did see how kids could have fun in the back of a car, even a Nash. I'm a great believer in relaxed circumstances. They just say 'Deliver,' and I say, 'In person, why should I send the delivery boy?' and if they don't say anything, I go. If they ask you to stay for a cup of coffee, three out of four times you can count on getting into the saddle. I've left more coffee standing in kitchens— Don't get me wrong, some of the timider ones take several visits before they get around to what they had in mind in the first place. That Mrs. Prinn, you wouldn't think it of her, would you? That's what I mean, the surprises. Her face looks like the Legion of Decency, and her legs and knees and thighs are thin, real thin, but that bag of bones is like drag racing, she comes so fast."

Elton at last gave Peter his change. Peter shoved it into his pocket without counting it. He wanted to try Elizabeth's number again, but another phone booth anywhere would be better than another moment in Elton's store. As he left, Elton actually waved bye-bye the way a child does. Could Rose possibly be on *his* itinerary? It was too ridiculous to imagine.

He had walked three blocks before he realized he had left the package sitting on Elton's counter.

"Forget something?" asked Elton, handing him the package.

If there hadn't been two customers at the counter, Peter would have said something.

"Don't forget what I told you," said Elton as Peter left the second time. "See you soon."

Chapter Thirteen

It was a time of nightmares.

Not just every once in a while, but every night, and sometimes several times a night, Peter would bolt awake, his pajamas drenched in sweat. He'd change, and then, getting back to bed, he'd marvel at Elizabeth, appreciating the fact that his nightmares didn't wake her and at the same time annoyed at her tranquil affection for her pillow, which she clasped to herself as if it were a lover.

His jealousy of her pillow was as ridiculous as his dreams: trying to get home, the buses and subways not running, taxi after taxi refusing to take him, slamming the door in his face and then taking someone else half a block away; or his mother standing over him, chiding him, warning him, lecturing him, while he wanted to get off to school, knowing he'd be late, wishing his mother would stop talking and let him go, and finally when she

did, finding in place of the school an empty lot; or the
recurrent riot, with one group in white helmets and
another in black helmets and he, helmetless, ducking the
stones from both sides, avoiding the broken glass, and
finally the billy club smashing down on his head as he
awoke.

He didn't try to make sense of his dreams. He just
wanted to sleep. He kept negotiating with God for just
one good night. And then he got it.

For the first time in weeks he had slept the whole night
through without waking. He recalled no dream and felt
miraculously rested.

He tested his body by stretching, careful to let his
heels lead. He tried a few sit-ups, eased himself out of
bed, windmilled around a bit, then turned the shower on,
brushed his teeth while the shower warmed up, and then
let himself under the needle spray, which felt delightful.
He was bathing in euphoria when he saw Elizabeth on
the other side of the translucent door. Turning the water
off just enough, he was able to hear.

She said, "What are you doing in the shower with your
pajamas on?"

He felt like a lunatic but handled the situation with
style.

"It feels different," he said, stripping the wet top off,
opening the door, and throwing the top at her, his bottoms following a moment later. He closed the door,
soaped himself, and sang *Oklahoma!* and World War II
songs, not caring that all those rousing words filtered
through a voice which his mother had warned "should
never sound a note out loud."

At his breakfast place were perched the usual coffee

and orange juice, and because he seemed to be feeling so good, Elizabeth asked if he wanted waffles, bacon, scrambled eggs, sausages, and he stopped the list at that point by saying yes, and she, enjoying it as much as he did, made waffles, bacon, scrambled eggs and sausages, putting them down on his greedy plate as each came off the stove, and he ate them all.

"Well!" she said when he had finished.

"Moderately well," he said, smiling.

In front of the mirror he admired the way his light blue cotton shirt looked with his black, soft-finish suit, his best, both the shirt and the suit, chosen to complement the day.

"How would you like to walk all the way to work?" he asked. Elizabeth was quick to agree. A fine idea.

Peter didn't use his usual brisk, near-trot way of getting to the next place fast; he sauntered, casually looking up at tall buildings he hadn't noticed before, pointing out stray leaves tenacious on a wintered tree, quickening to a remembered story out of childhood he had not told Elizabeth before, aware but not greatly concerned about the fact that they were taking in the city at a country pace and that they were already late for work.

It was a few minutes past ten when they got out of the elevator. There were a few glances as they walked together, not separately as they might have on a more usual day, down the aisle, past the secretarial pool to Elizabeth's office, where he wished her a good day, and then to his own.

He was startled: Paul was sitting at Peter's desk.

"Tried to get you twice on the intercom," he said,

"then thought I'd come by to see what was up. It's ten fifteen."

· "So it is," said Peter, trying to sound casual, but the first note of fear struck. *Paul had never made a fuss about the time.* His executives frequently worked late into the evenings and on weekends when necessary, and came in early if there was reason, never in fact stopped thinking about the job really, and normal working hours had never been an issue as long as Peter could remember.

His secretary, Nancy, handed him some incoming mail, mainly interoffice memos.

When she left, Paul said, "Maybe we'd better talk in my office."

Peter noticed the telephone message slip stuck on his pen, where he would be sure to notice it. In Nancy's handwriting it said, "Jonathan called."

"Could I make a call first?" Peter asked.

"Make it later," said Paul. Peter followed him. Paul's office door was closed behind them.

"Elizabeth is a nice girl," Paul said.

"Yes," said Peter, puzzled.

"And you're a nice fellow," said Paul.

"Thanks," said Peter.

"You nice fellows and girls ought to leave your picnic baskets and get in on time," said Paul, his voice honed to a slight sharpness. Paul was puffing away at his pipe. Peter liked the smell. His senses were still on the alert. He wanted to keep it that way, to stretch the day out calmly.

"I'm sorry we were late."

"Now," said Paul. He put the dummy of the TBC

brochure in front of Peter. "Why do you think they turned that down?"

"Well," said Peter, reflecting a moment, "the conception's fine, we know that. They okayed it with enthusiasm. The design is good, not great, but TBC never went for the visually conspicuous. The copy is straightforward, clear, the way Cary likes it, enticing only toward the very end. What do you think is wrong with it?"

"What's wrong with it," Paul said, "is that the client fired it back at us."

"I think I know why," said Peter.

"Go ahead," said Paul. "I'm waiting."

"Cary makes a big do about craftsmanship in mass production, but the fact is, he can't produce a competitively priced industrial scale with his present setup. Sales are off, way off. His consumer scale makes people hate to step on it. That no-slip surface Cary put on feels lousy to bare feet, and most people weigh themselves in bare feet. We've told him that a dozen times. You have. I have. He's sixty-six, insecure, and stubborn. His business is going downhill, and he's probably been fishing around for advice. And since he won't listen to advice that says his product line needs a drastic overhaul, he's finding people who tell him the advertising and sales approach is wrong. He's probably been interviewing agencies for a month or more. Maybe he's even decided on one. But he's also got a conscience. He's been with us eight years, and the first five or six of them were great all around. So he's decided to knock the brochure, and I think he'll knock anything else we show him, green, white or pink, until he's worked himself up to where he can overcome his instincts and fire us."

Paul was silent for a minute.

"Why didn't you say something before?"

"I thought you saw the message loud and clear. Besides, what can we do? Re-engineer his production line? Redesign his consumer models and tell him unless he bought our design he'd lose our agency? Paul, Cary and TBC are finished with this agency. He's suiciding, and I don't think either of us can stop it."

Paul's expression didn't change during the ten-second silence. Finally he said, "I think it's a lousy brochure."

Peter unfolded his handkerchief and blew his nose to give him a moment to think. "Paul, the ground rule when I came here was, we could con the client if we agreed it was the only way to get through to him, but we'd never con each other. You know damn well it's not the brochure!"

"Maybe," said Paul slowly, "if you weren't spending all your energies elsewhere, you'd have come up with a workable solution."

Peter started to say something and stopped. *Don't risk it.* Without Paul, no three hundred and thirty dollars every Monday.

"Maybe," said Paul, "we haven't been getting your best efforts lately."

"You know what the problems are."

"We've all got problems. We do our work anyway."

"I *have* been doing my work, Paul."

As he spoke, Peter remembered, out of the blue, how when he had first joined the firm, the hub of enterprise had been Paul, Big Susan, and a man named Finch. Finch was not only a gifted gabber, but a first-rate copywriter. Hadn't Paul and Susan and Finch gone on a client trip to the Coast and come back earlier than expected, and wasn't that shortly before Finch left without a word to anyone, packing up his wife and three kids and taking on a job somewhere in Virginia as ad manager for a small electronics company?

Hadn't the next triumvirate been Paul, Big Susan, and Bud Blacker? That had lasted a long time. And they had gone on not one but many trips together. And then Bud had had his heart attack, stayed away three months, and then retired to the Southwest somewhere.

Was *that* the pattern? It wasn't the brochure, it was the trip to Chicago.

"Peter, I think you and Susan and I ought to pay a visit to TBC and swing Cary around."

Cary wasn't swingable. *He* was.

Outside, pencil lines of rain were coming down, spotting the window.

"Take your time," said Paul. "Think about it."

"I don't think we can save that account," said Peter, the day cracking around him.

"I think we should *try*," said Paul. He paused for emphasis. "There's a lot at stake."

Peter knew how much there was at stake. Slowly he got up out of his chair. He thought for a moment. Thinking was useless. Could he threaten to reveal Paul's voyeurism? How? And who would care? Maybe if some clients—which?—heard Paul was kinky they'd be put off, but that's . . .

Peter thought the word "blackmail." Wasn't that what Paul was doing to him? Play my special little game of ball, or else you're fired? Also blackballed with other agencies? Anybody hiring him after ten years with Dale,

Bowne would want to talk to Paul, get his views on why Peter left. What would Paul say?

It didn't matter what Paul could bring himself to say. Peter couldn't talk about Paul to anyone else and live with it. Maybe Elizabeth, some day—but not a business connection.

He stopped at the closed door of Paul's office.

"I'm sorry, Paul, I can't make that scene."

"What scene?"

Don't kill it, came the warning.

"I mean, I don't think anything will change Cary's mind now."

"At least we'll know we've tried."

"No, Paul."

"If we lose TBC's billings, it'll be awfully hard justifying your salary."

"There are a helluva lot of other things around here that could use my time," he ran on, stopping only because he knew he was off the subject.

"Sure there are other accounts. But you're the highest-paid creative talent we've got. It doesn't make economic sense to use you on penny-ante accounts."

"I don't think you should. I think—"

"Last evening," Paul interrupted, "I ran into Mike Cohen. Very smart copy chief."

Peter nodded agreement. "He's young but very good."

"We stopped for a drink and ended up having dinner. I think he'd come over for about five thousand dollars less than you take down."

"You'd can me for five thousand?"

"I wouldn't dismiss five thousand dollars."

"What about everything I've done around here for ten years?"

"I wouldn't dismiss sentiment, either."

"Sentiment?"

Paul came around his desk and over to the door and put his hand on Peter's shoulder. "You're a good man, Peter. I'd hate to lose you."

Peter tried to disregard the hand on his shoulder, to concentrate on trying to understand. Despite Freud, it was still hard to see sex as the pivot. God's magnificent trick for procreating, the needle of desire bringing people together until they could find other common grounds for living together, or finding that the grounds didn't exist and so sex deployed them for another mate. How many turns could God's trick take? The cocksman, the table hopper who cannot sit still long enough to make a friend, much less a mate. The numberless Lesbians who married and even reproduced, making God's trick work both ways. And the homosexuals who settled for being wives to strong women, with an occasional excursion underground when the needling got strong. Well, that was all practically normal now, wasn't it, compared to the really kinky ones? Now here was Paul, the pitiful voyeur who was going to fire him when all Peter's defenses were down, when he couldn't take firing unless he played the kinky game.

Paul's hand came off the shoulder.

And why not play the game if you knew it was only a game? Millions did it, one way or the other. Look at the kids today; they tried everything and weren't struck down by bolts from heaven. The wife swappers were thriving in the middle-aged suburbs. Why not play the

kinky game with Paul and Big Susan, at least until the
mess at home quieted down, the economic pressure was
off? Would Elizabeth have to know, and if she found out,
would it make a big enough difference to change their
lives?

Would it change his life? That was the important
thing.

Paul seemed to be smiling. Was he sensing the possibility of a victory?

"Let me show you something," said Paul, turning
the lock on the office door. Paul opened the locked
drawer on his desk, took out an accordion file full of
photographs, and spread them out on his desk.

It was quite a collection. Peter had heard about the
collection, but he had never seen it.

The scenes of unorthodox sex shimmered in front of
Peter. *Kill it* came the cry inside his head, *kill it*, he's trying to show you how normal he is, how others do it. And
suddenly, with no clear notion of what was happening,
Peter found himself raising up the side of the desk until
the photographs began to slither off, with Paul clumsily
trying to catch them. And then, unable to stop, Peter
kept raising the edge of the desk until it was nearly verti-
cal, with a strength he didn't know he had. His arms
screamed with the effort, and then the desk was going
over with a tremendous crash, and instantly there was a
hubbub of voices outside Paul's locked door trying to
get in.

It was a miracle that Paul escaped injury. His face
glowed a fierce red. He spluttered sounds. Finally, "You
bastard, you dirty bastard."

Peter, his right arm now throbbing excruciatingly, a

sharp pain thrusting across the knuckles, thought of the irony of Paul calling *him* a dirty bastard, and maybe the truth of it, at the same time glad he—his instincts, perhaps his fear—had made the decision.

There was hammering on the door now, and Paul had to unlock it and open it a wedge to say, "It's okay, it's okay," and close and lock it again, but not before the eye-popping girls had caught a glimpse of the mess inside.

Without a word, Peter helped Paul right the desk. The edge that had hit the ground had cracked. They gathered up the photographs, and Paul stuffed them into the accordion file, but the locked drawer on his desk wouldn't lock now, and Paul cursed.

The pain in Peter's hand was a lot worse.

The men stood there, looking at each other. Finally Paul said, "We'll send you a check for the rest of the month. You'd better get your things out of your office now."

Peter couldn't help laughing; the month ended tomorrow. He saw that Paul misconstrued the laugh, but what could he say?

Paul righted his overthrown chair, sat in it, and swiveled away to stare out the window. Peter unlocked the door and, when he was out, closed it carefully behind him. At a distance, there was still a bit of a crowd, but Peter saw clearly only Big Susan. "I think you'd better go in to him," was what he said, and Big Susan, without a word, went into the office, and he could hear her lock the door behind her.

Then, behind the curious faces of the secretaries and some of the men who had now come out of their

offices to see what had happened, he saw anxious Elizabeth keeping as far back as she could.

He had already gathered his personal stuff into his
briefcase when she came into his office. "Can't talk about
it now," he said, then noticed the memo on his telephone
and called Jonathan.

The boy answered the phone very quickly. He must
have been waiting for the call all this time.

"Dad?"

"Sorry, couldn't call back sooner."

"That's okay." He sounded awfully grown up.

"What's up?"

"Mom's been crying."

"What happened?"

"Over Maggie," said Jonathan. "She doesn't understand about you and Mom. She's having trouble at
school."

Margaret had never had trouble at school.

"I'll try to see her today."

"It's too late today. She gets out at three ten. Can I
tell her you'll meet her at school tomorrow?"

"Is that what she wants?"

"She *asked* me to call you."

Why hadn't Maggie called herself?

"Gotta hang up now, Dad," he said, and his voice vanished with a click.

Peter threw the crumpled message slip into the waste-
basket. When he looked up, Elizabeth was gone, but
when he reached the street level in the elevator, she was
there waiting for him.

He carried his loaded case in his left hand. She took

his right hand in hers, but he winced with the pain and she let go.

As they came out of the revolving door to the street, she said, "Tell me about it."

On the way to her house, he told her.

Everything.

Chapter Fourteen

It was a calculated decision: Elizabeth would not accompany Peter to pick up Margaret in school. She'd be at her desk working, just in case Paul was looking for a reason to fire her also.

The school, as Peter came in sight of it, squatted like a white brick packing case three stories high, built before it was thought desirable for schools to be attractive. In front was the huge cage of the school yard, the ten-foot wire fence as forbidding as a prison. It was empty of children, the only sign of life some candy wrappers whipped around the yard by the wind.

Fortunately Peter had picked up Margaret at the school once early in the semester and knew exactly where to go. Through the side door, one flight up the clanging metal staircase, turn right and there was the back door to her classroom. He could see Miss Icardi in front of the green-gray blackboard. Miss Icardi was as he remembered her: plump, fiftyish, her shining black hair tucked safely in a bun.

Several of the children noticed him in the glass of the door. Their whisper telegraph worked instantly. Margaret glanced backward, spotted him, couldn't control a delighted wave. Miss Icardi saw him at the same moment. Peter didn't wave at Margaret, lest Miss Icardi think he was waving at *her*. Thankfully the jarring end-of-class bell rang.

Peter had to step aside as the calves stampeded out of the classroom, Margaret scrambling with the rest. When she reached him, he hugged and kissed her; they were like lovers greeting each other on a crowded railway platform, probably much too demonstrative, but why care?

"Mr. Carmody?" Miss Icardi's right hand and left fingers were intertwined in front of her, lest anyone be tempted to shake her hand.

"Oh, hello," said Peter, disengaging himself from Margaret. "Nice to see you again."

Miss Icardi took his proffered hand reluctantly. Peter winced with the pain of the handshake. Damn hand still hurt.

"The principal asked to have a word with you," Miss Icardi said, an official timbre in her voice.

"Oh?" said Peter, wondering what was up. He and Margaret followed Miss Icardi down the hall, encased in the stares of passing students.

The principal's name was Anderson. He was no more than thirty-seven or eight. His eyes seemed to float be-

hind tortoiseshell television-producer glasses. He pumped
Peter's hand once, demonstrating strength, efficiency, and
got to the point. "We have instructions in writing from
Margaret's custodian that she is not to leave school with
you."

"Her who?"

"Mrs. Carmody."

Peter tried to control the slight tremble that invaded
him.

"I'm her father," he said.

"You may go now," the principal said to Miss Icardi,
who looked very relieved and trundled off without a
word.

"I'm only obeying instructions, Mr. Carmody. I'm certain you understand I have no further prerogatives in the
matter once I've received instructions in writing."

Instructions? Prerogatives? What the hell was going
on?

"This isn't so unusual, Mr. Carmody," the principal
continued. "We've had other cases of this sort."

Cases?

"We are advised that you are no longer living in the
child's household, is that correct?" He didn't wait for an
answer. "In such cases, the mother is the head of the
household in which the child resides, and until custody is
finally determined, which is always the mother's in any
event, the custodian's instructions are followed with re-
gard to the welfare of the child."

"Maggie," Peter turned to her whitened face, "they
are wondering whether it is in your welfare to talk to
me."

Mr. Anderson let an official smile escape him. "We're not unreasonable people here, Mr. Carmody. You may talk to Margaret in my private office if you like."

"I was going to buy her an ice cream soda and walk her home."

Peter expected Anderson to make a crack about not having ice cream sodas on the premises. Anderson said nothing, led the way to his inner office, a simply furnished, large room with a desk, several chairs, charts all along one wall, and behind the desk, an American flag. "I'll just clear these things out of the way," he said, removing the papers from the top of his desk. He left them alone in the room.

Like visiting hours in a prison, was Peter's thought. He brushed it aside as Margaret put her head against him. He patted her hair, wished she wouldn't sob. Then when she did, he was glad of it, of course. He gave her time, then touched her tears with a clean handkerchief. It jolted him to see Anderson standing in the doorway so soon again.

"It's all right," Peter said to the principal. "I'm not hurting her." He hadn't meant the smart reply, but—the thought came as verse—*Peter is as Peter was and always will be.*

Anderson vanished.

"Tell me everything," Peter said to Margaret, who stuttered out the regiments of words she had stored in her armory. It was clear that she had had a delayed reaction to his leaving, wishing it into a very temporary matter. When too many weeks went by, it suddenly came through to her that her father might never be returning. Never, never! Rose, in the guise of consoling Margaret, would cry, too. Jonathan seemed to take everything coolly, isolating Margaret in her grief. She used none of those phrases, but that, in sum, is what she told him.

Finally she said, "Is there a chance you'll be back, Daddy?"

He looked at her lovely face, now red-eyed and tear-stained, a puffiness he hated to see there, and wondered how much he could lie to her and whether he should.

"Anything is possible," he said hesitatingly, "but I wouldn't give it too much hope."

She knew he was saying no. He felt better for it because it meant he had not really lied.

"Uncle Jack says you're going to divorce us, Daddy."

Damn Jack.

"Jack is a lawyer, Maggie dear. Don't pay too much attention to what he says."

She seemed puzzled. Peter, flooded with feeling, took her face in his hands.

"Maggie," he said, his cords not working right; the sound of her name came out garbled, unclear.

"Yes, Daddy?" she said, trying to help along.

"You—know—I love you?"

He hadn't intended the questioning inflection, but she knew, oh, she knew.

"And Jonathan, too."

"Yes," she said.

"You see," he said, wishing to Christ he could be articulate for ten consecutive seconds, "Mommy and I have a problem between us which we're going to have to, you know, solve. Solving it may—well, it means, probably means I will be living with someone else."

"Is Miss Kilter going to be your wife now?"

Why was he fudging? She was being so direct.

"It's too early to tell yet."

"Will Mommy have another husband?"

"Have you asked her?"

"I can't ask Mommy questions like that. Besides, she cries whenever I ask her *anything*."

Peter swallowed.

"The important thing, Maggie love, is that a father never, really never divorces his children."

And as he said it, he had his first knowledge that it was the biggest lie of all.

"Listen, how about that ice cream soda now?" Peter asked.

"We're not supposed to," she said, visibly delighted by the prospect.

"Let's see now," he said, "we could meet in Howard Johnson's. It's just two blocks—"

"I know where it is, Daddy."

"I'll be waiting in a booth."

She squeezed his hand.

This time there was a quick knock-knock on the door. Mr. Anderson appeared, displeasure reigning on his countenance. "I'm afraid you've taken advantage of the rules, Mr. Carmody. I regret that."

"What do you mean?" The instant Peter said that, he knew. The intercom on the desk had been left open.

Peter was livid. "You eavesdropped on my private conversation with my daughter?"

"It's a precaution we take. Warranted, it would seem."

"Why, you son of a bitch." Peter regretted not the words but that he had spoken them in front of Margaret.

"That will be all, Mr. Carmody. You may leave now."

"I will not be told when or where to leave my own daughter."

"I wish you hadn't decided to be difficult."

"I'm not being difficult. You're being inhuman."

"I'm glad Mrs. Carmody warned us of your eccentricities. Officer?"

The policeman must have been standing just beyond the open door. He looked large and stupid.

"What the hell is going on here?" asked Peter.

Margaret, frightened, was instantly at her father's side.

"Nobody wants any trouble, mister," said the policeman. "I'm taking your little girl home."

Margaret moved around behind her father.

"Who called the cops?" Peter shouted at Mr. Anderson.

"Please lower your voice," said Mr. Anderson.

"I'll shove your teeth down your throat. Who called the cops?"

"Nobody's shoving nothing," said the cop, taking Margaret's arm. "Mister, you better get out of here peaceably or I'll run you in."

"For what, having an ice cream soda with my daughter?"

"For breaking the law," said the cop.

"What law?"

It was insane, the policeman pulling on Margaret's arm, he holding onto her.

The policeman unhooked his billy from his belt.

"Not in school," said Mr. Anderson, his alarmed eyes counseling the law.

"No!" said Margaret.

The Husband

The policeman pointed the billy straight at Peter's face. "You take off, mister, or I'll get a squad car here in two minutes flat."

In his mind's eye, Peter saw himself punching Anderson, ducking the cop's billy, grabbing Margaret and running with her through the door and down the stairs and out and away, only to be stopped by the policeman's billy crashing down, then a court, a judge, and jail, perhaps no visitation rights at all because of violent temper; he couldn't win.

In seconds, Peter was out the door, without even —ashamed—saying good-bye to Margaret, rage thumping in his chest and brain.

He walked the streets of the city, refusing to believe he could not control the events of his life, that his daughter was not his own, that his conversation with her had been listened to, that Rose had written the letter, that Rose had requested that a policeman take Margaret home, that the web of his life was loose strings, all the connections disintegrating.

"Scotch," he told the barman as he settled on the stool. "Double."

The tavern was filled with construction workers. He was the only one in a suit. The others stared at him. *Fuck them*, he thought, bolting the drink and gesturing for another. The experienced barman served half a dozen beers down the line, taking his time before bringing Peter another double. This one, Peter noticed, just reached the line on the shot glass, not near the rim, as had the first one. He might have trouble getting another soon. He had enough trouble. He paid off the barman and went out onto the street, which seemed peculiarly ablaze with sunlight that hurt his eyes, and he didn't have his dark glasses with him. Why was it so bright so near the end of the day?

The second tavern he picked was one where he could sit at a table out of sight. He didn't want people staring at him. Not now. He tried to enunciate his order carefully. He was not a drunk. He simply needed another drink.

He imagined the lecture he would deliver if Jonathan, some years hence, caught with a marijuana cigarette, would say he wasn't an addict, you don't become addicted to marijuana, it was a clarifying experience, the pressures were on him, school, girl friend, problems. Marijuana cleared the air; he needed it. Would Peter understand?

Generations do not understand each other's vices. These new kids, the dropouts, the hippies, even the non-hippies who did the college bit—didn't they make sex and love and live with each other with a casualness that would defeat too-quick marriage, cut *down* divorce? Or was that an illusion? Or would they get divorced more often but more *easily*?

It wouldn't be the same.

Because his glass was empty, he ordered another drink. *Plus ça change, plus c'est la même chose.* True or false? The ends remain the same—power, accomplishment, freedom to say no or yes. It was the means that changed from generation to generation. And not the kinds of lies—lying was mankind's great tool for making do when the truth was useless—but the form the lies took. The lie about divorce was once necessary to conceal the fact that fallible men fouled their own most intimate arrangements, and if insight came, what a human being wants is a second chance.

Okay, divorce is no crime, not anymore, but the children business? What grim architect of marital warfare decided that children were the ultimate weapon?

Children were God's objective. Man's, too, when he found out immortality was a fake storefront: how go on if not through children? Part of me will live after me, feet walking the earth rather than pie in the sky. At least, they'll think of me when I'm gone, *or will they?* Do they? Some. Sometimes. Not much assurance there, he thought.

"I want one more double," he said, making the waitress a witness to his resolve.

Children weren't just for putting flowers on the grave, for wearing one's face around life, for keeping the name on mailboxes somewhere. The trick of children—a colossal trick worthy of God—was that they were really not children but *independent people*, independent of their parents often before they were independent of the customs, clichés of living—the umbrella called society. And as independents, some of them were lousy. I mean, let's face it, he thought, one could have kids that were just half good, or no good, or bores, or untalented, or mean or stupid. It's not likely they'd be very stupid or very mean if the parents were smart and the upbringing somewhat decent, but the world was littered with successive generations that seemingly had greater differences than similarities. Wasn't genetics itself a kind of freak-out, skipping a generation for important traits, or was that part of the master plan? Didn't the Indians have the grandparents teach the children most of the time? Was that a clue?

But some of those independent people—*new name for children*—were quicker, smarter, better, more talented, wiser, yes, by age twenty or thirty or forty, wiser than the parents whose passion play conceived them in the first place. Look at the kids, and their parents! If what mothers and fathers wanted of their children had propelled so many generations, what a fantastic centuries'-long self-delusion, what utter crap.

Baby animals found their independence so fast—they had to, their lives were so short. But humans took so long, needed someone to cajole food into one end of the alimentary canal and in due course wipe up the remains at the other end, and cuddle, love, care for—though wasn't an old blanket more lovable? Once out of babyhood, children weren't children; they were *new people*. If marriage fails and you get divorced, it increases the chance for independence of the new people. How's that for a home truth?

The newsreel of Peter's mind was flickering in black and white images of hostile experts, all wearing eyeglasses, badges of intellectual success, pooh-poohing his asinine insights.

The psychiatrists won't buy it. The social workers won't buy it. Not now, anyhow. Some day, to do someone else some good. The history of thought and science is the history of abuse and disgrace, of closed minds flapping their wings in the face of anything not in the literature.

"You can't fight City Hall," he said to no one in particular, as he left a dollar for the waitress, paid at the bar and hailed a taxi in the now near night.

The Husband

Elizabeth was home.

He gave her the short version of what had happened. She wanted details. He wanted a drink. Cautiously she poured him one.

"Little on the short side," he said, noticing the inch of liquid over the ice cubes. He took the bottle from the table and, with his unsteady hand, poured in more than he had intended. "I'll drink slowly," he said.

Elizabeth tried to get his mind off the afternoon by snaring him in chitchat, but the conversation was all one way. She wasn't even sure he was listening.

She tried the phonograph. She knew enough to avoid his favorites—Stravinsky, Schönberg, Bartók, cacophony. She tried Haydn. He wasn't listening. He said the noise bothered him.

She noticed he was pouring another drink.

She prepared some pasta in a way he particularly liked, but Peter swirled his fork in the plate without eating until she gave up and suggested they go to bed.

She helped undress him. She kissed his passive mouth. To no avail. It was the first time he had ever failed to respond to her.

When she returned from the other room and got into bed beside him, she thought for a moment that he was asleep. Then the lids of his eyes opened. She tried to touch them closed with her fingers and realized that he was crying without tears. Her head on his chest, she could hear the thumping inside.

She couldn't help, so she lay back on her pillow and must have dozed off after a time, because when she awoke with a start, Peter was slumped asleep in the chair at the opposite side of the room.

The Husband

Careful not to make any noise that might awaken him, she got out of bed, slipped her feet into her slippers, and it was only when she had crossed halfway to him that she noticed the peculiar insensibility of his sleeping expression, and a jolt of alarm thrust itself into her consciousness. He looked so strange.

With speed she went to the bathroom but there were none of the signs she was looking for, but then back at his side her eyes focused on the glass beside him. He had obviously poured himself another half tumbler of whiskey and drunk almost all of it, and then she saw the plastic medicine bottle with one red pill. It seemed stuck in the bottom of the bottle. There was another one on the floor near his foot. *Where were the rest?*

The fool, not with alcohol, not with alcohol. She tried to pull him up, to get him to walk. He was too heavy for her. She tried to wake him. It was impossible. She put up hot water for coffee, hoping to force some black coffee into him, trying to remember what else there was to do, but when she returned to the living room his breathing seemed to have changed to a barely audible internal lisp, and all the muscles in his face had relaxed frighteningly.

She tried pulling some clothes onto him, despaired, wondered who could help her drag him down to the elevator and outside to a cab, and then she did the only thing left—called an ambulance, invoking the God of her childhood, hoping against hope that Peter would live.

Chapter Fifteen

He felt the slight signal from the tips of his fingers first, a dart of barely perceptible sensation shooting through the pervasive numbness of his body.

He unstuck his eyes and saw the nurse busily fidgeting with a gadget at the left side of his bed. Why didn't she look at him?

"Nurse?" he said, glad to hear the drowned rumble of his voice.

"Don't move," she ordered, then looked up at last. "I'm not the nurse. I'll call her as soon as I'm through."

Peter now noticed the strap around his left wrist, with a wire leading to the nurse's machine. Right wrist also. There were straps around both ankles, he observed now, each with a wire leading to the same machine.

The nurse who wasn't a nurse opened Peter's pajama top and sloped it over his shoulders without moving him.

Then she took a suction cup, attached by wire to the contraption, and placed it on his chest. Then somewhere else on his chest. Then around on his left side. And all that time the machine buzzed away.

"EKG," she said. "Electrocardiogram." She was removing the straps from his limbs, unhooking him from the machine.

Of course. He had had one during an insurance exam.

"How's it look?" he asked.

"The doctor'll have to read it."

"Can you give me a clue?"

"It looks all right to me."

"You'd say that even if it wasn't."

"Right," she said. He wondered if she was a Lesbian.

As the technician wheeled the machine out of the room, the white-capped nurse came in, a metal name badge over her breast pocket, her teeth flashing a smile. Peter squinted at the name badge.

"It's Ceracki," she said, pronouncing it differently than it was spelled. "How are you feeling, Mr. Carmody?"

"I felt my fingers," said Peter.

"That's a good sign."

"Especially after they've been amputated," he said.

She quickly said, "Nothing's been amputated," then realized he was joking and laughed.

"I'm very thirsty."

"Sure." She got a glass from a cabinet across the room, along with a glass straw, ran some water, and held the glass for him while he sipped at the angled tube. The water was as good as the first drink after a rough day's work.

The thought of whiskey nearly made him gag. She thought it was her fault and readjusted the glass straw in his mouth. The effort of drinking was tiring, and he stopped.

"Could you just leave that near the bed?" he said, flicking a hand at the night table.

She shook her head. "Just buzz when you want more."

He realized instantly, of course, that the usual bedside items weren't handy because of "precautions."

"What's the matter?" she said.

He hadn't realized his expression gave so much away. "I haven't been a criminal before. It takes getting used to."

It was beginning to come back. The feeling in the fingers had not been the first sign of consciousness. But the other things had seemed like part of a nightmare, the few instants of wakefulness while his stomach was being pumped, the terrible retching in the emergency room. Why did he remember the screaming of the ambulance siren as *after* that?

"What hospital am I in?" he asked.

"Parkside Memorial," she said. "You were transferred from Roosevelt when it looked like you'd make it and they found out you weren't indigent. This is a private hospital."

"Thank heaven for Blue Cross," he said.

"Sometimes," she said. "Anyway, your bill's been guaranteed."

"Oh?" he questioned.

She showed him the calling card on the large bouquet of flowers which he had assumed to be a hospital prop. The card said, "We're with you." It was signed, "Paul."

He wanted to laugh. He wanted to cry. He felt like he was going to do both at the same time.

"Try to take it easy," said the nurse. "The doctor'll be making his rounds soon."

He thought of a young intern taking his pulse, trying to look older, official, authoritative, and failing. He was wrong. When the doctor showed up, he turned out to be the resident psychiatrist, who wasn't young or official-looking, and his authoritativeness all lay in a Central European accent.

The doctor delivered a little lecture about the hazards of mixing Seconal and alcohol, a little to-do about how lucky he was to have gotten medical help in time, and a few questions.

"I didn't mean to take my life," said Peter. "I just wanted to stop living for a while."

The "for a while" cracked the doctor up. "You nearly spoiled your plans. The mix you took wasn't a temporary formula, Mr. Carmody."

"What about that electrocardiogram?"

"Nothing to do with you. Nothing wrong with your heart. We're doing a study at the hospital, you know, the relation between suicide and other factors. We're checking on previous heart damage. You'd be surprised at the number of businessmen who've had heart attacks who try to commit suicide over something else later. God misses. They miss. Life goes on. Feeling better?"

"Better than what?"

"Okay, you're feeling better. See you later," he said. "I've got a couple of slashed wrists next door to talk to."

Peter reflected as to how inappropriate physical and mental medicine was to most ills of the human condition. How far more advanced were car mechanics, who could make a nonfunctioning car run and a poorly functioning car run better. White cap interrupted his reverie. ,

"The doctor says you can see them."

"Them who?"

"Three of them have been camping out there for some time."

Foolishly he tried to comb his hair with his hands and tidy the bed a bit, but he didn't have the strength for it, really, and slumped back onto the pillow as the door opened once more and Elizabeth stood there as if she expected to see a corpse.

In slow motion her expression loosened into a great smile, and she rushed across to the bed, holding his face, kissing his cheeks with an emotion he hadn't known, a fierce, possessive, almost furious clutching at the fact of his life.

Finally, when she raised her head, he said, "I smell like a hospital."

"It talks," she said gratefully. "You don't know how long we tried to get you to talk."

Behind her now he saw them, the most tentative, short creatures imaginable, boy and girl. Margaret took timid little steps toward him.

"Take a giant step," Peter said, and Margaret rushed to his bedside and he took her hand, squeezing it. Should he take Jon's hand, too? He looked at the boy's face. It was a boy's face, not a man's now, inexperienced, inefficient in dealing with matters of life and death. He held out his left hand for Jon, and they sort of shook.

"Hello, kids," he said, afraid for a moment to say more. Did they know why he was here? They must. What an example, finking out of life!

"I'm sorry," he said. They clearly didn't know about what. "How did you get here?"

Jonathan beamed. "In a limousine."

"The driver," Margaret exclaimed, "has a uniform. He's very handsome."

"All Paul's doing," said Elizabeth. "He phoned Rose. He told her he'd send for the kids and return them."

"Is he here?"

"Just the chauffeur. The hospital said only immediate family for now. And me."

"And you," said Peter.

"They asked me if I was fourteen," said Margaret.

"What did you say?"

"I lied," said Margaret, twinkling.

"I said I was fifteen," said Jonathan. "I don't know if the nurse believed me, but she let us in."

"That's a nice nurse."

"Look what the man in the car had," said Jonathan. He unrolled a giant-sized get-well card, held it high so Peter could see the flourishes of ten or twelve people from the office, including Paul's.

"The children have something of their own," said Elizabeth, stepping aside.

Margaret produced a Hallmark card with a fever chart on the front. Peter opened it slowly. Inside she had written: *Don't ever go away. I love you. Margaret.*

He knew she meant, Don't leave this life, and not, Don't leave this house.

Jon sidled up to the bed. "I'm not good at mush, Dad," he said. His card showed a man in a hospital bed, both arms and both legs in casts suspended by pulleys from

225

the ceiling. The printed caption said, "How was the skiing?"

Inside Jon had written simply: *Dear Dad, Jon.*

"Thank you," Peter said. He looked at his universe—Elizabeth, Margaret, Jonathan—and thought, what would his heart do now to that mad needle on the electrocardiogram?

They talked inconsequentialities for a few minutes and then the nurse ushered them out, promising them all a chance for a visit soon again and leaving him, the door closed, alone with his life.

Chapter Sixteen

Paul had clasped Elizabeth's hand and Peter's hand in his own as if giving them his blessing, which in fact he was: a week's paid license to go off together while Peter "convalesced."

As they waited for their rented convertible, Elizabeth said, "Paul has a lot of guts."

Peter looked at her quizzically.

"I mean, taking you back, loss of face, giving you this week, and—"

"And?"

"Adding me to the package on no basis he could rationalize from a business point of view. He's a nice man."

"He's celebrating, too."

"Celebrating what?"

"His relief. He must have blamed himself mightily, if I know Paul."

"You're being cynical, Peter."

"Just truthful."

She thought it best to let the subject end.

One of the nice things about renting a car, thought Peter, was the surprise of its color.

He threw their two bags in the back seat and slid in beside Elizabeth. "It's a hen's-egg blue," he said.

"Hens' eggs aren't blue."

"If they were, they'd be this color."

He checked the mileage. Not too bad. One of the tricky things about rented cars was the chance of finding five years' worth of mileage on a current year's car. The attendant was watching as Peter checked the front ashtray. It was clean. The attendant smiled. Peter checked the back astray. It was full up. The attendant lost his smile and hurried to empty it.

"Never mind," said Peter. He gave the attendant a quarter, put the car into gear, and they were off.

It was past the morning rush hour, and getting out of the city was easy. They were silent with their thoughts all the way up the East River Drive and onto the Hutchinson River Parkway. When they reached the Connecticut Turnpike, Peter broke the silence. "That's better," he said, accelerating to sixty.

He had quickly become accustomed to the car, found its rhythm, and had to control the impulse to let her rip faster than the speed signs cautioned. It was a boyish way to feel. Boyish, he thought, was a good feeling.

They made the Crabtree Inn a little after one. Peter was beginning to feel the first rumblings of hunger, which pleased him; he had lost six pounds during his week in the hospital.

The red-uniformed colored man escorted them to the bar, which was very nearly empty, presented the elaborate menu, took their order for martinis, and returned with their drinks before they had studied the appetizers.

"Take your time," he said, and they did, savoring each elaborately handwritten item as if they were pretasting it.

Elizabeth decided on lobster bisque to start with, and Peter ordered the avocado stuffed with shrimp.

"If you want shrimp," she said, "order shrimp. If you want avocado, order it neat. The combination is pointless."

"Yes, sir," he said to Elizabeth. Then to the waiter, "I'll have the avocado plain, with a wedge of lemon on the side."

If you didn't let your pride get involved, learning could be an added pleasantness.

She ordered the chicken curry and a salad. He decided on the beef, medium rare.

"Baked potato?" asked the waiter.

"Go ahead," said Elizabeth.

"Okay." He smiled.

"Sour cream and chives with your potato, sir?"

He considered a moment.

"Just butter, thanks." Then he added, "Could we get some of your famous popovers?"

"You get them if you asks for them or not," said the waiter.

All three of them laughed gently.

Peter could feel the mild effect of the martini coursing through the length of his arms and legs, stirring his appetite. The martini glasses had been prechilled. He liked that.

The Husband

"I think everybody ought to go to the hospital once in a while, just to lie and think."

"What have you been thinking?" asked Elizabeth.

"About you, me, the kids, life, love, work."

"No war and peace?"

"Not a thought," he said. "It was all very personal."

"Go on," she said, treasuring the measured pace of their conversation, the laxity that seemed so natural and easy in contrast to the jangled tempo of their recent lives.

"I've come up with a kind of personal order of battle. The sides change, relationships change. What doesn't change is that you're stuck with yourself."

"Sounds like a simplistic version of psychotherapy."

"Madame," he said, leaning across the table toward her, "history is littered with wise men rediscovering the obvious."

"Wise on."

"So, first is you. Meaning me. One comes to terms with oneself, and all that bullshit. But then life gets complicated. You can't do it yourself, 'it' standing for practically anything, even fighting. Your universe enlarges to include one other person, preferably one you can do a lot of things with, like talk to, fornicate with, fight, like choosing up sides, you and me being one side and the rest of the world the other. In union there is strength, provided the union is small—preferably two. Bigger unions lead to chauvinism, price fixing, monopoly, featherbedding, wanting to get paid for the six minutes it takes you to wash your hands slowly at the end of a day. The biggest union I'll go for is the tribe, but I'm afraid the space age has severely limited the scope of tribalism. Hence, I'm back to the union of two. Solve your own problem."

"Plural."

"Okay, solve your own problems. Find a mate you like to mate with, with all that implies. Everything else is as inflated as the United Nations."

"You'd de-politicalize the world."

"You have no idea how political, how hung up in power politics a simple twosome can get."

"And if the twosome isn't simple—"

"You follow me."

"I follow you, massa."

"You're the best-looking gun bearer I've ever had."

"Bear your own gun."

"You're the best-looking ammunition bearer I've ever had."

"Metaphor complete. Cut."

He put salt on the avocado, squeezed the lemon over it, savored a spoonful. She was right. If you're eating avocado, don't muck it up. He saluted her with the spoon.

"How's the bisque?"

She tried a spoonful from the far side of the bowl. "Too hot to taste."

"Take your time."

"Your priorities," said Elizabeth, "don't give much weight to hearth and home."

"Heart and home," he corrected her. "They do. Home is where one feels most comfortable. Right now my home is portable. Where we are. There's no place yet, no fixed place. Your apartment isn't our apartment. My hole in the wall isn't anyone's. But I don't feel homeless. Just house-less," he added, and she had to laugh.

"As for the kids, let's skip ahead. It's conceivable, not probable but conceivable, that three or four or five years from now, they might feel more comfortable with you than with either Rose or myself, even if they lived with Rose."

Elizabeth started to protest.

"No." He held up a hand. "I didn't mean *you'd* get custody in any sense. I mean kids pick their own crowd and their own people. After a time, inevitably, girls have problems with Mom, boys have problems with Dad— Freud itemized all that—so they pick more comfortable surrogates: a Dutch uncle, a teacher, a friend. Could be you. Get the point? Parents' relationship with children is very temporary."

He knew she was going to take exception.

"Sure there are exceptions," he headed her off, "but don't they come later, when the kids are no longer kids, when they fix up with the original father or mother as they would with a friend, a voluntary venture after the stress and strain is over?"

"You and Mao. He puts the kids in twenty-four-hour kindergartens, and you put them in left field."

"No!" Peter lowered his voice. That "no" had been louder than he had intended. "What I mean is, I'm not discarding families, I'm just trying to stop lying about the relationships. It's the one-two relationship, man and woman, that lasts if it works. Even in the best-managed families, when the kids are in adolescence, the one-two relationship is the only one that goes along as before. After the formative years, the kids are subject to as much guidance as the family dog. Or a friend. Or an employee. Yet look at the millions of bad, nonworking one-two relationships that are kept going because of a false notion of what's good for the kids. It's the most persistent middle-class delusion of them all."

"There's another."

"Oh?"

"I sometimes read the women's magazines."

"Shame on you," he said.

"Have to. Part of the job."

"That's no excuse."

"If you believe the women's magazines, divorces happen because the husband is a drunk—"

"Or the wife."

"Either way. Or the husband beats her. Or one or the other is unfaithful."

"Or both."

"They skip the biggest reason of all."

"Let me guess."

Elizabeth smiled. "Okay."

"Boredom."

"You *have* used that week in the hospital."

"Elf, I knew that one before the hospital. Every time I had a first-rate quarrel with Rose, it was over nothing. Nothing important, except the unholy boredom of our so-called lives. Boredom is the opposite of living. People want to live while they're alive."

"Try saying that in a women's magazine. The editor would get stomped to death."

"That's what I was getting at," said Peter. "To hide the truth, you turn on the myth-making machine. You make up a myth about people sticking it out for the sake of the kids. And if you find people getting divorces anyway, you change your pitch. You say okay, you divorce the wife, but you don't divorce the children."

"You're worried that in some sense you do."

"Sure, I'm uneasy about it. But it's beginning to dawn on me that as kids get into adolescence, they're in the process of getting their own divorces. In fact, that kind of divorce is indispensable for them, if they're going to grow up and become independent."

"What about young kids—three, four, five, six?"

"Haven't worked that out yet. Anyway, Maggie and Jon are both past that, thank heaven."

"You make it sound easier than it is."

"It's not easy, the law being what it is." Peter felt anger tumbling him again. "What the hell do the law, lawyers, judges—the courts are full of bored husbands serving boring time on the bench in court as well as in bed at home —what the hell has the law anywhere ever done to make marriage work?"

"Easy now," she said.

"Sorry," he said. "The law is a fink. It's got no more to do with justice than barbers had to do with surgery."

Peter and Elizabeth discovered themselves holding hands across the table and instantly withdrew them.

They had chocolate mousse for dessert and espresso afterward. Peter treated himself to a Jamaican cigar. It was after three o'clock. It had been a long, good lunch. He was glad they had talked.

"I guess we'd better make time," he said after a while.

"Finish your cigar," said Elizabeth. "There's no hurry. I told Barbara we'd get there Tuesday or Wednesday, that we were just sort of meandering up to New Hampshire, not breaking speed records. She said just to call a couple of hours before we got there so she could get the comic books off the living room floor."

Peter had almost forgotten that as a kind of New England beacon for their trip, Elizabeth had picked Barbara Estensorro, her best friend at Barnard, who had remained rich and single till she was twenty-eight and then married Fernando Estensorro, a Cuban sculptor of, as Elizabeth had put it, "famous people's heads, the Karsh of clay." They lived in elegant isolation near Keene, New Hampshire. Elizabeth and Barbara had kept in touch via Christmas and birthday letters and on Barbara's infrequent dress-buying sprees in New York. Elizabeth had had a standing invitation to come up ever since Barbara's marriage, and now, Peter in hand, was making her first visit.

"Why don't we camp here for the night?" said Elizabeth on a whim. "They have tourist rooms upstairs."

"It's only three-thirty."

"We could loll around, take a walk, take it easy. Wasn't that what we agreed to do? If you get bored with me, you've got half a dozen paperbacks in the suitcase."

"I'll let you know when I'm bored with you," he said.

That early in the day there was no problem about a room. They got the hostelry's best, what had obviously been the master bedroom when the inn was a private mansion. For $22 the night they got a huge bedroom, complete with match-ready fireplace, a pink- and black-tiled bathroom, plus a kind of anteroom, furnished in fake antique. It wasn't until their hostess left that Elizabeth noticed the mirrored ceiling in the bedroom.

"What the hell is that?" she exclaimed.

"Probably a vestige of the original owner," said Peter, "or installed by the innkeeper for the entertainment of his guests."

235

"Do you think it's a one-way mirror and they watch?" she asked.

If it was, thought Peter, what a perfect setup for Paul. He stood up on the bed and looked at the edge of the mirror. "Safe," was his verdict.

"I still don't like the idea."

"You could always ask her to change the room. You could say, 'Madame,' "—Peter fixed a falsetto in his voice —'my lady objects to the mirrored ceiling.' "

He kicked off his shoes and lay down on the bed. "I've never seen myself from this angle," he said.

"How do you look?" asked Elizabeth.

"Long."

She lay down next to him. "I look long, too." They laughed, Elizabeth's laugh stopping only when his mouth found hers. Perhaps because it surprised them both, it was the most exciting kiss they had experienced.

Both windows looked out on evergreens. A squirrel skittered along a branch. Elizabeth closed the blinds before undressing. In the nude, she looked exquisite.

"That squirrel is missing something," said Peter, finding his voice as he rose from the bed and kissed Elizabeth again. Then he lifted her in his arms and carried her to the bed.

"Don't move," he said and undressed himself without taking his eyes off her.

With the blinds drawn, the room was quite dark.

"Light the fire," said Elizabeth.

"Later," he said.

They must have slept for several hours afterward. When Peter awoke, the fire was roaring. Elizabeth was in his arms, wide awake. His upward glance caught the flickering image of the lovers in the ceiling mirror.

"Hello," he said to her.

"Hello," she answered.

"Thanks for lighting the fire," he said.

They stayed silent with their thoughts until the sound of cars signaled that people were arriving for dinner at the inn below.

"Shall we?" said Elizabeth.

"We shall," he echoed.

Peter hadn't worn an ascot in years, but he had put one in the suitcase and now put it on.

"I'd like to have a picture of you stark naked and in an ascot," she said.

"Okay," he said.

"Got it," the living camera said, blinking both eyes simultaneously.

Peter had a burnt-orange shirt to go with the blue ascot, gray flannel trousers and a conventional blue blazer. Elizabeth said, "I'm afraid all I've got is a dress."

When they first met, Peter had been somewhat puzzled by Elizabeth's attitude toward dress. She regarded it as unimportant as long as it passed certain minimum standards of taste and warmth, the way some people fed themselves to squash hunger till the next meal. At least that was the posture. But Peter had observed that Elizabeth usually dressed extremely well, simply, tastefully, even colorfully, with one difference from the many women he had observed. It was the total image Elizabeth went for, rather than *the* dress or *the* hat (Elizabeth never wore hats) dominating. Her consumption of clothes was not conspicuous; the effect was fine.

The Husband

The dress she put on now was really an elongated blouse, crisp cotton in what Peter thought of as a dark, quiet red, wine but clear, not a trace of lavender. She added her restrung pearls, and that was all.

In the dining room, the dozen or so people turned to look at them. Peter wondered why for a moment, and then realized that they had not come in the outside door but down the stairs. Elizabeth was not wearing a ring. Perhaps she would never choose to wear a ring, even if married.

Did it matter? It mattered to the police. One shouldn't be guided by the preferences of the police.

After the splendid dinner, they walked in the night air, pursuing what paths they could find by the moon's light until they came to a rivulet which might have been a brook in another season. Elizabeth picked up a small, polished stone and dropped it in. Peter picked up another stone and dropped it in also.

"We must come back to find those stones one day," she said, gathering her skirt a bit as she found the trail back, knowing that Peter was watching her every movement.

Inside, the diners had left, dishes had been cleared, and a few of the tables had been set for breakfast. The place had settled in a hush that seemed premature for city people at ten o'clock, but the peaceful lethargy in their limbs after the walk bade them climb the stairs. In the upstairs hall they heard voices from two of the rooms, meaning overnight guests, found their own, with the bed they had left rumpled now neatly turned down. They made love in the quietest way and were soon asleep.

* * *

They stopped for lunch the next day at a Howard Johnson's about a hundred miles from Keene because Elizabeth felt in the mood for their special version of fried clams. After lunch, she phoned Barbara and returned to the table with a puzzled expression.

"No go?" he asked.

"Oh, she's expecting us, and everything she said was fine, in fact excessive, but I felt a weird apprehension in her voice. I hope she and Fernando are getting on."

"You may have caught her in the middle of dishes."

"Of course." She tried to put omens out of her mind.

When they crossed the Massachusetts-New Hampshire line, Peter made a crack about the Mann Act.

He got no response.

"Doesn't it bother you, crossing a state line for immoral purposes?"

Still no answer. He wondered what Barbara might have said to bring on Elizabeth's silence.

The road map indicated they had to go through Keene and then head east. Halfway to Peterborough, a small road north brought them to the unpaved lane marked "Estensorro Private." Peter wondered what they did in heavy snows. The road wound through the trees on a path that seemed as much up as away, and it was nearly a quarter of a mile before a clearing burst before them and they saw the house a hundred yards ahead. They had to park their car in the clearing. Suitcases in hand, they climbed the smooth stone steps set in the hillside. Halfway up to the house they saw Fernando clambering down to meet them.

Peter was struck by how handsome Fernando was,

despite his thick beard, a cigar butt clamped in his teeth, and the baggy green overalls he was wearing.

"Let me help," he said as they exchanged greetings. "I was in the studio when I heard your car."

Fernando took Elizabeth's suitcase and offered to take Peter's as well, but Peter indicated he could manage.

"Where do you keep your car?" he asked. "Surely not up the hill."

Fernando gave a sly wink and pointed. Near the clearing, a small area had been bulldozed into the trees, but most of the trees there had not been cleared, their branches forming a kind of car-length shelter.

"Keeps most of the snow off," he explained. "Building a garage down here seems kind of pointless. Difficult to heat. This way, at least I don't have to scrape a foot of snow off a dozen times a winter. In snow season, I back in and keep a dozer blade on the front so I can make a path here in the clearing and down the road. Takes two hours. Good thing I don't commute to a job. Last year, January I guess, I didn't even try for the first couple of days, snow was so high."

Fernando seemed exuberant and, Peter noted, wasn't winded at all at the top of the climb, though Peter felt the full weight of his suitcase and was puffing mightily.

"It takes getting used to, I guess," said Peter.

"Sit-ups," said Fernando. "Eighty sit-ups, twenty-five push-ups, three minutes' chinning at a bar every morning."

Elizabeth flicked a look at Peter. He couldn't make out whether she was scoffing at Fernando's physical fitness program or reprimanding Peter for not doing the same.

Barbara was at the door, wiping her hands on an over-

long print apron, her dark blond hair gathered in the
back, a pioneer woman. She and Elizabeth kissed, Peter
was introduced, and Barbara stared in the most conspicuous way. She started at his face and wended her way
downward, taking him in a square foot at a time and
then the whole of him. He expected her to say, "So
you're Peter."

"Come in to the fire," she said. "Tea won't be a moment."

They settled themselves in chairs, Peter picking a
rocker.

"Can I get you anything else?" asked Barbara, serving
the tea.

"Nothing, nothing," emphasized Elizabeth. "Had a
good lunch. Let me look at you. You haven't changed."

Barbara blushed. "Older," she said.

"All of us," said Elizabeth.

"Elizabeth is a great relief to Barbara," said Fernando.
"Barbara was twenty-eight before she married, the last
in her class, except for Elizabeth. So Elizabeth is her saving grace."

Tactless, thought Peter, but he soon saw that the matter was an old one between the three of them, or at least
between Barbara and Elizabeth.

"You're married," said Fernando to Peter.

"Yes," said Peter. "A boy almost fourteen and a girl
almost thirteen."

"Ours is in boarding school," Barbara said apologetically. She showed a picture of a little dark-haired, un-
smiling boy who seemed much too young for boarding
school. "It's a special school," said Barbara. "He has an
emotional problem." Fernando silenced her with a look.

The Husband

Peter looked around. Elizabeth had spoken of the place as a "cabin in the woods," but it was far from that—a modern, large house on two levels, the rustic quality apparent only in some of the many antiques. He wondered if Barbara's inheritance or Fernando's sculpture had paid the way.

"Can I see your studio?" he asked.

Fernando was pleased. Elizabeth wanted to join them, but Barbara insisted on Elizabeth keeping her company. Soon the two of them were swept away in a babble of gossip about school friends and who was where with whom.

Through the kitchen a door led to an unheated, covered-bridge passageway to the studio. "This is recent," said Fernando about the passageway. "I used to find the twenty feet outdoors used to take away twenty minutes of warm-up time once I was in the studio."

The walls and ceiling of the studio seemed mostly glass. Peter noticed the glass was thermopane, which must have cost a packet. In one corner, there was a table littered with sketches, an electric coffee maker, cups; near the table, a couch with throw pillows. The rest of the room was devoted to platforms of various sizes, pedestals, and busts. Most of the faces were familiar and had one thing in common: the people had been in the news in recent years. Fernando's style, a rough, masculine quality, was common to them all, even to the busts of Maria Callas and Julie Christie. A strange collection. "If I were a cartoonist," Fernando explained, "I would draw every day the people of the day before. As a sculptor, I have a longer lead time. Fame animates me—unlike most artists, not *my* fame, but the fame of my subjects."

It sounded reasonable. The array of newsworthy busts just looked so peculiar. Stravinsky, General Lucius Clay, U Thant, Hubert Humphrey.

"Do you work from life?" Peter asked, sorry he had asked it.

"Oh, no, hardly ever. I find living models distracting. Besides, few would come here, and I like working in isolation, even from my subjects. These people, their photographs, are everywhere, and what I do—I have a darkroom in the main house—is make a composite, or rather a series of composites"—he showed several—"giving me the perspectives I need. I've never had complaints from purchasers, subjects, museums. Actually, the greatest market, from a dollar viewpoint, that is, is the reproductions. I get a royalty, just as an author would from a book—a book is a reproduction, is it not?—and people seem to want the likenesses of famous people around them. A photograph is too much—for an adult—but a sculpture, ah, that is art and the person, too. How is it in advertising?" he asked. "Do you find the work creative?"

"It's a reasonably unpleasant way of making a large living, I suppose," said Peter.

Fernando laughed.

"Surely you would not occupy your life in something unpleasant?"

"Well, no more unpleasant than a teacher supervising undisciplined children resentful of being in school, or writing for a magazine which finds its way into the trash can each subsequent month, or working in a foundation that gives away its money without perceptible effect."

Fernando laughed again.

"Actually," continued Peter, "the trick in advertising is to get enough power, to be enough use to someone, your client or your company, to have your own way about some things. I try to confine the ads I write to products about which I can tell the approximate truth. What I mean is—and this is hard for someone outside the field to understand—what I do is to describe the benefits or advantages of a product that really has some benefits and advantages. Some of our art directors—this will interest you—are actually quite talented painters, quite not being enough for a career in art. And so they use their skills, sometimes, I think, to the client's disadvantage. That is, they may design an ad that calls attention to its artfulness, attention that should be focused on, forgive me, the message."

"You are very frank," Fernando said, saluting.

"Frankness deserves frankness," said Peter, returning the salute.

They went back to the women.

"I have never sculpted an advertising man," said Fernando in the passageway.

"It is an anonymous profession," said Peter. "No one the public would know about."

"Ogilvy?" asked Fernando.

"What museum—or person—would want a statue of Ogilvy?"

They were laughing as they entered the living room, where the women were having a high time of it.

"We've been wallowing in gossip," said Elizabeth, pecking Peter on the cheek.

Peter noticed copies of *Partisan Review* and *Commen-*

tary on the coffee table. "Are you going to do Podhoretz?" he asked Fernando.

"When he makes enough money to buy the original," said Fernando.

Elizabeth joined their laughter, though Barbara remained conspicuously silent. Perhaps she didn't know who Podhoretz was. . . . That phone call from Howard Johnson's—why had it made Elizabeth apprehensive?

Fernando served the largest drinks he had ever seen anywhere, twelve-ounce tumblers filled to the brim with ice and Scotch.

"Salud!" he commanded.

They clinked glasses several times before all four of them managed to touch glasses at the same time.

Fernando unzipped a guitar cover, produced a magnificent instrument, and proceeded to sing several Spanish songs with a fair voice and remarkable verve. Elizabeth listened with fascination. Peter found it hard to keep his eyes away from Barbara. She seemed to be—he didn't know why he thought so, but he was certain—counting the minutes. Why? Were they unwelcome? Did she want them to leave? They had planned to stay the night.

"You are staying the night?" she said, as if reading his thoughts.

"Oh, yes," Elizabeth assured her.

Perhaps it was the music, or the weariness of travel, but Peter found the drink going fast and its effect taking hold even faster. He wanted to caution Elizabeth, who was drinking right along with them all.

"A small one," he said when Fernando offered a refill. The small ones turned out to be half-high in the glass, six ounces of ice and liquor. Peter took one sip and put the glass an arm's length away on the table beside the rocking chair so that he would not be picking up the glass unconsciously.

After a time, Elizabeth got to her feet a bit woozily. "Wow," she said, "that was a drink. I think I'll go lie down a bit. May I? Then I'll put on some slacks and a sweater and settle down for the evening."

"Sure," said Fernando. "I'll show you the guest room. Your bags are up there."

Which left Barbara and Peter alone for the first time. She brightened considerably.

"Elizabeth has told me a great deal about you," she said. "Of course, she had written before, but very discreetly. I'm so glad for her. She's the last unmarried in our class. Can you believe I was a virgin when I married?"

The assertion startled Peter.

"I've reached the point in life," he said casually, "where I can believe anything."

"It's very difficult for a girl with a great deal of money," she said. "When a boy makes a pass at you, you never know if it's you or the money. I thought I was frigid."

Peter looked at her face closely.

"Fernando changed all that," she said as he descended the stairs.

"Changed what?" he said, ready to refill the glasses again.

"Oh, never mind," she said, getting to her feet. "Peter, how about me showing you the grounds before it's completely dark? Out back there's a magnificent view if you go a hundred feet farther up. I wish we'd built the house higher."

"Perhaps," said Peter, looking at Fernando. "Actually," he said, putting his hand over his glass at the proffered bottle, "I'm as high as I ought to be."

"Go ahead, go ahead," volunteered Fernando. "I've got a drink to go, and I can fix the salad in the meantime."

There was a high color in Barbara's face. "Fernando fixed the chili. He's really the brilliant cook in the family."

Peter labored up the trail after Barbara. She waited for him at the top.

"Look there," she said. The view was indeed breathtaking.

When he turned, her face was closer to his than he had expected. Was it the drink?

"Do you enjoy sex?" she asked.

Surprise caught any answer he might have given.

"I mean with Elizabeth."

He didn't know what he could say except, "Yes." •

"Good," she said, taking his hand. She led him farther along the path until their view was again obscured. Down below, the house now seemed far away. Even the smoke from the chimney seemed an altitude below.

Peter realized that Barbara had taken his hand. "Just a bit farther," she said.

Where the trail seemed to end, there was a kind of lean-to. He searched for the view and found none.

"Not through the foliage," she said. "You have to look through the tree trunks, like this."

She lowered herself into the lean-to and motioned to him. He sat down beside her, realizing that his stiffness was unnatural. When his head was close to hers, however, he did see the view. Despite the gathering darkness, he could see the whole distance of the valley below, as if looking under the trees.

"That's Massachusetts," she said.

It was planned this way, he thought.

Barbara rested her head against his shoulder. And as she did so, her hand rested on his leg.

Barbara seemed to sense his momentary discomfort and removed her hand. She lay back, her head resting against the leaves, her right hip slightly raised, her right leg slightly over the left one. And then she stretched, a languorous action, and as she did so, Peter noticed she was stretching all four limbs, bringing her mound of Venus in conspicuous view beneath the dress.

First Paul and Susan, now what? Life in suburbia was supposed to be full of exotic arrangements, but here in the country? Was the whole world going kinky? Was Square Peter still lingering in the age of one-to-one relationships lasting a lifetime? Of course not. He had just left Rose for Elizabeth, hadn't he? But what was this? Was he imagining more than was actually happening?

"If the weather were nicer," she said, "I'd invite you for a moonlight dip."

"Where?" he said foolishly.

"There's a stream just there," she pointed. "It's like a shower under the waterfall."

"It's a great view," he said. "I think we ought to be getting back."

"Do I bore you?" she asked. "I hope not."

"No, no," he assured her, "it's just—"

He stopped his sentence because he had no alternative. Barbara was rubbing her hand across his middle, slowly, firmly, and her hand was slipping lower. *Yank her hand away, you fool,* he thought, but didn't, and wondered if it was good sense that was keeping him from acting precipitously, or whether he liked it.

In a moment, there was no mistake about what she was doing. It had happened to him once before. A whore at a bar had made her approach that way, but this was Barbara, Elizabeth's best friend at school; they were houseguests, they had just met . . .

He raised himself from the ground, not without difficulty, not without excitement, and with a thick voice suggested again that they should be going down.

Barbara raised herself to her knees and said simply, "I am down," and at once there were no secrets or ambiguities.

"Look," he explained to her, "I'm not a prude."

She laughed nervously. "I didn't think you were."

"You're an attractive girl," he said, not wanting her to be hurt by his unwillingness.

"Thank you," she said.

"I'm just not much for this sort of casual thing."

"I like you," she said. She seemed desperate.

"Elizabeth and I are just finding our way together. I don't want to complicate things." He was trying to say the least that would stop her.

"Please sit down again," she said.

He did, not wanting to be rude.

"You'll enjoy Elizabeth more afterward. It's always that way."

"Always?"

She was moving closer to him again. "It was Fer-

nando's condition that we could each have sex with someone else once in a while as long as there was no involve-
ment. To sustain interest in the marriage."

"Just like that."

"With friends we don't see too often. With people we
meet. We come together after each episode stronger than
before. It will be like that for you, too."

Not on your life, he thought.

She was undressing. He rose to his feet unsteadily.

"Oh, please don't go," she said. The pleading in her
voice threw the alarm switch. Fernando and Elizabeth
were down there. Would Fernando dare? *It was their
custom.* Would Elizabeth let him? It seemed inconceiv-
able. *Anything was conceivable.*

He ran down the hill, hearing Barbara calling after
him. He was running too fast for the terrain; he was in
danger of stumbling. He slipped, skidded, grasped
branches for support, but kept on going until he arrived,
his chest heaving for air, at the house.

Fernando, his face a snarl, was slouched with a full
glass and said only, "She's up there."

Peter ran up the stairs two at a time, but the door of
the guest room was locked. "It's me, Peter," he said, and
she immediately let him in. She locked the door behind
him and threw her arms around him. She was sobbing.

"I had no idea," she said. "I had no idea."

He pulled her face away just enough to look at her
and ask, "What happened?"

"Like a nightmare. I was dozing from the drink—it
was more than I'm used to, you know that—and suddenly
he was standing at the side of the bed. No overtures,
nothing. Just, oh, Peter, he wouldn't listen to anything I

said, he wouldn't stop. I hit at him and scratched, and it did no good till I—Peter, I had to kick him in the balls."

He didn't know if she was laughing now or still crying. "They're sick," she said.

Since Elizabeth had hardly unpacked, it took only a minute to fix their suitcases. Peter led the way down the stairs. Barbara had returned. Her back was against the front door. Whatever Fernando was saying, he stopped the minute he heard footsteps down the stairs.

"Please excuse me," Peter said to Barbara, his voice firm. Barbara looked at Fernando for instructions.

"They're not even married," said Fernando. "You'd think they were an old married couple." He gulped at his glass. "*Your* friends," he said, underlining his contempt.

Peter didn't want to touch Barbara. He motioned her out of the way.

"They're useless," said Fernando. "Let them go."

Out the door, Peter and Elizabeth warily descended the stone steps into the darkness.

"You'd better give me your bag," he said.

"It's okay," she answered.

They didn't say another word until they were in the car. Peter locked all four doors, sealing off the outside world. The engine started instantly. He backed up carefully, then swung down the dirt road, following his low beams. The woods were full of limbs and eyes.

"How often do you think this happens?" Elizabeth asked.

"I don't know," said Peter. Thinking of the reported orgies of the ancient world, of the gossip of monasteries, of what he had heard in the Army—even if only a hundredth were true—he said, "I guess oftener than either of us thought."

Peter noticed with alarm how low the gas gauge was, and not a station in sight. He hoped, he prayed they wouldn't run out of gas. Not here. He wanted to be a long way away before he stopped driving.

Chapter Seventeen

The only car they passed on the treacherous road was a green Mustang driven by a blond boy of eighteen or nineteen, laughing away with his girl friend beside him and not paying enough attention to the road, Peter thought. How much attention had he paid to the road when he was that age? He hadn't had a car. Now all the kids have cars. Adolescents will inherit the earth.

"There's a gas station," said Elizabeth.

The two pumps stood like mechanical men, each with a hose arm raised in rigid salute, each lit by a large bare bulb under a metal overhang. An old gas station with old pumps; didn't see many of them along the roads anymore. Any pumps that pumped gas were welcome.

Behind the pumps was a clapboard house. The instant they stopped, a light went on inside, and an elderly woman came to the screen door.

The Husband

Peter stepped out of the car so he wouldn't have to shout. "Tell the boss we want a tankful of high test, please."

"I'm the boss," said the woman, wrinkling her crow's-foot face and wiping her hands on her apron.

"Hope we're not too late for you," said Peter.

"When them lights are on, I serve gas. When they're off, I'm asleep."

She filled the tank but not brim full. It could easily have held another gallon or more, gas she could sell to him this time only. Most of her customers must be transients. How many gallons did she miss selling by not filling to the brim? Enough gallons in a year to give the house the paint job it badly needed?

"Oil and water okay?" she asked.

"Okay," he said, not knowing whether they were okay or not, but not wanting a woman that old to lift the hood, check the stick; man's work. Bad enough she had to pump gas. The rental agency probably checked the oil and water before the car went out. Head stuffed with trivialities. Better than thinking about what had happened back on Kinky Mountain.

He paid the woman.

"How far to Keene?" he asked.

"Not far," she said.

Helpful. He slid in beside Elizabeth and was happy to see the needle on the gas gauge swing over to the right when he turned the ignition on.

As he turned onto the road, he wondered why he hadn't seen the green Mustang pass. They'd been at the station five minutes surely. The kids probably pulled off to the side of the road to neck. They didn't call it necking anymore, did they?

Elizabeth said after a while, "That's a lonely place for a widow."

"How do you know she's a widow?"

"Oh, a woman can tell."

"Be specific."

"I just can tell."

"The way you can tell if a woman sitting in a bus is married or not?"

"Yes."

"Very unscientific."

Elizabeth said nothing.

"Maybe she has children in the house with her."

"No children," said Elizabeth. "Maybe once, but not now."

"Oh, sure," he said. "Anyway, it's too far East for Bonnie and Clyde."

"She could get robbed," said Elizabeth. "She could get raped. Eighty-year-old women get raped."

The thought seemed suddenly very funny to them both. They were laughing when Peter saw the police car on the side road. Instinctively he checked his speedometer. They weren't going too fast; they were okay.

"If they're trying to catch speeders, they ought to pull off the road a bit more," said Peter.

He had hardly finished the words when he heard the unmistakable sound of metal on metal somewhere behind, a squealing of tires, a thump, a prolonged crumpling sound, the scrunching of broken glass, and a final silence.

Peter's foot had come off the accelerator instantly. He

braked hard. The tires screeched. Making the U-turn took four tries on the narrow road. A side glance at Elizabeth's face: it was white.

You could have driven on, a voice said in his head. You could not have driven on, the same voice said.

The sounds, carried on the night air, had seemed to come from just behind them, but it was at least two hundred yards before his high beams caught the tangled scene of the accident which blocked the road. The front bumper of the police car was locked into the back bumper of the Mustang, and the front of the Mustang had smashed into—or been pushed into—a tree. Had the police car accelerated too fast just as the Mustang's driver, spotting the police, had slowed down? The Mustang had swerved and smashed. Its windshield had vanished. The front and vent windows on the driver's side were shattered. The girl sitting next to the driver was screaming.

Peter thought to keep his lights on the scene of the accident. He and Elizabeth were out of their car and running even before the policemen got out of their car. Peter reached the Mustang first. He could see the boy's neck, a vast length from open collar to chin, his face straight up at the roof of the car. Unnatural angle, he thought, remembering the war and how in picking the wounded you skipped the ones with unnatural angles: broken neck, broken spine. The boy's hands gripped a broken-off piece of the steering wheel. The steering column with the rest of the wheel was hard up against his chest. Peter wished Elizabeth wouldn't see; she was at the other side with the girl.

The girl didn't stop screaming. Elizabeth didn't know whether to slap her face or not. How could you slap a face covered with blood, blood running from the hair, over the eyes, and from gashes in the cheeks and chin?

Both policemen were out of the car now, obviously shocked. One of them was bleeding at the side of the head. The other limped.

"She must have hit the windshield," said Peter. The seat belts flapped uselessly. How do you stop bleeding in the head? You can't put a tourniquet around her neck. She was bleeding from so many places in her face and head. Elizabeth put her hand to the girl's face and withdrew a large sliver of glass.

The policeman who was bleeding at the side of his head said, "Get her to a hospital."

Peter came around to the other side of the car. He and the policeman tried to get the girl out. If only she'd stop screaming. Maybe broken bones. Don't move if she has broken bones. Have to move. Have to get to a hospital, she's bleeding to death.

"Hospital six miles ahead in Keene," said the policeman.

The policeman with the limp said to the other, "You pulled out too fast. You hooked his back bumper."

"Shut up," said the other policeman as he and Peter managed to get the girl out. They carried her, a writhing sack, to the police car.

"Use your car," said the limping policeman. "We'll never get the bumpers untangled in time."

They put her in the front seat, where Elizabeth had been sitting. Blood all over the car. Peter couldn't help thinking: it's a rented car.

"He's breathing, I can hear him breathing," shouted the other policeman bending over the boy. "I'll radio."

The limping policeman radioed for help. The radio worked. "Get going," he said to the others.

Elizabeth got into the back seat of their car with the policeman whose head was bleeding. He couldn't be too badly hurt. He seemed all right, except for the head wound, though his face was chalk. "I'd drive, but I might conk out. I'll just give directions."

Peter backed up and swung around, leaving the accident scene in darkness. He drove seventy miles an hour, thinking, that's dangerous on a road like this. He realized the girl had stopped screaming. Turning to look, he heard the policeman say, "Keep your eyes on the road. She's passed out." Elizabeth held a handkerchief tight up against the girl's forehead, where the bleeding was worst. The handkerchief was quickly soaked in blood and useless. Peter handed over his own handkerchief. "God," Elizabeth whispered, "let her live."

When they reached the populated area, the policeman instructed him, in the absence of a siren, to keep honking his horn. The first red light, Peter started to brake.

"Keep going," said the policeman.

Peter looked right and left and accelerated again. "Next light, turn right."

It seemed an eternity; too long, too long.

The light was a red blinker. Another car was approaching the intersection from the opposite direction.

"Flash your lights," said the policeman. "Flash them again. Turn right."

Peter felt like an automaton.

"Just a bit more," said the policeman. "Okay, turn left up the hill."

Peter saw the hospital sign and, almost immediately, the hospital itself. He followed the red emergency signs around to the rear. They carried the limp girl into the emergency room just past the wide doors.

"I'm okay," the policeman said to the hurrying nurse. "The girl's lost a lot of blood."

"Put her on the table," the nurse instructed and pressed a buzzer. Within a minute, it seemed, the plasma stand was alongside, the bottle upside down, leading into the tube, the tube to a needle, a quick swab of the girl's arm, the needle inserted.

A second nurse—where had she come from?—was damping up the blood from the girl's head so she could see where the blood was coming from. The resident doctor appeared. He seemed to Peter no older than the boy who had been driving the car.

"Lot of stitches," said the doctor to himself. "Call Surgery," he told the nurse and busied himself about the girl's head as Peter, feeling he could do no more, stepped backward, took Elizabeth's arm and led her, trembling, to the other side of the room.

"Why can't they work faster?" he said to Elizabeth.

The second nurse was filling out forms. Ridiculous!

A stretcher on wheels was put alongside the table. The girl was gently transferred, the apparatus still in her arm, the empty plasma bottle replaced with a full one.

"Pretty girl," said the nurse with the forms. That nurse had never been pretty. She asked Peter, "Car crash?"

"Yes," interjected the policeman.

Just then several policemen, including the limping one, came in, carrying the boy on a stretcher. Peter felt curiously outnumbered. The form nurse put her clipboard down and looked at the boy. Dispassionately, Peter thought.

The nurse put her head down on the boy's chest. She felt his pulse. The limping policeman looked at her questioningly. "DOA," said the nurse.

Elizabeth was crying. One of the policemen led her into the waiting room. Peter followed. The policemen asked them both questions, filling out a questionnaire. Peter told them everything he had seen and heard.

"Anything else?" The policeman directed the question to Elizabeth.

She shook her head.

The policeman took their addresses, checked Peter's against his license, phone numbers where they could be reached if necessary, asked him to sign his statement. Then, "You can go if you want to."

"What about the girl?" asked Elizabeth.

"I'll check."

The policeman went out and didn't return for a full ten minutes, while Peter and Elizabeth thumbed sightlessly through the magazines in the waiting room.

"She'll live," he reported, "probably. We've reached her parents. They said the boy is her steady. Since first term high school."

"The boy's dead?" asked Peter fruitlessly.

"I guess so."

Fifty thousand people a year die this way, thought Peter as they wandered out. A lot of blood to mop up in the rented car. He took Elizabeth by the arm back through the wide doors and asked a passing nurse if there was a coffee shop in the hospital. She directed them. He'd mop up later. Too late to count on a motel on the road, but ought to be plenty of tourist homes in Keene. They'd find a place to sleep. Ha, thought Peter, sleep.

The coffee was very hot. They had Danish with the coffee. The waitress didn't seem to mind that they were both a mess. All she said was, "Accident?" They nodded. End of conversation.

After a while, Peter said, "If only the police car had come out two seconds later."

Then he said, "If only the boy hadn't braked immediately."

"It was probably instinct," said Elizabeth.

"Probably," he said, holding the coffee cup with both hands. "It's very temporary, isn't it?"

"What is?"

"Life," he said.

He put the coffee cup down. It was time to attend to the car.

Chapter Eighteen

If a holiday refreshes because of the change, the next four weeks passed as a holiday for Peter and Elizabeth. They worked throughout. But they also savored what they did. The closeness of death, first Peter's, imagined and acted, and then the actual death of the boy, made breathing, showering, walking, eating, listening, reading —the events of a lifetime—welcome, relished, consumed, appreciated. And the exposure to aberrant Paul and Susan (was Susan aberrant, too, or only accommodating?) and also Fernando and Barbara, perhaps not so kinky by the standards of the age, nevertheless made simple face-to-face heterosexual union, one man, one woman, a delight worth inscribing on stone.

While Peter and Elizabeth had worked on the same account on occasion, they now for the first time were put on an account together at inception, he handling

copy, she handling art. And what an account! Paul had
made a presentation to a beer company that was sixteenth
or seventeenth in the New York area—and that mainly
by accident. If a grocer's hand happened on that brand
when someone ordered a six-pack of beer without speci-
fying, they got Brew, for that was its unfortunate name.
Unlike the brands with a history, its life had been short;
it had been advertised with obvious rhymes like "true"
and "new," which sold nothing to anybody. The brewery was owned by Hans Christian Seitz, an immigrant,
self-made, who admitted to Paul during their first interview that more than half of Brew's dollar volume came
from his truckmen passing bills to tavernkeepers to get
them to take in kegs. Seitz himself was perfectly content to go on in this way, using bribery as his main advertising medium, but was increasingly incapacitated by
multiple sclerosis and was gradually turning over active
command of his small brewery to his son, Hans Christian
Seitz II, just twenty-seven and only a couple of years out
of Harvard Business School. Seitz II had devoted his post-
Harvard time to studying the business by riding the
trucks with the men, visiting bars, and seeing what actually happened at the point of sale. He had told Papa Seitz
that the company's problems would be a classic case at
the Business School, and that unless the old man found a
new way of selling his product, the business would stagnate. Papa hadn't taken too kindly to "stagnate," even
after the word was explained by Seitz II as meaning lack
of growth. After all, hadn't he raised a family in comfort
on that kind of stagnation? But what was the point of
sending your son to Harvard Business School if you
didn't listen? And anyway, the old man was halfway to

helplessness, and he didn't want his son taking an executive job with a competing brewery. So he agreed to listen to marketing presentations from several interested agencies. Paul saw Brew as a possibility for an experiment he had wanted to try for a long time.

Paul's pitch was hard to beat. He agreed to try a radically different campaign, and if sales didn't increase by at least 25 percent by the end of that period, Paul would refund the agency's full commission, and since the agency would obviously incur costs against that commission, it would take a bath. It sounded "challenging" to young Harvard. What sounded even better to him was Peter's part of the presentation.

"Sir," said Peter, addressing the young man in his father's office in the brewery, figuring that since he was going to tell him how to run his business, he'd start with "sir." The boy took it well. "I haven't tasted your beer, and I may not before this campaign is over. I don't like beer very much, and in any event, I have never found any appreciable difference between the brands that are bottled in Brooklyn. All the campaigns I've seen blink the fact that beers made locally taste the same. What I'd like to do is come right out and say that."

"Go on," said the tolerant young man, who actually felt in a panic about how to deal with that home truth.

"I'd like to prepare a TV commercial which says right out all beers made with the same water taste pretty much the same. That's the attention grabber. Then we'll show them the new Brew bottle, which isn't a bottle at all but a glass with a lid."

Peter unveiled for both Seitzes—but playing to young Harvard—Elizabeth's grand contribution to the scheme, an attractive glass with a lid like a jam jar, not a bottle cap. "All you do, says our commercial, is get it from the fridge, take the lid off, so, and drink. Don't reach for a glass and a beer, reach for a Brew. And if you don't drink beer from a glass, wouldn't you rather drink out of a Brew bottle than a beer bottle? Moreover—and this little point will appeal to the women who buy the beer at the supermarket—the glass you get with Brew becomes a permanent asset in the kitchen. If the children break glasses frequently—actually it's the women who break the glasses, but we don't say so—you'll have a constant new supply of glasses when you buy Brew beer. Brew costs the same as other beers, but you get six free glasses with every six-pack."

The kid from Harvard was stunned because he had heard all the stuff about creativity in business, but this was the first concrete example that had excited his glands.

D-day for the campaign was the first day the new bottle glasses were distributed, and nobody had to wait ninety days for the results, which were immediate and astonishing. The problem was not how to sell enough Brew, or even to brew enough Brew—they put the brewery on three shifts to meet the demand—but how to get enough of the new bottles fast enough.

"With the profits you'll make this year," Paul told Harvard, "you'll be able to buy a glass plant. After all, that's what people are buying from you—glass."

Success makes laughter easy. They laughed together, and Peter, enjoying the triumph, even drank a glass of Brew, which, as he had said, tasted no different.

To celebrate, Paul took Peter and Tony Cavallo to lunch at the Baron.

The Husband

"You know," said Paul, looking around at half a hundred tables of executives lunching mostly with each other, "anybody in this room who's not in advertising knocks it as a lousy business to be in. They just don't know the feel of finding a client with a big problem, dreaming up a solution and watching it work. Some of these guys have been canning tomatoes for twenty years. Same tomatoes, same cans."

"Boring," said Tony Cavallo.

"Right," said Peter. "Here's to advertising, the great horse race." He raised his water glass for a toast.

"Hey, we can do better than that," said Paul, signaling the waiter, who turned on a quick fawn. "Three bottles of Brew." He had to explain twice more before the waiter understood it was a brand of beer. Finally Paul said, "Check the bartender," and the waiter vanished, only to return a minute later with the news that they had "Budweiser, Schlitz, Heineken, and Löwenbrau. Which, please?"

The three of them had a good laugh. "Oh, well," Paul said to the uncomprehending waiter, "we do well enough with the six-packs. Let's have three Beefeater martinis, which is what we wanted in the first place."

"On the rocks," said Tony.

"With peel," said Peter.

"Three Beefeaters on the rocks with a twist," said Paul, sending the waiter off to the bar.

"We really should have Elizabeth here," said Tony. "That glass she designed is a beaut."

A moment elapsed while Elizabeth's name registered its different thoughts in each of them.

"It takes a good art director not to let the bright ideas get by," said Peter.

"I noticed you didn't let her get by, either," said Tony.

All three of them laughed nervously.

"They say you're going to marry her," said Tony.

"Who's they?"

"You know, the office, talk."

"Maybe that's personal," Paul chimed in, trying to be helpful.

"Yes," said Peter, "marriage is kind of personal. Actually," he continued, "I'm still married."

Tony and Paul laughed at that.

"Let's leave eventually for eventually," said Paul.

"You're going to get thrown out of the union if you marry her," said Tony as the waiter put the drinks down in front of them.

Paul raised his glass. "To Brew, the unobtainable," he said.

"What union?" asked Peter.

"The union of all us fellows who have a broad on the side," said Tony. "It's finking on the fellows to ditch the wife and marry the broad."

"You mean the married Mafia will get me?" asked Peter.

Any reference to the Mafia always angered Tony.

"Why don't we order?" said Paul, noticing that Tony was already halfway through the oversized martini. He signaled for menus.

He and Peter both knew Tony's wife. Tony had married her while he still lived in Little Italy up in the Bronx. He was just out of Evander Childs High School, messengering for an agency and studying art at Pratt Institute at night, too busy to date lots of girls and so concentrating on one, the only daughter of near neighbors, who assumed in time that their daughter would marry nice-looking Tony Cavallo. Not to disappoint their assumptions, or those of his parents either, Tony married Mary and they had five kids in eight years, by which time Tony was making his name as a commercial artist and his wife decided that they needed something more reliable than the rhythm method.

By the time Mary and Tony officially stopped procreating, Mary, to whom spaghetti was soul food, had broadened in beam, chest, and chin to the point where Tony was embarrassed to be seen publicly with her. She looked so much older and, in professional company, so inappropriate.

Mary was recuperating from Cavallo number five when Tony met the Widow, which is how he always referred to her. Actually the Widow was about twenty-five then, pretty as hell, safely Italian, and no children; her husband had been killed in an accident on the Queensboro Bridge. The Widow appealed to Tony's aesthetic sense—a lithe, quick body, black eyes in a beautiful dark face.

"Tony," said Peter, "how often do you see the Widow, once a week?"

"Who do you think I am, that old creep in *Any Wednesday?* Three, four times a week, sometimes every day."

"Weekends?"

"Sometimes."

"You still have time for a mercy fuck for Mary once in a while?"

"Listen, you're the guy that's getting the divorce, remember?"

"Why don't we order?" said Paul, whose arrangement with Big Susan had never involved marriage or divorce.

Paul ordered a sirloin on the rare side, Peter a junior steak medium, and Tony gave the waiter an elaborate order in Italian for his own special formula of fettucini.

"No hard feelings?" asked Tony.

"Of course not," said Peter. "Nothing intended."

"Sure," said Tony.

"Do you see the kids often?" Peter asked.

"Sure," said Tony.

"I mean, aren't they asleep when you get home from the Widow?"

"Who comes home?" said Tony, laughing mischievously. "Listen, they know who their father is. That's what counts."

"Doesn't the Widow want any kids?"

"She's got enough on her hands at confession. What do you want, a couple of bastards to get the priest all upset?"

Lightly, lightly, Peter cautioned himself.

"Does Mary know about the Widow?"

For a moment, Peter thought Tony wasn't going to answer. "Sure," he said, "you think she's stupid? Better that way," he said, twirling the fettucini between fork and spoon. "It keeps me off her back. I mean her front," said Tony, laughing it up, Paul joining in but wishing the conversation would stop. "Listen," Tony went on, "I must know over a hundred guys in this business, or some other business, I mean know personally, who got a woman on the side. What's so unusual?"

"Nothing," said Peter. "Just old-fashioned, I guess. Tony?"

"Yeah?"

"Do you love the Widow?"

"I think," said Paul, "the company is indebted to you both for a first-rate campaign for Brew."

"I'll drink to that," said Tony, and the conversation about wives and widows and children was laid gently to rest, except in Peter's mind, which, as they talked about how the principles of the Brew campaign could be applied to other products, tumbled mercilessly with the thought that he had a 2:30 appointment with J. P. Hill, the lawyer he had hired to negotiate the separation agreement with Jack.

They were still over coffee when Peter excused himself. "I have a two thirty date on the outside," he said, getting up.

"Good luck," said Paul.

"What luck?" asked Tony.

"Oh, he's seeing that lawyer about the property settlement."

Peter wished Paul had kept his big mouth shut. Tony motioned Peter back to the table. Peter wanted to continue out, but knew that Tony was quite capable of announcing his message across the Baron's dining room. He came back to the table but didn't sit down.

"I tell you," said Tony, "my way is a lot easier on the nerves."

Hill was a little man with rimless glasses who had been recommended for his savvy on marital affairs, his willingness to take on husbands, sure losers under the law, and most particularly for his cool, which Peter welcomed as an offset to his own lack of composure.

Peter was only a couple of minutes late, and Hill saw him right away.

"Look," said Hill, pumping Peter's hand and gesturing toward a chair, "this isn't going to be comfortable for you. I don't mean the chair, I mean what we've got to talk about. But it'll go a lot better if you let me lead, you follow, and try to keep calm even if you don't feel calm. I've got the facts. I've had my meeting with what's-his-name—"

"Jack Baxter."

"Right, and what we've got to do now is work out the strategy. You been a soldier?"

"World War Two," said Peter, feeling uncomfortable.

"Well, this battling's different because you can't win. No husband does. The law for husbands stinks, but it's the law. The wife gets custody. You get visitation rights, but they have to be negotiated, and she's going to make visiting the kids as difficult as possible. She'll use every loophole to block you. Remember that for later, too. She'll also get most of what you've got—I'm talking property now, and money—and you'll get nothing of what she's got. She can be the most able-bodied woman in the world. She can work; it doesn't matter. You continue to support her. That's alimony. And you support the kids until they're twenty-one. That's child support. If you miss alimony payments or child support, you can be locked up in jail. You're not supposed to go to jail for debt, but the jails in this country are full of husbands who don't or can't pay alimony. That's the system. You can duck the system by going abroad, changing your name, and maybe she can't find you. Maybe. But you've got a life to pick up here, so you stand your ground. What we do is try to keep her from getting everything she wants to get. If you think that's all unfair, I agree with you, but until the divorce laws become fairer—and you and I will both be dead by that time—we play it this way."

Hill gulped air.

"The first thing I'm going to suggest is the hardest."

"Shoot," said Peter.

"You're okay," said Hill. "I hope you hold up. What I want you to do is not to see the children for a while."

Peter didn't understand why that was necessary.

"You've been in plenty of business negotiations," said Hill. "Their trump card in this negotiation is the children. The more they know you're desperate to see them, the more they'll twist."

"This isn't a business negotiation," said Peter, wondering if he had chosen the right lawyer.

"I know," said Hill. "But if you could see it that way, it'd make things easier. What we're trying to do is make a deal. The problem is this lawyer your wife's got—"

"Jack Baxter."

"Right. Baxter seems to take all our discussions personally. Sometimes he sounds like *he's* the aggrieved husband."

Peter explained that Jack had always had a bit of a hang-up about Rose.

"That may account for it," said Hill. "Your wife's found herself a new boyfriend, and her lawyer seems as unhappy about that as he is about you."

So Rose had a friend. That was quick.

"His name," said Hill, "is Leluc. He's a French business man now living in the States, twice divorced, no
children of his own, and intensely interested in a third
marriage equipped with suitable children. He's not a fag.
He's not an alcoholic. No police record. According to
Baxter, Leluc's around the house all the time, evenings
and weekends, taking charge. He actually sat in on the
meeting I had with Baxter."

"He what?" asked Peter.

"That's okay," said Hill. "It helps us. His presence
threw Baxter off. Also, if Leluc's serious, that's in our
favor. When she remarries . . ."

Peter had a sudden sense of everything happening
much too quickly.

"When she remarries," continued Hill, "the alimony
stops. Of course, she won't get married till she's got a
property settlement out of you."

"Can't we hold off then?" asked Peter.

"You can't get a divorce without a settlement. She can
haul you into court, and the court will gladly serve as the
instrument of her revenge. If they try family court,
you'll get an impartial social worker, impartial except
she's a woman, and an impartial psychologist, impartial
except she's a woman. You'll have to keep away from
your new friend because Baxter'll put a detective onto
you. Of course, we can put a detective onto her and Leluc, but it won't get you anywhere. How long can you
take not seeing the children?"

Peter thought, *not long.*

"I don't know," said Peter.

"I think we ought to go for the settlement."

"Is it permanent?"

"Probably. It sticks even if she gets married fast."

Peter fumbled with the pack of cigarettes on Hill's desk. He took one. He lit it, even though he didn't smoke cigarettes.

"It's a free country," said Peter finally.

"Yep," said Hill. His rimless spectacles jiggled as he laughed.

Gradually Peter came to see the threats and counter-threats—and there were many—as the legal game it was, and though it was still painful, like all things it went down easier as the weeks passed. Finally the negotiations reached a point where Hill was able to recommend, "Let's take the deal."

Rose got most of what she wanted—money, house, car, furniture—and Peter got, for the first time, the legal right to see his children every other Saturday, 10 A.M. to 7 P.M.

Peter couldn't help wondering what Leluc looked like. In his mind's eye, French came with a neatly trimmed mustache, wavy hair, tall, thin, elegant, something like a maître d', with a voice like the man who read Air France's commercials on the radio. He wondered if Leluc had hair on his chest (Peter had none). He wondered if Leluc had hair on the back of his hands (Peter had none). Or —and the thought hit him with a shock—would Leluc look like Peter, because people were said to repick the same style in mates?

The first Saturday after the settlement was signed, Peter found himself as nervous about the visit as he had been about his first job interview out of school. (How does a father visit his children, what does he do, how does he behave, how—?) Though Peter wanted Elizabeth along for necessary comfort, to feel that someone else was on his side, on Hill's advice he left her in a coffee shop several blocks away and went to the door alone, intent on controlling what he said and felt, if that were possible.

As he approached the house, slowing his pace a bit because it was still a few minutes to ten and he wanted to be there precisely at the time indicated in the agreement, Peter found himself anxious about Leluc.

Maybe Leluc wouldn't work out, he thought, and Rose would have to find someone else. No, Rose was too skilled. If Leluc was eligible, she wouldn't let him get away. This was it.

He pushed the familiar doorbell. It might as well have been the door to Tibet.

Chapter Nineteen

Be civil, Peter gave himself a final instruction as Leluc answered the door.

Though Leluc, standing on the threshold, was a step up from Peter, Peter found himself looking down at Leluc, who was short indeed. Of course, Frenchmen were short. No mustache. In fact, no wavy hair, very nearly no hair at all, just a vestigial ring of fuzz above the earline where the grass fire had ended.

"Leluc," said Leluc, extending his hand. They shook.

"How do you do?" said Peter. He felt ridiculous.

"Won't you come in?" said Leluc in a markedly French accent. Peter wondered whether Rose would pick up the accent in time.

He took a step or two inside the house—*his* house, he thought, then immediately squashed the thought. Truthfully he hadn't expected to be invited in, but to be left waiting for the kids at the door.

Past Leluc, he could see how much the living room had changed. The furniture had been rearranged, the wall blazed with radical paintings (Leluc's, or just Leluc's taste?), and the burnt-orange drapes had been replaced with white chiffony stuff Peter would have permitted only in a bedroom.

This is not your home, he told himself, *not anymore.*

"I will get the children," said Leluc. He went up the stairs, which seemed to Peter an undue familiarity, and soon came down with Margaret and Jon in tow. Both children were "dressed up" and nervous as hell.

"Hello, Dad," said Jon very formally.

Maggie seemed prepared to be formal also, but it didn't work, and she and Peter embraced, not without embarrassment, in front of Leluc.

"Seven o'clock," said Leluc.

That was unnecessary, thought Peter. And wasn't Rose going to make an appearance? He had to get used to the idea that he might not see Rose again, unless the law required a confrontation at some point.

As soon as they were out of sight of the house, Jon relaxed his formality, which pleased Peter. The boy's stiffness was not for him, but for the others. They chatted about school and the Little League until they reached the coffee shop, where Jon slid in beside Elizabeth in the booth and Maggie opposite. Peter ordered coffee for himself, a refill for Elizabeth and chocolate milks for the children. *They seemed less like children than they ever had before.* While Elizabeth was doing a brilliant job of getting acquainted with the kids and making them feel comfortable with her, Peter was thinking: What to do?

Finding a solution to Brew's sales problems seemed minor compared to filling the emptiness that loomed in the next few hours. When he had seen the children regularly, day in, day out, it was easy to suggest a movie on the weekend, or bowling, or just a walk. But he had a sense now that the movie itself counted, that if it turned out to be less than great, he would have created a disappointment for them. They weren't dressed for bowling; in the future that would have to be arranged in advance. It seemed absurd to have to make arrangements for something like bowling in advance. What to do?

"What would you like to do today?" he asked, feeling somewhat like the aimless characters in Paddy Chayevsky's *Marty*. He fully expected Jonathan to answer, "I don't know. What do you want to do, Daddy?"

Which is exactly what Jon did.

Peter looked to Elizabeth for help.

"Why don't you do something reckless?" she suggested.

"Such as?"

"How would you kids like," she addressed them, "to try the Ferris wheel at Palisades Amusement Park?"

Peter thought the idea of the amusement park brilliant. With dozens of different things to turn to and not more than minutes to spend at each, the kids could be kept whirling, safe from dragging time, safe from boredom with him.

"I think Palisades is a great idea," said Peter.

"It's hard to get to," said Jon matter-of-factly.

"Oh, we could rent a car, zip across Manhattan, through the tunnel, up the other side. An hour tops."

"It's too long," said Jon.

"Last Saturday," said Margaret, "Mommy took me shopping to Saks and Bloomingdale's, you know, not for anything special, just to see what they had."

"Browsing?" asked Peter.

"Something like that. We didn't finish Saks, so we couldn't get to Bloomingdale's. Could we go to Bloomingdale's?"

"That's no fun," said Jonathan with finality.

The kids glared at each other.

Elizabeth touched Peter's hand across the table in reassurance, then immediately withdrew it, lest the kids see.

Peter quickly weighed the facts of visiting life. Margaret would want to do some kinds of things, Jon others. Would that mean they'd have to separate, perhaps Elizabeth going off with Margaret and he with Jon? Would that be interpreted as Elizabeth's having visiting rights? Would it be better for him to take Margaret for one Saturday a month and Jon for another? Was once a month enough to maintain a relationship with your own children?

"Surely," said Elizabeth, "there is something we'd all like to do together."

There were all kinds of "good" things they ought to do, thought Peter—the Metropolitan, the Museum of Modern Art, the Museum of Natural History, the planetarium—but the kids had been to all of them, and were they old enough to explore in depth? And if they got bored, would it allow time for someplace that was fun, so they wouldn't on this first visiting day conclude that a day with the old man was a drag? Obviously alternate Saturdays now had to be planned in advance, very, very carefully, specific places, with a timetable.

As the best bet for a holding operation, he got them all onto the subway headed downtown without telling even Elizabeth where they were going. When they passed Times Square, Jon and Margaret's interest perked. When he motioned for them as the train pulled into West Fourth Street, they both lit up. Daddy was taking them to Greenwich Village.

The Village had the allure of the offbeat, the not-quite-prohibited, the semi-scandalous. Boys with beards, beatniks, hippies, the streets a walking museum of characters to look at, and then, on Eighth Street, the shops, which pleased Margaret and Jon, who found the book and record stores fascinating. They accumulated packages at a rather fast rate, but Peter gratefully paid, buying the day's grace.

They ate in a pizza joint, ordering a large-sized sausage pizza for the four of them, Cokes for the kids, and Chianti for themselves. Jon said he was still hungry, so they ordered a supplementary pizza, this time with anchovies. Jon ate one slice, decided he didn't like anchovies on pizza. Peter offered to order a third, plain pizza, or a small sausage pizza, but Jon said he wasn't hungry anymore. Peter found himself staring at the uneaten pizza in front of them, angry not because of the waste, but because the pizza lay there as a symbol of his failure to work things out.

"Did you enjoy it?" asked Elizabeth, swinging to the rescue of Peter's downhill mood.

The kids nodded, and so they paid the bill, gathered their armloads of packages, and off they went. Peter thought it would be heavenly to rest a bit, but the two movie houses they passed had shows "for mature audiences only." It was just after the disappointment of the second movie house when they spotted the leather-craft store, its small window filled with sandals, hats, handbags made of supple leathers. It was Elizabeth who led them into the shop, her eye on a handbag in olive leather, a beautiful, simple thing, a pouch really, but fashioned with great taste. While she was deciding in its favor, Jon disappeared into the back of the shop and emerged wearing a vest covered with brown fur.

"Crazy," he said. "It's called a bear vest."

The proprietor, a very thin Indian Indian, turned on the hard sell in a way which convinced Peter that the bear vest was a dog to be disposed of. Jon gloried in it. The price was twenty dollars. Twenty dollars for a gag? The pressure from the Indian was great but resistable. The pressure building all day inside Peter was not resistable. He gave in.

"You sure it's not too expensive?" asked Jonathan.

"I'm sure it is too expensive," said Peter, trying to smile as he handed over the money, only to see Margaret, taking her cue from Jon's triumph, trying on a leather Greta Garbo hat.

"You've never worn a hat, Maggie," he said in self-defense.

"Always a first time," she said, shaping it in front of the mirror.

The Husband

Peter pulled Elizabeth aside and whispered frantically, "She'll wear it *once*."

Elizabeth shrugged her shoulders helplessly. She knew the fit of the trap.

Peter paid for the hat, which Margaret insisted on wearing out into the street so that, in her words, "Some of the kooks will look at me now."

They were a distance from the store when Peter realized that Elizabeth had not purchased the handbag. The day had cost them over seventy dollars.

Elizabeth walked on ahead with Margaret, which gave Peter an opportunity to talk to Jon alone for the first time.

"Do you think, Dad, that Vietnam will still be on when I'm old enough to go?"

Peter remembered his war, how everyone was certain it would be over before Peter was old enough to be drafted. That was a laugh. Two years in uniform. But the risk had been *his*, and he hadn't been sensible enough to believe that death was possible. Death or dismemberment. But Jon?

"Do you think it will still be on?"

The first real question he had ever been asked by his son.

"I don't know," said Peter.

They were all tired, and the packages were getting to be a drag, so they took a cab back, a last luxurious fling and, Peter decided, a worthwhile one, because in the nest of the back of the cab the four of them sat, tired, enjoying the glow of a hard day's effort. Was the day a success? Peter studied the children's faces. He couldn't tell. Should he suggest taking only Jon the next time, split-

ting them up, as he now knew would be inevitable in
time? He'd try once more, the two of them together.
He'd plan carefully. He'd map an itinerary. He'd work
out everything ahead of time. It was like planning a marketing campaign. It lacked spontaneity. Is that a built-in
handicap of visiting days?

The cab let them out. Peter overtipped the driver,
hoping Jonathan would notice. Elizabeth hung back on
the sidewalk while Peter and the kids, arms loaded, went
to the door. It may have been open, but the kids rang the
bell. The establishment of formalities had now begun.

Peter had taken a step or two back quite unconsciously,
fading out of the picture. As Leluc answered the door
(would he *ever* see Rose again? And why the thought?),
the kids turned to half-wave at him, but their attention
was now clearly on home, the house, and Leluc, who put
his arms around them and conspicuously kissed Margaret on the cheek and shook Jonathan's hand. Peter had
never shaken hands with Jon.

Is Leluc taking them for his own?

Did you divorce children also?

He joined Elizabeth, and they walked toward the subway. He slowed his pace, then stopped.

"Anything wrong?" she asked.

"Nothing," he said, suddenly buoyant. "Let's go for
a ride. It's only seven."

Peter fished in his pocket for his credit cards, came up
with Hertz.

Twenty minutes later they were on their way, across
the Queensborough Bridge, Fifty-seventh Street, down
Ninth Avenue to the Lincoln Tunnel, and she knew.

"Palisades Amusement Park," she said.

"Clever."

"Haven't been in fifteen years, maybe more."

"Thought we'd give it a dry run, see what might interest the kids next time."

She looked at him, relaxed now behind the wheel. Man and boy, she thought, she loved him.

As they walked from the parking lot, they passed families with children coming out of the amusement park, the day done. On the way in with them were teen-agers, mostly in twos.

"Feel middle-aged?" he asked her.

She squeezed his hand.

"Hungry?" he asked as they passed the first hot dog stand.

"Yes, but if we're going to try any of the rides—are we?" He nodded. "Then let's wait till afterward."

Practical woman, he thought.

"How about the tunnel of love?" he asked.

"Closed years ago. Old-fashioned."

When she saw where he was headed, she felt the first twinge of fear. She had suggested it for the children, not herself.

She thought he might ask her first, but he went straight up to the booth and bought two tickets. She looked up at the Ferris wheel, a huge full circle rimmed with lights.

"I thought we were going to explore, to see what the kids might like," she said.

"That," he said, "was the excuse."

She remembered what he had said about necessary risks. But was this risk necessary? The wheel seemed fragile as well as high, so few supports, so much dead weight.

The attendant took their tickets, strapped them into a swinging seat side by side. Nearly half the seats above were filled; half to go. The attendant motioned the operator, who moved them off the ground so that the next couple could get on.

It was an exasperating ten minutes as their seat moved up eight feet at a time. Then they were at the very top of the circle; beneath them the dizzy fairground blinked away.

"Just look at it," he whispered close to her ear.

She hadn't realized her eyes were closed. It seemed a very long way down, much farther than from the ground looking up. Peter and herself and the wooden seat and sides obviously must have weighed three hundred pounds or more. Yet it all hung so loosely from the skimpy circular frame. And how many times three hundred, how many other couples had now added weight to the spindly circle of the skeleton wheel? In looking down, she had shifted her weight, and just that slight movement started their seat rocking, wildly it seemed in relation to those few bolts holding it up in the air.

"There doesn't seem to be much holding us up," she said. "Are you sure it's safe?"

She saw his expression and laughed at her own question. How would Peter know if it were safe? Amazing that the whole spidery apparatus would stay upright when massive steel bridges sometimes collapsed in a wind. They would circle faster than any bridge ever swayed, spinning like a wheel, with the individual seats swaying back and forth as well as moving around, she thought, secured by bolts subject to rust or metal fatigue or an attendant's careless inspection, the failure to adjust a single nut that had come loose.

"I remember reading somewhere," said Peter, shouting to be heard above the new level of noise, "the first of these contraptions had more than thirty cars carrying forty people in each of them." He pointed a finger at his fact-filled temple. "Nuts," he said.

"Why aren't we moving?" she said.

They could see the lineup of couples now waiting to get on the Ferris wheel; the line wasn't moving. No one was being put on, though there were still a couple of empty seats.

"We're probably overweight with passengers," said Peter, not knowing what he was talking about. "Too many fat people aboard."

The operator and the attendant seemed to be talking busily, like a pitcher and a catcher at the mound. Why talking? Why were people gesturing upward? What was wrong?

Suddenly the wheel started to move, not slowly as before, when passengers were being put aboard, but in a great lurching motion that sent Peter and Elizabeth sprawling against each other and very nearly flying out of the seat despite the strap across their laps.

Elsewhere on the wheel, girls were screaming from the shock of the lurch. What had happened? Why all the milling around down below?

The wheel lurched a second time, this time worse. The screams from passengers were louder. One could hear, "Let me off! Let me off!" carried on the wind.

A great panic seized Peter. *I want to be living when I die*, he remembered.

Elizabeth's face had whitened. Why was she looking at him that way? She hadn't screamed as the other women had, but that expression of ultimate fear on her face . . . Oh, the foolish chances people take in a life filled with hazard. Was she blaming him for what was happening?

"Brace youself," he shouted, "before it happens again." The nails of her left hand dug into the flesh of his right.

Down below, they could see a car with a red light flashing on its roof moving, insectlike, through the crowds, its siren carrying sound to them up high. The car inched as close as it could to the crowd and two uniformed ants got quickly out, conferred with the operator and the attendant, pointing first at something on the driving mechanism, it seemed, then up at them. How could they be removed? A crane? And if a crane, how?

There must have been a thousand ants now staring up at them, the biggest spectacle of all in the amusement park. "Don't move the wheel!" someone shouted from somewhere nearby, and a contrary cry was picked up by others suspended on the wheel. "Let us down!"

Was this their last view of the world, Saturday night at Palisades, rides, twenty-five, thirty-five and fifty-cent thrills, hunger pangs for a greasy hot dog, and finish, now?

Would it help to pray? Peter thought. *If I knew how. If I meant it.*

Suddenly a terrible machinery grating came from below. A great hush vented from the staring crowd. The huge wheel swayed. Then it lurched, only a few feet around this time, and stopped, swaying them again. Dear God, what was happening?

The Husband

From their new angle, Peter's vision of the ground immediately below was blocked, and he had to lean over the side to see.

"Don't lean like that!" she said, immediately sorry.

And then the wheel moved, not a lurch as before, but in a smooth pattern, slowly turning them backward toward the ground. The crowd of onlookers applauded wildly.

As Peter and Elizabeth came down to ground level, wanting desperately for the wheel to stop so they could get off, they found themselves being raised again. The Ferris wheel turned. They were not going to be deprived —deprived?—of their ride, as the wheel, now working, circled them over the top again, and again, and again, fear, relief, fear, relief.

"Looks like they're going to give us the fifty-cent ride anyway," he said.

It seemed unendurably long until the couples were let off, two by two. Elizabeth and Peter touched their feet to the ground.

Some of the people who had been stuck up there stayed to argue with the attendant. What was the point? Holding Elizabeth's hand firmly, he pulled her with him through the gaping earthlings, who were disappointed that the apparatus had not come crashing down for their enjoyment.

"Excuse me," he said as they worked their way through the mob now beginning to disperse. "Excuse me."

They had a life to lead.